His breath was warm on her face. "You are full of commands this morning, Vivian. I, however, am not of a mind to heed them. I will give you a choice. Either I kiss you, or I turn you across my knee and paddle you soundly for being a reckless little fool."

She opened her mouth to give him a proper dressing-down. She never had the chance.

"Wise choice," he announced, and covered her lips with his.

The kiss was nothing like the one before, except for the instant reaction it sparked within her. He was not gentle this time, but fierce and demanding. His lips were firm, and unrelenting, and, as before, seemed to fit perfectly against hers. Even as she tilted her head to give him better access, she knew she was teetering on the edge of something ruinous. This was not some insipid, harmless dandy. This was St. Helier, of the decadent speculations and wicked tongue.

By Emma Jensen
Published by Fawcett Books:

CHOICE DECEPTIONS
VIVID NOTIONS
COUP DE GRACE*

*forthcoming

VIVID NOTIONS

Emma Jensen

FAWCETT CREST • NEW YORK

A Fawcett Crest Book
Published by Ballantine Books
Copyright © 1996 by Melissa Jensen

All rights reserved under International and Pan-American Copyright Conventions. Published in the United States by Ballantine Books, a division of Random House, Inc., New York, and simultaneously in Canada by Random House of Canada Limited, Toronto.

http://www.randomhouse.com

Library of Congress Catalog Card Number: 95-96157

ISBN 0-449-22396-5

Manufactured in the United States of America

First Edition: June 1996

10 9 8 7 6 5 4 3 2 1

1

How quickly time doth fly, its wings a-beat,
And go I must to climes less fair of sky.
Long years might pass ere once again we meet;
My weighted heart in yearning heaves a sigh,
Good morrow, love, good memory, and good-bye!
I turn my gaze to days not yet begun,
And lo- what Vision greets my teary eye?
Now flits away as rays of evening sun;
I yearn! I burn! I follow, Vivid One!
　　　　—Newstead's *Heart's Notions*, canto III, xxii

THERE WAS NO doubt about it. She was dying.

Death was not, she decided, at all what she had imagined. No peaceful passing, this. Nor was she facing it with courage or dignity. She had never been one to whimper in life, and she silently cursed the ignominity of her behavior in the face of demise. And groaned aloud as a new spasm racked her slender frame.

"Easy now, Miss Vivian. You must save your strength."

For what? Another day like this one—so ill and weak that an imminent demise seemed the greatest of blessings? She was a thousand miles from her home, virtually alone, and guaranteed of nothing more than continuing wretchedness.

"Esther," she moaned, lifting a pale hand from the coverlet.

Her maid scurried to her side and bent over the bed. "Yes, miss?"

"Quickly, the basin!"

Moments later, with admirable strength for one hovering on the threshold of the hereafter, Vivian hauled herself over the edge of the bed and cleared her stomach of what little was left there.

"Serves you right," Esther muttered as she plied a cool cloth to her mistress's forehead. "Crossing the Channel in February."

"What would you have had me do? Remain in Le Havre till spring? I would have thought you pleased to be done with the place. That sailor was quite determined to see what you wear under your skirts."

"Whsst. Sick as a dog and still with that mouth. Why, I can only imagine what your mother would say!"

Vivian wearily pushed lank hair off her forehead. "Mother," she said bleakly, "is presently comfortable in Boston. Should she be here, experiencing the horrors of this heaving deathtrap, I would gladly accede her right to complain."

"There is nothing wrong with this ship, miss. Your father would never put you on an unworthy craft."

"He *owns* this ship. Of course he thinks it worthy."

The maid clucked her tongue as she bustled about the room. "If you are well enough to talk so, you are well enough to do something about your appearance." She added another bucket of hot water to the hip-bath. "A good thing indeed you weren't born a hundred years earlier. The fine folk of Massachusetts would've taken one look at you and had you on the scaffold for witchcraft."

The sight of the hot water was enough to get Vivian out of bed. She paused on her shaky way across the room to peer into the mirror. "I imagine you are right," she announced ruefully. "I am indeed a sight."

Her hair, a tangled cloud of midnight black, surrounded a face made ashen by the hated and humiliating sea-sickness. Several days of not eating much had brought her high cheekbones into sharp relief and painted shadows under her jade-green eyes. Had the reflection not been so familiar, Vivian herself might have thought she was facing a witch.

"Did you know, Esther, that the English are known for disposing of their witches by burning them at the stake? Perhaps I ought to change my plans."

The maid chuckled as she helped the girl out of her nightrail. "You're far too lovely to be mistaken for a witch. Into the tub with you."

The heat of the water was enough to temporarily still the churning of Vivian's stomach, and she sighed with pleasure. "Do you know what I wish to do the moment we arrive in England?"

"Kiss the earth?"

"Well, after that. I intend to have a good, long soak in a full bath."

Esther was busy picking up clothing from the floor. "Might be a bit difficult, seeing as we're to be on a coach out of Devon tomorrow."

"Must you remind me? Mother goes to all the trouble of sending me to distant relations in England and I am to pass the first month rusticating in Cambridge."

"Perverse girl." The maid planted her hands on her ample hips. "You know full well you have no interest in London. Your weak stomach has put bile in your tongue."

Vivian gave her best cajoling smile. "Yet you tolerate me nonetheless. You are a saint, Esther."

"Hmmph. I've half a mind to agree with you after these past days."

She turned back to the task of tidying up, and Vivian grinned. Esther had been her mother's abigail before becoming her own, and was as dear as family. True, Vivian's headstrong character and frequent escapades were responsible for much of the gray in the older woman's hair, but she was endlessly devoted.

Vivian wondered idly what her hostesses would think of the maid's impertinent mien. Never having met the

3

widowed sisters, she could only hope they were not so rigid as those stiff-lipped matrons who ruled Boston Society. She rather doubted she would be so fortunate. From what she knew of it, British aristocracy appeared to be rather high-in-the-instep regarding servant-employer relationships.

Well, Lady Fielding and Mrs. DeLancey had been effusive in their letters of welcome. They were in for quite a shock if they expected a meek and tractable miss. At twenty-three, Vivian was a good twenty-two years past tractability.

As if reading her mind, Esther announced, "You will be on your best behavior these next months, missy. Your mother wanted you to have a real English Season, and I will not have you sent home in disgrace before spring is over!"

Vivian groaned as she reached for the soap. "Not to worry, Esther. Nothing on God's green earth could make me act so badly as to merit another ocean crossing before July."

On cue, the boat gave a mighty lurch.

"Bleagh," Vivian said, and reached for the basin Esther was holding out.

"Ah, the most recent installment. Good man, Tare! I knew I could count on you to have a copy still warm from the presses."

Noel Windram plucked the slender volume from his friend's fingers and dropped into the facing chair. White's was uncustomarily empty for late afternoon, no more than a half-dozen members scattered throughout the room. Even Brummell's Bow Window seats were vacant. And it was all due to the book—scarcely half an inch thick even in its embossed leather cover.

"That copy," Jason, Viscount Tarrant, said tersely, "is to be in my wife's hands before supper if ever I wish her to speak to me again."

"Rubbish. Aurelie worships the ground on which you tiptoe. She will forgive you the lapse."

4

"She will not have to." Tarrant reached out and deftly retrieved his precious possession. "I stood in a queue at Hatchard's for a good half hour waiting to purchase my copy. I fully intend to reap the benefits of the torture."

Noel sighed in resignation, then comforted himself by taking his friend's brandy. "You plan on her reading it to you in bed, then?"

"Not at all. I plan on her reading it anywhere but in my presence."

"You were ever the literary snob. I fully intend to read the thing."

"Enjoy your sojourn at Hatchard's" was his friend's dry response.

"Really, Tare . . ." Noel gave a sly grin. "I shall not be passing within a hundred feet of the place." He raised his hand mere inches from the table and seconds later a liveried servant appeared at the table.

"Lord St. Helier?"

"Harris, my good fellow. Pop over to Hatchard's, will you, and purchase a copy of Mr. Newstead's latest for me."

Coins changed hands—a bit more, of course, than the book would cost—and Harris gave a short bow. "I shall return directly, my lord."

Noel nodded benevolently at the man's quickly departing back. "There, you see how simple that was? I shall have Canto IV of *Heart's Notions* in my hands before the hour."

His friend waved for another glass and poured some of Napoleon's finest. "It is a sad commentary on our society that this absurd work should so enthrall the ton. To the best of my knowledge, the only person missing from Hatchard's was Prinny himself. And that only because I am certain the publisher delivered the first copy to Carlton House."

"Come now. Better for people to trample each other over literature than war."

Both men had served as officers on the Peninsula, and both were well aware of the present situation in France. Neither was inclined to return to battle.

"I will agree with you there," Tarrant said, staring into

his brandy. "Now we can but hope Wellington tramples the Corsican for good."

"Here, here," Noel replied fervently, raising his own glass.

They sat in silence for some minutes. Then he offered, "You really have not read any of Byron's latest?"

Tarrant's dark brows rose. "I believe Byron's latest is *Hebrew Melodies*. I read those upon their release as Nathan's libretto."

"Do not play dense. Why, everyone knows *Heart's Notions* is Byron. The cantos positively reek of *Childe Harold's Pilgrimage*."

"Do you not think he would have published under his own name? After the success of *Childe Harold*, he has become quite famous. And his notoriety grows with each subsequent year."

"Precisely! The man thrives on his reputation. What better way to set the ton once again upon its ear than by releasing such pieces under a pseudonym? Look around you, Tare. White's has quite been emptied by the need to possess *Notions* as soon as possible. And the dance floors shall be quite as vacant this eve. Everyone will be crowding the parlors to whisper and speculate on Newstead's identity."

"The identity of Newstead's latest quarry is more to the point."

"Even better!" Noel said delightedly, slapping his hand on the table. "The 'Vivid One' mentioned in the final verse of III is bound to make her appearance in IV."

"I pity the woman, whoever she is."

"Why? She will be quite the most talked-about lady in Town should she be known."

"Yes, well, there you have it. Chances are she is some innocent young thing who caught Newstead's passing fancy. Speculation will do nothing good for her reputation."

"Perhaps not," Noel agreed, "but entering into the speculation will be far more entertaining than discussing the fortune someone will attain by marrying Lord Idlesby's horse-faced daughter." His eyes strayed back to the book

6

now cradled protectively in Tarrant's lap. "He is in Town, you know."

"Idlesby? I would imagine so if he is to fight off his daughter's legion of suitors."

"Not Idlesby, man. Byron. He and his wife have taken a house in Piccadilly Terrace."

"Hmm, yes, I had heard he married."

"Really, Tare, it was some months back. Where on earth have you been?" He grinned knowingly. "Of course. You are relatively newly wed yourself. I imagine East Sussex was rather warmer than usual this past winter."

Tarrant allowed a quick grin of his own. "It was a delightful winter, to be sure. I recommend marriage, St. Helier. It is turning out to be an agreeable state indeed."

"Well, you caught a gem. Apparently Byron is not nearly so blissful. Rumor has it he took his wife to Cambridge before arriving in Town. To Six Mile Bottom, Augusta Leigh's home."

"For God's sake—you don't believe that rot about his having an affair with his half sister, do you?"

Noel casually shoved a lock of ash-brown hair from his forehead and reached again for the brandy. "Of course I do. I have read all three cantos, after all. 'The Lady of Lithe and August Charms' of Canto III impresses me as being a decidedly crowing admission."

"I still do not believe it to be Byron at all," Tarrant muttered.

"Ah, well, we are all entitled to our own opinions. Perhaps I shall accompany you home and ask Aurelie what she believes. Your wife is an immensely astute woman."

He smiled anew as his friend all but swelled with proud pleasure. Ordinarily the sight of a man in love with his wife inspired a sort of amused pity. In Tarrant, however, it was acceptable. His viscountess was a smashing creature, warm and intelligent. Tare was lucky to have found her.

"Aurelie is indeed astute. She is also, at present, not at home."

"No? I thought she was eagerly awaiting Newstead."

"She is spending the afternoon with Lady Fielding and Mrs. DeLancey. Apparently they have a young woman residing with them for the Season. American heiress. She has been with them for the past six weeks in Cambridge and makes her Town debut tonight at the Symington fete. Mrs. DeLancey sent Aurelie a rather frantic note. It seems the girl is resistent to wearing white."

"Good heavens! How utterly intolerable! Next it will be locusts and frogs."

Tarrant smiled ruefully at his friend's sardonic pronouncement. "Yes, well, the good lady is in quite a state over it. Aurelie went off to see what she could do."

Noel leaned back in his chair, stretching his long legs in lazy comfort over the Aubusson carpet. He had just returned from a long visit with his mother, and it was a relief to sit in a chair that did not threaten to collapse under his weight. He found himself wondering if George Hepplewhite had himself been a puny man. His own well-muscled, over-six-foot frame tended to quite dwarf his mother's delicate parlor furniture. "An American heiress who refuses to wear white for her debut. Perhaps there will be more to talk about than Newstead, after all."

"I thought you were not planning to attend."

"I was not. I am fond of the Symingtons, to be sure, but as I have no need to seek out a bride, I thought to avoid the crush."

His friend gave him an amused, slightly pitying smile. "You really ought to think about marrying one of these days. Even the ancient and affluent St. Helier earldom requires an heir to continue."

"Oh, but I have an heir—Cousin Derwood." He chuckled at Tarrant's dour expression. "Do not fret, old man. You will never be subjected to Derwood's presence in the House of Lords. I fully intend to marry—next year, perhaps. I shall find some pretty, tractable country miss, settle her in Devon with a few children, and be done with it. For now, perhaps I shall take Byron's place as bachelor roue of Society."

Tarrant sighed. "You are a thoroughly heartless creature, Hel."

"Not at all. I am a romantic to the core. Now, give me that book. I shall occupy myself with it till Harris arrives with my copy."

Felicity DeLancey's tight, gray curls had become somewhat loose over the course of the afternoon. She shook her head yet again and surveyed her charge with sad eyes. "Would you not at least consider the cream silk?"

Vivian had grown extremely fond of the sweet-tempered widow during the past six weeks, but she was not to be swayed. "I have already swept the royal floor with white muslin for the Queen, madam. I am set on the blue for tonight. Why, you yourself said it was a flattering color for me."

"Yes, dear, I did say that." The older woman sighed. "And my opinion has not changed. It is just that the cream would be so charming and ... appropriate for the occasion." When Vivian did no more than smile patiently, she turned to her sister for support. "Do you not agree, Constance?"

Lady Fielding was as fashionable and handsome as her sister, but much more candid and bold of character. "I do not. The girl is quite right. She looks exceedingly well in the blue."

Vivian quite adored Lady Fielding, too. While Felicity was far the sweeter of the two, Constance was a kindred spirit. Her stern mien and sharp conversation had been intimidating for all of two hours. By the end of their first evening together, the three had been conversing like longtime acquaintances. In fact, Vivian wished the two widows had been present in her life as much as her stolid American relations. They were far better company.

"Aurelie?" Mrs. DeLancey implored their guest. "Would you please repeat what you wore for your Introduction to Society?"

"White," the young lady replied promptly, "and it was

9

utterly dull. Besides, Miss Redmond's coloring is far better suited to the blue than the cream."

Vivian regarded the lovely viscountess with some envy. Lady Tarrant's chestnut hair and delicately flushed complexion were what she might have wished for herself. In her experience, she had found her own black curls and dramatic eyes drew far too much attention to her impetuous character. Perhaps had her parents given her softer looks and a different name, her digressions would have passed with less notice. As it was, she seemed destined for inevitable comparisons to the feckless, faithless woman who led Merlin astray and turned Camelot on its ear.

"Thank you, my lady," she said sincerely. "I am a disaster in white." With a rueful smile, she added, "I take on the appearance of a statue whose head and face have been defaced with paint."

"Rubbish," Lady Tarrant said with a laugh. "Your skin is fair, but hardly colorless. Nor is the gown so inappropriate. It is, I think, the color of a smoky sky. You will look charming."

"There, you see, Felicity? Aurelie has given her approval, and her opinion carries a good deal more weight in Society than yours." Lady Fielding tempered her words by patting her sister's hand. "Look at it this way—Vivian might have set her mind on the purple."

Vivian's eyes promptly swung to the wardrobe and the beautiful, deep-violent gown hanging there. She sighed.

"Oh, dear," Mrs. DeLancey said plaintively. And sighed.

Lady Tarrant laughed. "I predict you are going to be a smashing success, Miss Redmond. There is something about you that will quite attract the eyes of Society. Something . . . vivid."

Vivian had attended her share of balls in Boston. At the age of twenty-three, she was, in fact, well accomplished at the art of dancing gracefully, chatting with animation, and pretending great interest in conversation—all without displaying the fact that she was bored to tears. This night, however, her heart was pounding with trepidation.

She was not overly concerned with her reception by London Society. She would be going back to Boston in a matter of months, after all. She did not, however, want to disappoint her hostesses. They had been beyond kind and encouraging. Were she to make an utter cake of herself, they would be the ones to live with the ton's disapprobation.

She knew she looked well enough. Esther had tamed her hair into some semblance of order, piling the midnight curls high on her head. The gown did suit her, far better than any pastel would. Perhaps, she thought as she surrendered her wrap to one of the Symingtons' footmen, the bodice was a bit too revealing. It had certainly looked modest enough in the modiste's book.

There was nothing to be done about the lushness of her form—it had been much the same for a good six years now, but she took the time to ruefully recall the marvelous meals that the widows' Cambridge cook had provided. True, she had been a bit gaunt upon her arrival in Devon, but several weeks in the country had restored what weight she had lost.

"I told you we would be more than fashionably late," she heard Mrs. DeLancey scolding her sister.

"Well, I am sorry, Felicity, but my gown was creased." Lady Fielding smoothed the rose silk. The dowager baroness was nothing if not fashionable.

"You could have worn the green."

"The green is a season old. It would not have done at all."

As the two older women commenced with their affable bickering, they were slowly moving toward the ballroom. Vivian saw, as they crossed the threshold, that the huge room was packed with what must have been all of Polite Society. It was a sea of glittering jewels and bright fabrics. Pausing at the top of the stairs, she gazed in awe at the most dramatic display of wealth she had ever seen—and she had seen the best Boston had to offer.

"The Dowager Baroness Fielding," the butler intoned from his position on the landing. "Mrs. DeLancey. And Miss Vivian Redmond."

"Come along, dear," Mrs. DeLancey whispered, and started forward. She stopped after a moment, however, and glanced curiously from the assembled guests to the space behind them, as if expecting to see someone of importance. "I wonder . . ." she began.

"Do not be a goose, Felicity," her sister snapped. "They are not looking behind us. They are looking at Vivian."

She was right.

Vivian felt what color she possessed draining from her cheeks. No less than two hundred pairs of eyes were fastened on her unruly curls, not-white gown, and pale face.

2

iii

As fleeting glimpse of heaven doth cajole
A mortal man to dream of feasts unknown,
So hath a Vivid Visage struck my soul.
All shadows of past paramours have flown
And left my heart to yearn for her alone.
O Nimuë! her beauty so enthralls,
Her sorcery so far exceeds my own—
That should I be imprisoned by her walls,
Gladly would I languish 'neath the stone.

iv

O tell me—is my strength enough to breach
Your alabaster wall, ebon rampart?
And will my cry soar high enough to reach
Your ears and send my longings to your heart,
Or am I doomed to failure ere I start?
Two sentinels guard oe'r you as you stay;
With fearsome eye do keep us well apart.
Have you arrived from lands so far away
To taunt and haunt me only to depart?
                    —Newstead's *Heart's Notions*, canto IV

VIVIAN'S FIRST IMPULSE was to turn on her heel and flee. She had no idea why the assembled revelers were staring at her, and she did not like it in the least. If this was how the English greeted each new arrival, one American was very pleased not to be English. No wonder young ladies of the ton were reputed to swoon with astonishing regularity during the Season. Their nerves were very likely shredded the first night.

She felt the two older ladies stepping in to stand at either side. Strengthened by their support, she straightened her shoulders and raised her chin.

"Good girl," Lady Fielding commended her.

"Why are they staring so?"

"Perhaps news of your loveliness has spread through Society already," Mrs. DeLancey offered helpfully.

"Word of your fortune, more likely" was her sister's gruff rejoinder. "Nothing like an heiress to turn heads in the city." She nodded decisively, setting her towering ostrich plume into motion. "Shall we descend?"

The buzzing below took a marked rise in volume, and Vivian realized there had been a moment of almost complete silence. Her fortune had never caused nearly so dramatic a response in Boston. She wondered if perhaps whatever rumors had circulated had not been a bit exaggerated.

None of the recent visitors to her hostesses' townhouse had seemed overly impressed with her importance. She certainly did not believe Lady Tarrant would have spread anything untrue. The gazes still fixed on her, however, were rife with ill-disguised interest. Even as her knees knocked together, she kept her pace stately and her chin high.

"We shall continue straight on," Lady Fielding whispered as she nodded to several acquaintances. "I spied Aurelie across the floor. Perhaps she will be able to shed some light on the matter."

It was an odd sensation, having the crowd part before them as they went. Vivian had not, in her most fanciful moments, imagined a reception half so theatric. "Does this happen often?" she asked through gritted teeth.

"Often enough, dear." Mrs. DeLancey smiled at a cluster of matrons. "I do believe Constance is right. Someone mentioned your wealth."

14

"Beasts to the kill," Lady Fielding muttered.

Vivian nearly stopped dead in her tracks. "I beg your pardon?"

"Best not to cavil, I said. There is nothing to be done now but proceed."

Lady Tarrant materialized in front of them. She immediately reached out to grasp Vivian's hands. "Did I not tell you?" she queried brightly. "You have already turned heads. My own debut was not nearly so gratifying." She stepped back then, drawing the other girl with her. "Come along. You must meet my husband. I have told him all about you."

Vivian followed, uncustomarily tongue-tied. Lady Fielding, however, was having no such problem. "What is the meaning of all this? It felt as if we had walked into a royal wake and Vivian was the king's mistress."

"Constance!" her sister gasped.

"Well, it did! Fortune or no, that reception was decidedly unusual."

Aurelie laughed. "Yes, it was rather daunting for Miss Redmond, I imagine. It has been quite the oddest evening. No one seems to want to talk of anything other than Mr. Newstead's latest canto. It was released this morning."

Lady Fielding sniffed loudly. "More of that rot already? A disgrace, I say."

"Really, Constance," Mrs. DeLancey remarked, "I find the verses rather dashing and romantic."

"You would."

Vivian was lost. Lady Tarrant's warm and unconcerned greeting had banished some of her apprehension, and she found her voice strong enough to ask "Who is this Mr. Newstead? I am afraid I have not heard of his work."

"Oh, it is a marvelous series," the viscountess replied. "He writes of a new infatuation every few weeks. I have not had a chance to read today's installment, but Jason did purchase a copy for me. It was ever so chivalrous of him to brave the hordes."

She had stopped and was smiling saucily up at a tall,

darkly handsome man. "Miss Redmond, this is my husband. Jason, may I present Miss Vivian Redmond of Boston."

Lord Tarrant promptly bowed over Vivian's hand. "It is my pleasure, Miss Redmond."

"Lord Tarrant." Vivian had never met a future earl before and, despite Mrs. DeLancey's careful instructions, could not remember if a curtsy was appropriate. The state of her knees had improved, but she thought it wise not to take a chance. "Lady Tarrant has been more than kind in her warm welcome."

"Not at all," Lady Tarrant insisted. "I am delighted to have a new friend. Jason, you have not complimented Miss Redmond on her gown."

"Please, it is Vivian, and I do not think Lord Tarrant . . ."

"How remiss of me." The viscount's tawny eyes flashed in amusement. "May I compliment you on your gown, Miss Redmond? I myself am prodigiously fond of blue."

Vivian wondered for an instant whether she ought to be offended. She promptly decided it was not worth the trouble. She liked Lady Tarrant and was quite certain she would like her husband. "Thank you, my lord. I fear this gown was white when we left the house. You see, there was an unfortunate encounter with a wagon carrying barrels of blueing . . ."

The viscount's laugh was every bit as comforting as his wife's greeting had been earlier. Feeling much more the thing, Vivian laughed with him.

She was rather a smashing creature. The silvery sound of her laughter carried across the room, and Noel felt the corner of his mouth turn up in a smile, wishing he could have heard whatever quip had amused Jason.

"Well, the Tarrants seem to like her," his companion commented sourly.

"Yes, Lydia, they do."

Lydia Burnham had attached herself to his coatsleeve sometime past and was now pressed rather intimately

16

against his arm. "She certainly timed her debut carefully. How very artful—arriving late to the ball on the night canto IV was released. I wonder if Byron will be arriving next. Of course, he might not have been invited. That nasty affair with his half sister has quite put him beyond the pale."

"Really, Lydia. You do not believe that rot, do you?"

"Why, I most certainly do. He all but admitted it in canto III . . ."

"Lord and Lady Berringdon," the butler intoned in the distance.

"Anyone can see the 'Lady of August Charms' is Augusta Leigh," she continued. "How utterly outrageous of him, and how repugnant . . ."

"Was that not the Byrons who were just announced?"

"Was it?" Suddenly she was patting at her hair. "La, I do believe I see . . . Eleanor beckoning. If you would pardon my desertion, my lord, I must attend her."

"You leave my abandoned heart in tatters, madam," Noel muttered dryly as she disappeared into the crush.

Lydia Burnham was an unmitigated jade, with neither the beauty nor the charm to soften her sharp tongue. She was full determined to marry a title, and flitted among the peers with the stamina and resolution of an iron moth. He glanced down to see if there were any holes in his indigo kerseymere coat. It appeared to be intact.

He pitied Eleanor Symington the visit she was about to receive. True, Eleanor did regard Lydia as something of a friend, but she was invariably kind to everyone and did not deserve the pique to which Miss Burnham would undoubtably succumb once it became clear she was not to encounter the Byrons after all.

Another peal of laughter carried over the floor. It took him a moment to locate the girl's midnight curls amid a cluster of male heads. So, Byron's Vivid One was heading for success after all. He could not remember her last name, but *Vivian* echoed in his ears.

Had he not read the better part of Canto IV, he might not have responded to the name. But he had read it, as had more than half of those present. Clever man, Byron, with his thinly cloaked clues. Anyone with any knowledge of British folklore would recognize Nimuë, the brazen beauty who had seduced Merlin and then led him to an eternal trap under a great boulder.

Nimuë, of course, was better know as Vivien.

Well, the Vivid One had come to England from across the sea and had arrived at the ball with her two sentinels. Noel reached up to adjust his cravat with a smile. Perhaps Byron had been unable thus far to get past the two old viragos, but Noel felt no apprehension. Lady Fielding and Mrs. Delancey were lifelong friends of his own mother and were decidedly fond of him. Gaining permission to pay his addresses would be no problem whatsoever.

It was time to meet Newstead's Latest.

"No, my lord, I do not know George Washington," Vivian said, struggling not to laugh aloud. "To the best of my knowledge, he never resided in Boston. Besides, he has been deceased these past fifteen years or so."

"Has he?" Baron Something-or-Other asked, a careful study in precious foppishness. "I had not heard. Of course, things do arrive from the Colonies with such extreme delay."

The crowd of men surrounding her nodded in agreement with this sage pronouncement. "Yes, certainly," she agreed with deceptive sweetness. "Why, it has been near three whole months since I myself departed Boston Harbor."

"How do you find England, Miss Redmond?" another young man asked. Surveying his cravat, Vivian wondered how he managed to speak past its tight knot.

"Damp" was her ready response.

At this veritable pearl of wisdom, a good half-dozen heads bobbed up and down. A half dozen more were prevented from bobbing by impossibly high collar points.

"Did you enjoy your sojourn in Cambridge, Miss Redmond?"

Her gaze flew up to the speaker's face. She was certain

she had not been presented to this man. She knew this because, after any number of introductions, he was the only man besides Lord Tarrant whom she felt she would recognize at a second meeting.

There was none of the fashionable dandy about him. His ash-brown hair, rather than being styled in the popular Brutus, was on the long side, thick, and brushed carelessly away from his forehead. And his cravat, while being neat to a fault, sported a knot that would not, she surmised, require a mathematician to fashion. He was passingly handsome and looked as if he could reside in Boston.

She gave him a bright smile. "I enjoyed Cambridge immensely, Mr. . . . ?"

"Windram," he offered, politely elbowing Baron Whomever out of the way to bow over her hand. "My pleasure, mademoiselle." He straightened then, his height putting him well above the scowling peer. "I have myself visited Boston and found it a charming place. Unfortunately, my time there was sadly limited. I would like very much to return at some point."

"As would I," Vivian replied saucily.

He had a lovely laugh, deep and resonant. "May I have the honor of this dance, Miss Redmond?"

He captured her hand again and was drawing her forward before she could demur. She thought it would be pleasant indeed to dance with him, but remembered enough of Mrs. DeLancey's lessons to cast a questioning glance in that lady's direction.

"Ah, not to worry. I have already presented myself to your estimable guardians." He inclined his head toward Mrs. DeLancey who promptly smiled and nodded her approval. "They are bosom bows of my own dear mother."

Pleased and reassured, Vivian allowed him to guide her onto the floor. "You do realize this is my first dance in England," she informed him. "You might well be leading yourself into a minuet with a veritable elephant."

"I have no doubt you are as graceful as you are charming."

Noel noted that she did not flush with pleasure at the compliment as most girls would have done. Instead, she raised one winged black brow and countered, "Perhaps it is I who ought to be concerned then, Mr. Windram."

"I shall contrive not to tread upon your toes."

"And I shall contrive to keep them out of your way."

He smiled in appreciation. No simpering chit was Miss Vivian Redmond. She was delightful. He had met many far more beautiful women, but was ever ready to exchange beauty for a keen mind. Not that she was unattractive. Byron had done well to label her the "Vivid One." Under the tumble of black curls, her green eyes sparkled with vitality, and he wondered if the lustrous rose of her lips was gift of nature or cosmetics. There was certainly nothing artful about the rest of her face. The tip-tilted nose and determined chin hinted at indomitable vitality and frankness.

He planned to enjoy their association immensely.

"You know, Miss Redmond, you have brought a flash of something literary to my mind."

"Have I?" She stepped away with the pattern of the dance, her skirts swirling in a graceful arc around her slender form. "I am afraid that is a sadly common occurrence."

So, the chit was openly admitting it, was she? Splendid. "Sadly?"

"Yes. The references cannot help but be a bit on the nocuous side."

He noticed as they moved into the allemande that she was smaller than he had first thought, her head just reaching his shoulder. There was something formidable about Vivian Redmond that obviously had far more to do with spirit than stature.

"You do not relish being the talk of the town?"

She tilted her head and regarded him through jade-green eyes before whirling away again. "I have scarce been here long enough for that, sir."

Upon her return, Noel held her hand a beat longer than

was appropriate. "Perhaps your reputation has preceded you. News travels fast through the ton."

"Ah, but very slowly across the Atlantic, it seems." When she smiled, a pair of puckish dimples appeared beside her mouth. "Has your mother perchance been conversing with my hostesses of late?"

"Not to my knowledge. Why do you ask?"

"It seems the only reasonable explanation. You hint at knowing of my character, Mr. Windram, and invoke Vivien, yet we have never met."

"Ah, but how do you know it was Vivien to whom I was referring?"

This time, the steps took her from his side for some minutes. Above her head, he spied Lydia Burnham in the neighboring set. She did not look at all pleasant. In fact, the gaze she had fixed on Miss Redmond was amusing in its chill.

"Everyone familiar with Arthurian lore," she replied eventually, "has made the ludicrous comparison at one time or another. I did not expect matters to be different in England. I simply hoped to be granted a longer reprieve."

As they turned, Vivian spied another lady watching them with what could only be termed a frosty gaze. She wondered if perhaps Mr. Windram was in some way attached to this woman and stifled a flash of disappointment. She was certainly not in the market for a husband, but it might have been nice to indulge in some harmless flirtation.

"Are you married, Mr. Windram?"

His brows, which were, strikingly, several shades darker than his hair, rose in twin arcs. "No, I am not."

She staved off a pleased smile. "You sound very proud of that accomplishment."

He looked proud as well, though his expression was but part of the effect. There was a sculpted elegance to his face that hinted at impeccable bloodlines and no small amount of arrogance. She had seen similar strong, bold noses and stalwart jaws on classical statues. Even his eyes, deep set and silver-gray, reminded her of a heroic noble's graven image.

"I would not say pride describes my attitude. Bachelorhood is not, after all, a state to which I dedicate my life. No, I am merely content for the time being."

Thinking perhaps she had just been warned off, Vivian gave her best debonair grin. "I understand you perfectly, sir. There is nothing in the world to compare to freedom. I am more than content in my own."

"Yes" was his leisurely reply. "I rather thought you would be."

His hand was very large around hers, and she wondered if, were he to employ both at her waist, they would span the slender circumference. She could only imagine what her mother and Esther would have to say about that vastly improper thought.

Well, her thoughts were hers alone.

"I imagine I would agree with you, Miss Redmond." Her eyes snapped up to his and she lost a step. "If only I knew what you were thinking."

"I—I beg your pardon?"

"Obviously you were considering something satisfying. Would you care to share the thought?"

"No, I would n . . . What I mean, sir, is that it was nothing of import. Certainly nothing that would be of any interest to you."

His slow, lazy smile banished all thoughts of cold stone. "If I may be so bold as to say so, my dear, I imagine whatever you do will be of great interest . . . to the ton . . . and to me."

A faint and completely unfamiliar tremor rippled from their joined hands up her arm. It was not unpleasant in the least, but neither was it particularly comfortable. Vivian vaguely heard the final strains of the music fade away and she pulled her hand from his. "I . . . er, thank you." He stared down at her, making no move to leave the dance floor, and she cleared her throat nervously. "I believe you are meant to escort me back now, Mr. Windram. The dance is over."

Again the smile, and again the tremor, though their hands were no longer joined. "I expect you are half right there. I should escort you back to the sentinels." He offered his arm and she took it gingerly. "But the dance is not over."

He said nothing else as they approached Mrs. DeLancey.

Confused, and more than a little disconcerted, Vivian searched for any appropriate retort. All she could come up with was "Thank you, Mr. Windram. I enjoyed the dance."

"As did I." He brushed his lips across her hand. "We shall enjoy a good deal more," he added softly. "I admit to having found you more vivid than even the verses imply. I look forward to experiencing firsthand what Newstead has but imagined."

With that, he disappeared into the crowd.

"He is a lovely young man, is he not?" Mrs. DeLancey patted Vivian's cheek. "So very gallant."

Vivian was not certain gallant was the word she would have chosen, but she was loathe to disappoint her kindly hostess. "Yes, very," she conceded lamely.

"And so handsome. His dear mother was a renowned Beauty in her day, and St. Helier . . ." She paused. "My goodness, Constance, whatever is the matter?"

Vivian turned to spy Lady Fielding bearing down on them, Lady Tarrant in tow. Neither looked particularly cheerful.

"We have gotten to the bottom of it at last," the former announced grimly.

"Bottom of what?" her sister queried.

"The scene on the stairs, of course, and the hordes who flocked for introductions." Lady Fielding turned to Vivian. "No offense, dearest. You are a remarkable young woman, but the attention reeked a bit of excess."

"None taken, madam. Do tell me the reason for the . . . excess."

It was Lady Tarrant who answered. "Remember how we were speaking of Mr. Newstead's verses earlier?"

"Yes, but . . ."

"And how he writes of a new woman in each?"

"I . . . yes, but . . ." An odd and discomfitting thought flashed into her mind. "You are not saying . . ."

The viscountess nodded. "The ton," she announced with a sigh, "has embraced the notion that you are Newstead's most recent infatuation. He calls her the Vivid One."

"Why would anyone possibly think I am she?"

"That I cannot say, not having read Canto IV. From what I can gather, however, it has something to do with your name, the fact you come from abroad, and your recent stay in Cambridge." Lady Tarrant seemed a bit disconcerted by that last bit. "You see, Byron was in Cambridgeshire last month."

Vivian narrowed her eyes. "Lord Byron?"

"Of course. It is common knowledge—or common speculation, at least—that he is Newstead. The style is his, the . . . topics suit, and Newstead Abbey is the Byron estate in Nottinghamshire."

A series of rather unpleasant speculations formed themselves in Vivian's mind. "The same Byron who is reputed to have had an affair with his half sister?"

"Vivian, really!" Mrs. DeLancey reproved.

"I am sorry, madam, but the man's reputation has managed to cross the Atlantic. In fact, that is only one of many such rumors I have heard." She turned back to Lady Tarrant. "I take it then, any 'subject' of this Mr. Newstead would provide a great deal of fodder for the gossip mills?"

"Well, yes . . ."

"And might perhaps hence be regarded as a challenge for other men?"

"I suppose so, yes, but in your case it is not nearly so . . ."

"That bounder!"

"What did you say, my dear?" Lady Fielding asked, elegant brows raised.

"That shameless scapegrace!" Vivian quickly warmed to the tirade. "That officious, arrogant, two-headed worm!"

"Yes, that is rather what I thought you said."

"Constance!" Mrs. DeLancey flapped her fan in her sister's face. "Vivian, dearest, are you referring to Lord Byron?"

"Byron?" Vivian scowled. "Not at all. I am speaking of Mr. Windram."

"Who is Mr. Windram?" Now Mrs. DeLancey's eyebrows shot up. "Surely you do not mean St. Helier?"

"St. Helier?"

"Noel Windram. The Earl of St. Helier."

"Earl?"

"Why, yes, dearest. Did he not tell you?"

"Oh." Lady Tarrant smiled slightly. "Noel neglects to mention his title at times. He seems to find it amusing to do so."

"Amusing." Vivian was nowhere near calm, but she had regained admirable control over her voice. "He finds it amusing. Am I correct in assuming the *earl* seeks amusement on a regular basis?"

"Yes," the viscountess replied, "he does, actually."

"Right." The next word out of Vivian's mouth prompted a shocked squeak from Mrs. DeLancey, a gruff chuckle from Lady Fielding, and a dropped jaw from Lady Tarrant.

"Did he ... er, contrive to offend you somehow?" that lady asked, her lips curving slowly into what appeared to be a wry smile. "His tongue can be a bit loose on occasion."

Vivian managed a smile of her own. "I shall bear that in mind, my lady." *When I stuff Mr. Newstead's latest canto down his lordship's elegant throat!*

3

VIVIAN SET THE book down and grimaced. "I still think the concept absurd."

"But possible?" Aurelie handed her a cup of tea. "I daresay Mr. Newstead has quite caught your essence in his verse."

"Not mine. Someone else's."

The viscountess smiled gently. "I believe the whole point of a man admiring from afar is to keep his admiration secret. Really, Vivian, it is entirely feasible you were being observed without your knowledge."

"Rubbish. I would have known had someone been close enough to see"—she retrieved the book and flipped through the pages—" 'celestial orbs of verdant green.' " She sniffed. " 'Terrestrial' is a far more appropriate word to use with 'green.' Correct me if I am wrong, but celestial implies *blue*."

"Poetic license?"

"Poetic ineptitude." Vivian reached for another book. "I have been rereading *Childe Harold's Pilgrimage*. True, the style and versification are similar to *Heart's Notions*, but the comparison stops there. Byron is anything but inept. In fact, I am beginning to think him rather brilliant."

"You are being overly critical, I think. Even Byron has bills to be paid. Releasing *Notions* in cantos might hurry the craft a bit, but it undoubtably increases the sale of the piece. No one lined up in such a manner for *Lara*."

"That," came Vivian's tart response, "is a commentary on the reading taste of Society, not the merit of the poet."

Aurelie laughed but made no reply. Moments later, the salon door opened and the viscount entered. "Hello, my love," she greeted him as he bent to kiss her. "I am glad you have returned. Vivian and I have been discussing—"

"Newstead?" Jason groaned. "I have just left White's to avoid further discussion of the piece." He turned an engaging grin on Vivian. "Should I apologize for my untempered tongue there, Miss Redmond?"

"Not at all, my lord. I am in complete agreement." Her own smile faded as a second figure appeared in the doorway.

"Hullo, Aurelie." The Earl of St. Helier breezed into the room to bow over the viscountess's hand. "You are looking stunning as ever." He turned to Vivian. "Why, Miss Redmond, what a pleasure to meet you here. I thought to pay a visit to the home of my mother's dear friends, but the crowd spilling through the door was far too intimidating."

"The crowd," Vivian muttered, "is the reason I am here." She pulled her hand back before he could raise it to his lips. "I have been forced to flee from *unwanted* visitors."

One black brow lifted a notch, but St. Helier gave no other indication that he might have comprehended the insult. On the contrary, he flashed his now-annoying, easy grin and said, "I trust I am not one of the unwanted."

She had not noticed before that two of his upper teeth extended below the rest, giving him a decidedly leonine appearance. Upon their meeting three days past, she might have found the feature enticing. Now she merely found it gratingly apt. "I would venture to say, my lord, that unwanted guests seldom recognize their status."

She was gratified to see his eyes widen in surprise and comprehension. Unfortunately, they were not alone, and Aurelie's awkward cough lessened the satisfaction of the moment. The stinging tirade she would have liked to loose on St. Helier was left to simmer on her tongue.

Then, to her utter chagrin, the man had the nerve to laugh. "Are you in the habit of informing those sorry indi-

27

viduals that they are not welcome? Or do you simply sneak away to safer climes?"

She had, in fact, been reduced to climbing out the retiring room window. The steady stream of curious faces and prying tongues had not lessened in the days since the Symington affair, threatening both her patience and her sanity. It was not that frank speech was beyond her. On the contrary, she had wanted very much to clear the house of its nosy visitors with a few choice words. She had, however, been unable to decide whether the entire crowd ought to be basted, or merely a choice few. It would not have done at all to insult any of the widows' true friends.

Hence, the window had seemed the lesser of evils.

"Vivian was but accepting my invitation to tea," Aurelie announced smoothly. "She cannot be expected to stay in every afternoon." Vivian noticed she had managed to drape the edge of her wrap over the pile of books and was delighted to have such an ally. "As you"—the viscountess cast a pointed glance at the men's feet—"can always be counted upon to track mud over my carpets. Go deal with the matter."

Both Tarrant and St. Helier looked startled but, to Vivian's relief, promptly took themselves off to deal with the matter. "My goodness," she remarked in awe as the door shut behind them, "that was impressive. Would you possibly consider doing the same at my hostesses' home?"

Aurelie retrieved her wrap and set the books out of sight. "I will no doubt have to explain all of this to Jason later. I tend to bring more mud into the house than he does."

"I do not suppose you would consider not saying . . . No, I suppose not." Vivian sighed. "I do not wish to cause any scenes. I merely wish to be spared the effort of being pleasant to Lord St. Helier."

"Ah, yes, how good of you to bring up the subject. Would you care to tell me what he has done to cause such antipathy?"

"He was . . . forward upon our first meeting."

Aurelie's eyes narrowed shrewdly. "You seem the sort of woman well able to handle forwardness. Does this, too, have something to do with Mr. Newstead?"

Vivian slumped inelegantly against the cushions. "At the moment, *everything* seems to have something to do with that wretched book. You were there that night. I could not move without treading on someone. Last night at the opera, every glass in the hall was trained on our box. There has not been a quiet moment in the house for three days! And it is all because of some woman who bears the most trifling resemblance to me."

Aurelie said nothing for some moments. Then: "Has it not occurred to you there might be some enjoyment to be gained from the experience?"

"Enjoyment? Good Lord, how?"

"You are not a dull creature, Vivian. The London Season can be all but intolerable in its dullness. With all the attention you are receiving, you have it in your power to make the next several months quite lively."

"But I do not want lively! I do not want attention! I wish to spend the Season in sweet, anonymous tranquility. Then I wish to go home—where, I feel compelled to mention, I have not had a quiet day in years. I deserve a respite from chaos!"

"Well," Aurelie said, plying the teapot again, "I fear you are to be disappointed. The ton seizes sensational events with the tenacity of a pitbull. Besides—as *I* feel compelled to mention, you have thrown out a challenge for our dearest Noel. He adores a challenge."

"I believe I can avoid his lordship easily enough."

"Ah, you do not know Noel. In fact, I would expect him to reappear any moment now, charm at the ready." Just then, the sound of boot heels rang in the hall.

"Oh, dear." Vivian stared uneasily toward the door. "Do you have a convenient retiring room window?"

Aurelie grinned and patted her hand. "No, but I imagine we can find an acceptable alternative."

* * *

Noel surveyed the empty parlor with far less disinterest than he was showing. He had been looking forward to a good sparring match with Miss Vivian. Her absence was exceedingly disappointing.

"Sly creatures, women," he commented dryly to Jason.

"Aren't they though?"

"I thought there was something a bit off about the boot thing."

The corner of his friend's mouth twitched. "Well, you did not complain."

"*You* went first." Noel stalked across the room to the satinwood cabinets. "Hell, man, where is the brandy?"

"In my study. Aurelie drinks it otherwise."

Noel suspected his friend was not entirely jesting. "Marvelous woman, your wife. What a shame you met her first."

"I imagine she will be quite flattered you said that."

"I imagine you will not tell her. What if she should decide to abandon you for a better situation?"

Jason, never one to take him seriously, grinned as he replied, "One of my wife's greatest strengths—and greatest blindnesses—is her acceptance of this mere mortal. I do not deserve her."

Noel grunted. He was in no mood to discuss the marvels of the female heart. He was far more interested in different parts altogether. He had thought to begin with Vivian's agile mind and work from there. "Where do you suppose they went?"

"Not far, I suspect" was his friend's laconic response. "Miss Redmond seemed quite content in Aurelie's presence. I believe it was you she meant to avoid."

"Well, thank you for the gentle tidings. I was doing rather well till she went all high-in-the-instep on me. Can't imagine why."

"No? Fancy that."

Noel studied Jason's face carefully. Damn the bounder for having a perfect poker face. He knew from experience that it was far more advantageous to be paired with Tarrant at games than sided against him. "I would ask what you

30

meant by that, but I am afraid I do not want to know." He stalked across the room, stopping when a small pile of books next to the settee caught his eye. "I'll be damned." He plucked a familiar volume from the top. "The minx was reading about herself."

"She was reading Newstead," Jason corrected. "It is only your supposition that she is the subject."

"Mine and a good half of the ton's. Here." He thumbed through the first few pages, seeking a now familiar passage. "Listen to this: 'Could I but see your face in morning's light/ As oft as it appears to me in dreams—/ Celestial eyes of verdant green so bright/ Would my days and lonely eves unite.' " He snapped the book shut. "What say you to that?"

"I say it is rather appallingly bad poetry."

Noel stifled a growl of annoyance. "It is a perfect description of Miss Redmond's eyes."

"Is it? I thought her eyes were blue."

"They are *green*, you dolt! Verdant, vivid, emerald green!"

Now Tarrant had the audacity to look smug. "Perhaps you ought to be the one composing odes to Miss Redmond. Unless, of course, you already are."

This time, Noel did growl and chucked the book at Jason's head. "I do not know why I bother talking to you at all these days. Marriage has rattled your brains."

"Entirely possible. But it allows me to compose bad poetry to my wife's eyes with impunity. Now, did you describe Miss Redmond's orbs as verdant, vivid? Or was it vivid, verdant?"

That did it. "I do not give a bloody damn about Miss Redmond's eyes! They can be orange for all I care. What I wish to examine is the part of her not visible for public inspection. I wonder if her skin is as luminous all over?"

"Now, Hel . . ."

"Tell me, do you think her legs are of the longish variety? It is so dashedly hard to tell through all those petticoats. I should like to know whether they would wrap around a man's flanks with length to spare."

"St. Helier . . ."

"Of course I have a fairly good image of her breasts . . ."

"Enough!" Jason shook his head in wry amusement. "I do not believe you wish to speak of Miss Redmond so. No"—he raised a hand before Noel could respond—"I amend that. I do believe you wish to speak so. I simply think it unwise."

"Unwise?" Noel repeated, wondering if marriage really had rattled his friend's brains. Tarrant had always been a bit stuffy, but never prudish. "I am not married. I may admire any fair form I choose."

"Of course. How silly of me." Jason dropped Mr. Newstead's book onto the table. "Perhaps we should repair to White's. If you ask very nicely, Brummell might give up his seat, granting you the entire window through which to admire any fair form bold enough to stroll down St. James."

"Not a bad idea," Noel muttered. "Not a bad idea at all."

Jason paused in the doorway. "Just a moment. Allow me to leave a note for Aurelie."

Noel shook his head sadly. As much as he liked Aurelie and appreciated the connection she shared with his friend, he could not help but bemoan the loss of Tarrant's unfettered conscience. In fact, he decided as they reached the street some minutes later, he would be damned if he would allow himself to ever be so shackled that every move must be reported. Tarrant might not mind the effort, but Noel found the concept galling. A man's time was his own. If one needed regimentation, one could bloody well join the army.

"Have they gone?"

Aurelie peered from behind the draperies. "Yes. The coast is clear."

It had been a bit stifling, hiding behind the heavy velvet curtains, but it had certainly been illuminating. Vivian had been hard put to stay still when St. Helier commenced his mental perusal of her figure. In fact, she had gone so far as to wonder whether Lord Tarrant would have allowed her to cosh his friends over the head with a fireplace poker, or whether he would have interfered.

"The nerve of the man," she fumed as she shook out her creased skirts, "discussing me as if I were some common doxy!"

Aurelie was busy settling the drapes back into place. "Yes, I am afraid he went too far. I do apologize. You should not have had to hear that." She gave the velvet a last twitch and crossed the room to pick up her husband's note. "Considerate man," she said with a smile.

"Oh?"

"Yes. He tells me he shall be home for supper."

This seemed no more than common courtesy to Vivian, but she refrained from commenting to that affect. "How nice."

"There is also a postscript." Aurelie's eyes sparkled as she looked up. "He tells me I should not hide behind the curtains as dust makes me sneeze."

Vivian wore the cream silk that night. It was, she decided, more flattering than stark white, but still an unfortunate sight. Her first impulse had been to pull the violet gown from the wardrobe, but prudence triumphed. The ball was to be held at the palatial townhouse of the Earl and Countess of Heathfield, not an event to be approached with defiance.

True, she had never met the Heathfields and hence could perhaps justify a bit of brazen spirit. The problem was, quite simply, that the earl and countess were Lord Tarrant's parents and the ball was for his younger sister, Grace. Vivian had met the young lady at the Symington fete and had found her delightful. There had been no mention of the blasted Newstead in their conversation, nor had Grace regarded her with anything more than sincere pleasure at making a new acquaintance.

All in all, Vivian felt she owed it to their family to present herself with a modicum of respect.

"You look like you just stepped out of the schoolroom," Esther said critically as she shoved the last pin into her mistress's hair.

"Perhaps," Vivian replied, surveying the neat knot in the mirror. "But it is better than looking as if I had stepped out of Mr. Newstead's verse."

The maid sniffed. "Doesn't mean you have to rig yourself out like a girl. There's nothing so terrible about what the man wrote, after all."

"You mean at least he stopped just short of calling me a feckless hoyden? The references to Nimuë were more than enough, I should think."

She had arrived home the night of the Symington ball to find Esther fully apprised of the situation. It seemed news traveled more quickly through the ton's staff than through the ton. The maid had even managed to get a copy of the volume somehow. Vivian had not asked. She had firmly refused to so much as look at the thing until the following morning, and only then to skim the beginning. After her time with Lady Tarrant that very afternoon, however, she felt well acquainted with Mr. Newstead.

She still thought the poetry less than Byronic and the whole situation absurd.

"For tonight at least," she announced primly, "I shall be as unvivid as possible."

"I'll believe that when the next book comes out," Esther retorted. She, unlike her mistress, thought the situation rather entertaining. "Your mother would be in raptures to know Lord Byron is writing poems to her daughter."

"My mother would have a fit of apoplexy. She warned me to—oh, how did she phrase it? Try to keep my immoderate passions tightly reined?"

"If I remember correctly, missy, her word was 'excessive,' not 'immoderate.' And this is a different matter."

"Why? I did nothing that last week in Boston to draw undue attention to myself either."

34

Esther slapped her shoulder lightly with the hairbrush. "You attended a costume ball dressed as a soldier!"

"I was being patriotic. Uncle Thomas's old gear fit perfectly."

"You left the house in breeches!"

Vivian shrugged. "Olivia Cabot went as Diana. At least *my* legs were covered."

Esther threw up her hands in resignation. "Don't know why I bother."

"I don't either." Vivian jumped to her feet and planted a kiss on the woman's wrinkled cheek. "I shall give your best to Lord Byron when we waltz."

"You are a hopeless hoyden."

"And you are a silly goose. Don't wait up for me."

Mrs. DeLancey smiled in approval as she reached the landing. "You look lovely, my dear."

"Why, thank you, madam." Vivian dropped into a demure curtsy. "I am not vivid this evening."

Lady Fielding, resplendent in claret satin, gave a short laugh. "You would be vivid in sackcloth, girl." She surveyed Vivian's ensemble with a critical eye. "I daresay you will pass muster, but a few more jewels would not hurt. I shall send Betty upstairs for my tourmalines."

"Thank you, madam, but I think not. The pearls will suffice." The simple choker accentuated the graceful length of her neck but was unquestionably the most modest piece in her collection. "If I might accept your kind offer of the ivory wrap, Mrs. DeLancey, we can depart."

The Heathfield house was, if possible, more crowded than the Symingtons' had been. To Vivian's relief, she made it all the way to the receiving line before the familiar buzzing started. And even then, it was far quieter than before.

"Hello, Miss Redmond," Jason's sister greeted her. "I am so glad you could attend."

Her second brother, Rickey, was standing by her side. "Well, Gracie, your success is now complete. I thank you,

Miss Redmond, for coming. No ball is complete these days without the Vivid One's presence."

He yelped then, and Vivian suspected Grace had pinched him—hard. "I am so sorry," the girl said. "Rickey has the sense of a toad at times."

It would have served no purpose to agree, so Vivian merely gave the pair a serene smile. "It is quite all right. I expect I shall be able to tolerate the misapprehension until the correct identity comes to light."

"But were you not in Cambridge these past weeks?" Rickey asked. This time, his sister limited herself to rolling her eyes. "Oh, I say. Sorry, Miss Redmond. Dashed rude of me. A toad, Grace says. She's quite right . . . perfect toad."

Vivian found it impossible to dislike any of Jason's family. At the moment, however, young Rickey was not among her favorite persons. "I am holding up the line," she offered after a moment. And fled.

Noel had been watching her since her arrival and was by her side before she had taken ten steps. "Good evening, Miss Redmond. You are looking lovely this evening."

She stopped in her tracks and turned to face him. He waited for her to speak, very much looking forward to whatever might spill from her delectable lips. She blinked once, again, took a visible breath, and walked away.

"Giving me the cut, mademoiselle?" She kept walking. "Of course, stupid of me to ask if, in fact, you are doing so. But you see, I am thoroughly resistent to being snubbed. The truth is, I do not believe I recognize the action." He followed her as she beat a path toward Lady Fielding. "Ah, splendid. Your estimable guardian is conversing with Lady Cowper. Fortunate, that. I am certain she will give you permission to waltz. She is ever so much more accommodating than the others. Sally Jersey has been known to slight a girl simply because of her eye color."

The mention of a waltz had slowed Vivian's steps. He matched her pace and continued, "Perhaps you ought to take lessons in the cut direct from dear Sally. She is really quite magnificent at it. The lovely Emily is another matter entirely. She is endlessly gracious." He raised his hand, "Lady Cowper . . ."

His voice was not loud enough to reach the countess, but it was loud enough to bring Vivian to a dead stop beside him. "Stop it!" she hissed.

"Why? I should like to waltz and you need permission."

He studied the charming flush of her cheeks and wondered anew if other parts of her anatomy would pinken so delightfully.

"I have no wish to waltz with you, now or ever. Why will you not leave me alone?"

"Leave you alone? What an unpleasant concept. I like you, Miss Redmond."

Now her eyes were flashing with the deep fire of finest emeralds. "I do not like *you*, Lord St. Helier. You are rude and arrogant, and I would sooner dance with the odious Mr. Newstead himself!"

With that, she took several angry steps backward and nearly upset a gentleman passing behind her. She spun about, horrified to see him stagger slightly before regaining his balance. "Oh, oh, I am so terribly sorry! Did I hurt you?"

"Hurt me, madam? Not at all." His brief smile enhanced an already handsome face. "I am certain one as lovely as you could never do injury to another."

Vivian was too concerned with her clumsiness to respond to the compliment. "You are favoring your leg, sir. I fear I have . . ."

He silenced her with a raised hand. "A longtime affliction. Think nothing of it." Under the shock of dark curls, his vividly blue eyes were sincere—and amused.

"If you are certain, sir . . ."

"I assure you, madam, the encounter was my pleasure."

With that, he bowed briefly over her hand and continued on his way, still limping slightly.

"Oh, hell," Vivian said softly.

"Yes, I would say you have quite done it now."

She turned to find St. Helier not two feet away. "Is not even deliberate cruelty beneath you?"

"Was I being cruel?"

She resisted the urge to kick him in the shins. "I have just caused some poor, kind man to limp, and you make it worse with your callous comment."

His brows rose dramatically. "Poor, kind man?" When she gave no response other than to set her jaw and glare at him, he asked, "Are you such an accomplished actress or are you simply blind?"

Vivian closed her eyes and counted ten before replying, "At the moment, I am embarrassed with myself and furious with you."

"Well, you are lovely in both states. I imagine it will make for fine verse."

"What *are* you talking about?"

In the following seconds, she felt as if his strange, silver eyes were boring into her very soul. "All right, my dear, I will play along for the time being. The man you just very nearly sent flying onto his impeccably attired rump? That was Lord Byron."

4

"**I** SHOULD HAVE worn the violet."

Noel did not think he could possibly have heard her aright. "I beg your pardon?"

He noticed her face was the same color as her gown and took a step toward her. He did not expect the vivid Miss Redmond to be a fainter, but it was not a chance he wanted to take. She did not seem to notice when he took her arm, but merely stared off somewhere past his shoulder.

"It would not have mattered after all. And I went to all this trouble to be inconspicuous."

As if she could possibly be inconspicuous. Her very presence raised the level of energy in the room. At the moment, however, she seemed utterly drained of her vitality. "Miss Redmond?"

"Hmm?"

"Could I perhaps fetch you something to drink? Lemonade?" *Scotch? Brandy?*

"I . . . no. No, thank you. Maybe a bit of air . . ."

Now he was not about to pass up either the suggestion or the sudden acquiescence. The Heathfield house had a marvelous, shadowed terrace. The gardens were even better. He tightened his grip on her arm and steered her toward the French doors. She went with him, docile as a lamb.

And stopped suddenly, mere feet from the doors.

He tugged lightly. She resisted. Her eyes, he noticed with foreboding, were no longer vague. They were narrowed, and sharp as green glass.

"I must be mad," she announced clearly. It was all Noel

could do to keep from howling his frustration. "Witless, rattle-pated . . . *stupid*!"

"Really, Miss Redmond," he said quickly, taking a last stab at getting her delectable little form outside, "it is perfectly acceptable for two friends to take the air. Very common, actually . . ."

"What *are* you babbling about, St. Helier?"

"You requested a breath of air. I am merely offering my escort." Yes, cool logic might work. "You cannot very well go outside on your own."

The single, flat laugh would have shredded the ego of a lesser man. "You must stop taking yourself so seriously, my lord. And you really ought to consider taking me more so." She shook off his hand. "Now, if you would excuse me . . ."

She executed a lissome turn and Noel was momentarily distracted by the sight of her skirts swirling around her legs. How far below the high waist of her gown would he have to go to reach her hips? A handspan? Less?

By the time he regained his senses, she was a good twenty feet away. He nearly had to sprint to catch up with her, no mean feat considering the crush. In fact, had the crowd not parted as she went, he would not have caught her at all.

"Miss Redmond, wait!" She kept going. "Vivian, damn it . . . Pardon me." He shoved past the elderly Duke of Marlborough. "My apologies, your Grace. Vivian . . ." He caught up with her at last and grasped her elbow. "Are you always so contrary?"

She did stop walking and fixed him with a cool gaze. "Are you always so irksome?"

He resisted the urge to shake her—then the urge to haul her into his arms and kiss her senseless. "Where are you going? You are in no condition to do anything rash."

"I am perfectly fine, my lord. And I have no intention of doing anything rash."

"Well, I am prodigiously glad to hear it." He waited for her to answer his first question. To his surprise, she did.

"I am going in search of Lord Byron, of course."

"What?"

"I am going in search—"

"Yes, yes, I heard you. Why, for God's sake?"

Her expression was now of the variety one might give a slow child—patient and slightly pitying. "I should think it would be rather obvious."

Noel thrust both hands into his hair and pulled. "Humor me, if you please."

Now Vivian wanted nothing less than to humor him. She had already given him far too much amusement as it was. "Humor yourself, St. Helier," she said tartly. "I do not wish to play."

One advantage, she found, to being less than six feet tall, was the greater ease in moving through tight spots. It took a bit of twisting and dodging, but by the time she paused and turned, the earl was nowhere to be seen. She smiled as she congratulated herself on nimble feet and agile mind.

"Vivian, dearest, I do not mean to question your wisdom"—she spun about to find Mrs. DeLancey standing in front of her—"but speaking with Byron has done nothing to help your cause."

"No," Vivian replied with a resigned sigh. "I suppose it has not. It was not intentional, though."

"On your part, perhaps. I suspect little happens accidentally to Byron." The older woman patted her cheek affectionately. "Come now, I would like to present you to Lady Cowper."

"Not now, madam, if you do not mind. I need to speak with Lord Byron."

The lady's blue eyes widened almost comically above her rosy cheeks. "I beg your pardon?"

Vivian wondered if she were perhaps slurring her words that evening. "I am on my way to speak to—"

"Yes, I heard you, dear. I simply thought I had not heard correctly. What on earth would possess you to do such a thing?"

Now she wondered why such an obvious concept seemed

clear only to herself. "I will obtain a public announcement from him, of course. No one is willing to believe what I say. Should *he* explain that he is not Mr. Newstead, however, and that I am not the Vivid One, the *ton* would have no choice but to listen."

"What makes you believe he will do anything of the kind?"

"Why would he not? He seemed an entirely reasonable sort. He was far more concerned with my own distress than with his."

"You discussed the poems?" the older woman asked, shocked anew.

"Of course we did not. I did not realize to whom I was speaking at the time."

"It might be best if you explained, dearest. I am afraid you have quite lost me. What was . . . er, distressing him?"

Vivian was loathe to replay the entire dismal scene, so she chose the briefest possible explanation. "Well, I trod upon him. Did you not see?"

Mrs. DeLancey shook her head. "I saw none of the exchange. Lady Walthering informed me of it. She was, I fear, a bit vague with the details."

"Who is Lady Walthering?"

"Merely an acquaintance. Of course, she did not see the event either. I believe she heard it from Mrs. Clarke. Or was it Lydia Burnham? I believe it was Miss Burnham who said Byron appeared quite beside himself in your presence. I could be mistaken. By the time the news reached me, it had come through countless mouths."

"Oh, bother." Vivian's shoulders slumped.

Mrs. DeLancey had, after all, been standing no more than twenty feet from the entire scene.

"Yes, well, what's done is done. Now, dear Emily is waiting, and one should never make a patroness wait."

"But I must speak to—"

"You must *not* speak to Byron," the lady interrupted with uncustomary sharpness. "It is all well and good for the man to be composing verse to you; the poems have been of unrequited admiration to date. But should it be suspected that you are encouraging his attention, you will have tongues flapping anew."

Vivian started at her, appalled. "*Encouraging?* Madam, I have met the man but once, this eve, and no introductions were made. How could that possibly be construed as encouragement?"

Mrs. DeLancey got a firm grip on her elbow and began determinedly steering her through the crowd, all the while beaming like an aged cherub at the people around them. "Do not be a goose, dearest. Everyone believes you met the man in Cambridge."

"But—"

"Oh, Vivian, do hush! Now smile. Here we are!" She pulled Vivian to a stop in front of a young, sweet-faced woman. "My lady, may I present my ward, Miss Vivian Redmond of Boston. Vivian, Lady Cowper."

"Ah, the Vivid One!" the lady announced gaily, and Vivian winced. "Oh, dear. I see I have offended you, Miss Redmond."

"Not at all, my lady." Vivian forced a weak smile, understanding the importance of receiving the nod from a patroness of Almack's. "I simply do not wish you to be under a misconception."

"A misconception?" Lady Cowper gave an impish smile. "Now that would be unfortunate, would it not?" True to St. Helier's description, she appeared entirely genial. "You do not believe yourself to be Newstead's Muse? Or you do not believe yourself to be vivid?"

"I do not believe I am anyone's Muse, madam."

"But you do find yourself vivid?"

"I . . . er, no . . . well . . ." Vivian felt herself floundering. *Curse the Brits for their ridiculous rules and requirements!* It was hellishly difficult not to offend when one was being roasted, albeit charmingly. She took a deep breath and a bigger risk. "Perhaps if the verse were less precious, I would be more inclined to take credit."

There was a moment of weighty silence. Then, eyes

43

sparkling, Lady Cowper laughed aloud. "Brava, Miss Redmond! Newstead's Vivid One or no, you well deserve the title. I shall look forward to your presence at the Assembly Rooms."

When she had gone, Vivian turned to Mrs. DeLancey, who looked as if she would like to leap into the air and click her heels together. It was a diverting image, to be sure. "Well, madam?"

"Well, my dear, you were splendid. I suppose you could have worn the purple after all."

The stream of callers the next afternoon completely surpassed all previous days. Stevens, the widows' butler, informed her that the crowd outside the house quite blocked the street. The young visitors were, without a doubt, a lively and silly bunch. The ladies arrived with invitations to tea and ill-disguised envy, the men with flowers and undisguised admiration.

Vivian took it all with good grace—until one young woman arrived with a book. Newstead's cantos. She all but thrust the thing under Vivian's nose as she took her seat. "I would be ever so pleased if you would inscribe it for me, Miss Redmond."

Vivian recognized her as the Miss of the Icy Stare from the Symington ball and tried desperately to remember her name—if, in fact, she had ever known it. She gently pushed the book away from her face. "Would it not be more appropriate to ask Mr. Newstead for the inscription, Miss . . . ?"

"Oh, perhaps I shall do so another time. Fancy that, having both the author and subject blessing my little volume."

There was something pettish and calculating about the lady, and Vivian thought momentarily about blessing her with the water from one of the countless vases of flowers. "I am certain it would be. All the more reason for me to demur, Miss . . ."

"Do not tell me you are being coy on the matter. It hardly seems necessary at this point. Why, after your encounter with Lord Byron last night . . ."

"Lord Byron," Vivian interrupted as pleasantly as she could, "was merely being kind enough to excuse my elbow in his chest."

The other woman pursed her thin lips in an eloquent expression of concern. "Oh, dear. Did he say something untoward that provoked you to such measures?"

Vivian tried not to grind her molars into dust. Everyone crowded into the widows' parlor was now listening with rapt attention. "He said nothing at all. He merely had the misfortune to be behind me when I stepped backward."

This very simple, very uninteresting pronouncement brought a hushed buzzing to the group. "Really?" Miss Whomever queried, looking rather like a startled rodent with her pursed lips and round eyes. "Standing behind you? How fascinating." The others present seemed to agree, if more murmurs were any indication. "Was he perhaps observing your conversation with someone else?"

The possibility had not occurred to Vivian, and she did her best to dismiss it out of hand. He had been walking by, had he not? To be perfectly honest, she could not say.

"If memory serves, there was nothing particularly interesting to be observed," she said calmly. "In fact, I confess I cannot recall the conversation myself."

"Ah, you wound me, Miss Redmond."

Her eyes slewed to the doorway. Never could she have imagined being so pleased to see Lord St. Helier. He was lounging against the jamb, blocking the way of the diminutive Stevens, who was bobbing up and down behind his shoulder, clearly trying to announce his arrival. He was dressed casually, almost carelessly, only the faint sheen of the cream silk waistcoat and impeccable cut of the russet coat belying his wealth. As always, one errant lock of overlong hair arced over the angled brows, giving him a decidedly roguish air.

To her eyes, he appeared an angel of salvation.

"How kind of you to arrive so promptly, my lord." She darted a quick look at the clock. Twenty past three. An odd time to have set for an engagement, but no one seemed to

45

notice. "Though I am afraid it would be unforgivably rude of me to abandon my guests for our ride." She hoped he had, in fact, arrived on horseback. "I have been so entertained that I have not had time to prepare."

There was no mistaking the message in the verdant eyes. Miss Redmond was a damsel very much in need of rescuing. For the briefest of moments, Noel debated playing ignorant. Her response would no doubt be vastly entertaining, but he abandoned the notion quickly. A ride she was requesting; a ride she would have.

He bowed to the room, noting as he did that Lydia Burnham was glancing peevishly between Vivian and himself, all the while patting discreetly at her hair. "I am sure everyone will understand if you were to excuse yourself, my dear. I have, after all, been awaiting our engagement with all eagerness."

One sweep with his narrowed eyes sent the men scurrying to their feet. An equally potent smile at the ladies had the same effect. It was marvelous, he mused with no small amount of irony, what an earldom and an obscene amount of money could do for a man's influence.

The fawning boys queued up promptly to say their goodbyes. Young Meriton, bolder than the rest due, Noel speculated, to the assurance of his own earldom someday, bowed longer than necessary over Vivian's hand. "Perhaps we shall meet in the Park, Miss Redmond."

Her eyes swung once again to Noel, but he was not going to help her there. He was far too busy wondering whether he could grasp enough of the man's impossibly intricate cravat to strangle him with it.

"It is a very large park, my lord," she offered at last, not without a nearly imperceptible flash of raillery.

Meriton nodded as if she had graced him with the keys to the kingdom. "And again at the Vaers' this eve?"

Vivian nodded and Meriton stepped away. Into his place went one pup after another, each wearing a twistable cravat, and each nearly stumbling over himself in his eagerness to

46

be clever. The ladies were far quicker and far less effusive in their farewells.

Lydia, ever the contrary jade, rose leisurely from the settee and waved a now-eminently recognizable book in Vivian's face. "Are you certain I cannot persuade you to sign this, Miss Redmond? I daresay Lord Byron will be all the more willing to add his name if 'tis below yours."

Violence against women was not among Noel's repertoire, but he allowed himself the brief mental image of his boot connecting with the woman's bony posterior. From the look in Vivian's eyes, he surmised she was having similar thoughts. She remained coolly gracious, though, pushing the book away with less than appropriate force.

"I am very flattered. And, should we discover it is you of whom Newstead writes, I shall be the first in line for an inscription."

Noel wanted very much to laugh at Lydia's flushed face. He contained himself and sent the last of the boys off with a jerk of his head. "Perhaps you ought to go get ready, Miss Redmond. We do not want to be caught in the crush."

"Of course." She rose gracefully to her feet. "If you would excuse me, Miss . . ." When Lydia gave no response, she shrugged and headed for the door.

He caught her in the hall. "If memory serves me right, there are no horses here suitable for riding." Her guilty flush told him all he needed to know. "I will see to it. Do not think to evade me, Vivian. Go upstairs, put on something appropriate, and be back in fifteen minutes. If you do not, I will come after you and carry you out over my shoulder."

She opened her mouth to deliver what would undoubtably be a stinging setdown. However, she seemed to think better of it, and hurried up the stairs. He took a moment to enjoy watching her ascent, then turned toward the door. Lydia, looking more than a bit peeved, flounced out of the parlor.

"Leaving so soon?" he quipped.

"Stooping so low?" she shot back.

"And what, if I may ask, does that mean?"

She gave him a deceptively sweet smile. "Really, St. Helier, I would not have thought you the sort to chase after another man's leavings—especially not Byron's."

This time, he very nearly seized the absurd little reticule and stuffed it into the smug mouth. Instead, he returned her smile with a cool one of his own. "It is fortunate we are old acquaintances, Lydia, or I might be tempted to call you a shrew."

Her lips drew into a tight line. "You can be such a boor, St. Helier."

"Was that boor or bore? I rather like the former. The latter, however . . ." He grinned as she pushed past him. "A good day to you, Miss Burnham."

He was out the door himself some minutes later, speaking to the boy holding his horse. Coins changed hands and the lad set off at a run toward Berkeley Square. Noel handed his mount over to one of the widows' grooms and, whistling, returned to the house. He half hoped Vivian would defy him. It would undoubtably cause her hostesses immediate heart failure, but he liked the idea of pounding up the stairs to fetch her from her chamber.

Vivian expected him to come through the door at any second. She did not doubt for a moment that he would do it. "Please, Esther, you must hurry. He will not wait long."

The maid ignored her as usual, calmly putting the finishing touches on the elaborate ensemble. "We can't have you going out without a hat."

"Oh, blast the hat! I will surely lose it anyway."

"Not if you value your hide, you won't! 'Tis a work of art I've created, and I'll not have you ruining it with a wild gallop."

Vivian had to admit Esther had indeed done a marvelous job. Her hair was sleeked into an elegant coil at the nape of her neck, the jaunty little cap perched so its ostrich plume swept artfully down to curve near her cheek. "Somehow I do not think it was quite what Michelangelo envisioned as art," she said tartly, leaping up to avoid being

48

swatted with the hairbrush. She grinned at the glowering maid. "Ah, you threaten your sainthood with those thoughts!"

Unable to resist the affectionate teasing, Esther broke into a reluctant smile. "Off with you, then. And try not to fall off. I don't fancy having to get the dust out of that velvet." She gave a last sweep with the brush as Vivian breezed past her.

True to promise, the earl was there, waiting at the foot of the stairs. His curly-brimmed hat dipped rakishly over his brow, and she was once again reminded of a dashing rogue. She was so intent on studying him that she nearly missed the first step and her heels hit the second with an audible thump.

"Well, it is about t—" he began, and cut himself off midword. "Good Lord."

Vivian managed to make the rest of the descent with her feet in the right places and her chin high. "You do not like blue, my lord?"

It seemed an inordinately long time before he replied, "You are blinding, my dear."

She knew he was not referring to her beauty. True, the peacock blue riding habit was a bit on the bright side, but the modiste had assured her it was all the rage. Besides, she *liked* bright colors.

His gaze narrowed slightly as he surveyed her from head to foot. She knew she ought to be insulted by his slow perusal. Instead, she found herself inexplicably hurt by the feeling he was wincing at the sight. "You told me to change, my lord. I will not be sent upstairs to do so again."

"I would not ask." *God,* he thought as she took his proffered arm, *she is glorious!* Hyde Park suddenly seemed a very poor idea, indeed. They were bound to be swamped by her admirers within minutes, and he wanted her to himself. He sighed. "Shall we go then?"

As commanded, a second horse had been retrieved from his own stables and stood next to his gelding. "Vivian, may I present Guinevere."

She had been surveying the mare with obvious pleasure. Now her head snapped around to face him again. "That was cruel, my lord!"

"It was true." To prove the point, he softly repeated the name. The mare's ears pricked up and she shook her silky mane. "I am afraid even my stables are not without limit, my dear. Not knowing your skill in the saddle, I chose the only mount of whom I had no reservations. You may blame her name on the previous owner."

For a moment, he thought Vivian was going to spin on her heel and leave him in the street. Then she straightened her shoulders and approached the mare. "She is lovely," she said, running her hand over the glossy black nose. Ever the kitten, Guinevere all but purred in pleasure and sidled closer. "Yes, my love, you are a beauty. Let us just hope I do not have to speak your name in public." The mare bobbed her head appropriately.

Vivian allowed Noel to help her into the saddle. He stepped back as she arranged her skirts to savor the picture. Her hair was the same midnight color of her mount's sleek coat, and, with the striking blue of her habit and fairness of her skin, Miss Vivian made an entrancing portrait indeed.

"I trust, my lord," she said as he swung up into his own saddle, "your horse is named neither Arthur nor Lancelot."

He grinned as he patted the gelding's neck. "Not even close. This is Jason."

She blinked. Twice. "Jason? After the Greek hero?"

"Jason. After the man who saved my life on the Peninsula. You had the right thought the first time."

"You mean to tell me you named your *horse* after Lord Tarrant?"

"Certainly. As I said, he dragged me from the fray when I had been hit. It seemed an appropriate gesture. I am very fond of my horses."

She tilted her head and gave a wry smile. "Is it not customary to name one's firstborn after a personal hero?"

"Perhaps." He shrugged. "But as there was no way of

knowing when that firstborn would arrive and as my gratitude was excessive, I chose the easiest option."

He clicked Jason into a brisk walk, and Guinevere followed. He expected Vivian to continue roasting him on the
matter of names. She did not.

"You were wounded, my lord?"

"It was but a scratch," he replied, "but the impact
knocked me from my horse. I would surely have been
trampled had not Tarrant risked his own life to get me out."

The truth was slightly more dramatic, but unimportant.
He had his life and his horse. Jason had his life—and a
wife.

They rode in silence for a time. Then he offered, "I am
sorry Lydia was such a jade. Her redeeming qualities tend
to hide themselves for the duration of the Season."

"Lydia?"

"Lydia Burnham. The shrew with the book."

Vivian had to laugh. She could not have described the
lady more aptly. She sobered quickly enough, though. So
that was Lydia Burnham, the one who had passed on the
gem about Byron's attentions the night before. "Does she
dislike everyone, or have I been singled out for her antipathy?"

St. Helier chuckled. "Lydia does not particularly like
other women, especially not those who possess the wit and
beauty she lacks."

"Hmm." Vivian chose to let the compliment pass. "She
clearly likes you well enough."

"She likes what I am, not who."

"Honestly, my lord—I daresay she is half in love with
you, perhaps more."

This time, his laugh was humorless. "Lydia," he informed her, "is angling after a title. Mine seems to be the
target for this week. Last month was Lord Darrowby. She
even set her cap for Jason some years back, though he was
supposed to have an arrangement of sorts with Eleanor
Symington."

"Truly? Mrs. Symington and her husband seem so happy together. As do Lord and Lady Tarrant."

"Yes, well, hearts do not often follow expectation." He turned in the saddle. "Have you lost your heart to some young fop yet, Vivian? Newstead appears to have lost his to you."

"Rubbish," she retorted. "All of that nonsense shall be refuted soon enough."

Her emphatic nod sent the ostrich plume curving across her face. She reached up to push it away but St. Helier was quicker. He deftly swept it to the side, letting his hand brush across her cheek in the process. Startled, she jerked away from his touch.

He grinned at her. "How glad I am to hear that. I would hate to have competition for your attention."

Annoyed yet again by his presumption, Vivian snapped, "You are competing, sir, with my disfavor. It is a mighty foe indeed."

He was not cowed. "Only disfavor? Ah, you give me hope. If it were repugnance I might be concerned. Disfavor is a fleeting thing."

"I think not in this case," she replied primly. "I thank you for coming to my aid this afternoon, my lord, but I trust you will not view my presence here as encouragement. I simply did not wish to have a scene in the midst of my hostesses' home."

"You think I would have made a scene?"

"You threatened to come after me and carry me out of the house!"

"Only if you tried to renege, my dear. It would not have been me making the scene, but you."

She counted ten. They were entering the Park now, and the presence of a healthy percentage of the ton spared her the effort of shouting at him.

"You did not answer my earlier question, Vivian. Is there some carbuncle-faced fellow pining away for you in Boston?"

"Yes, my lord, as a matter of fact, there is." The words

were out before she could consider them. Apparently chicanery was to be the order of the day. Well, the first deceit had gone nicely enough. "He is hardly carbuncle-faced. He is quite handsome, endlessly charming and gallant, and I shall be prodigiously happy to return to him at the end of the Season."

There, that ought to take some of the wind from his sails.

"A fortunate man, to be sure. Tell me, what is this paragon of malehood's name?"

"Name?" *Oh, dear. Name.* "It is Daniel."

"Daniel. Apt, I would say, my dear. Sparring with you does tend to leave a man feeling as if he had faced a den of lions." He appeared not to notice her scowl. "So, what is . . . Daniel doing in your absence? Composing tercets to your toes? Gazing moodily across the Atlantic, crying your name to the wind?"

"I imagine he is occupying himself with far more useful projects, my lord. We have an understanding, you see. We are to be apart only for these few months—then never again."

"How sweet." St. Helier led the way onto the wide promenade. "But you do have these few months, after all. Do you not think it might be wise to experience a bit of life? Never again is such a very long time." He reached out to snare Guinevere's reins, drawing the little horse to a stop. "I would be glad to offer my services as . . . guide, mademoiselle. You might find that you return to your Daniel a different woman." He flashed his feline grin. "If, of course, you return at all."

There was nothing she could do short of climbing down and walking home, so she fixed him with a cool gaze. "I would sooner attach myself to a crocodile, my lord."

His grin widened perceptibly to show yet more teeth. "Come now, Vivian. I can be charming on occasion, gallant even. In truth, I am not such a bad fellow."

Some annoying little voice in the back of her mind reminded her that he was, in fact, exceedingly diverting company. Her eyes certainly fixed themselves often enough on his face and form.

Her mind, however, was not to be swayed.

"I am certain you are right in saying so, my lord. Why, when compared to the devil, I'm sure you are not a bad fellow at all."

His muttered response was lost in the arrival of Lord Meriton and his band of earnest dandies.

5

VIVIAN WAS AMAZED by the speed with which the following weeks passed. Balls, soirees, evenings at the theater—all whirled by in a blur of pleasant, if not exciting, activity. At each event, she scanned the crowds for Lord Byron. She thought she spotted him once at a ball, lounging nearby in the shadows of several potted trees, but when she looked again, he was gone.

Heart's Notions was still the literary talk of the town, and no less than twenty people had requested her inscription in their copies. She was fast running out of polite reasons to demur. Discouraged by her hostesses from making even the most discreet of inquiries, she was left with little more to do than dodge waving pages, wait, and squint at every distant male figure.

One male figure was never distant enough. Lord St. Helier appeared at her side with vexing regularity and impressive determination. Vivian soon grew weary of having to deflect his sly wit and invitations to dance continuously, but she could not repress a twinge of admiration at his blithe demeanor. He never seemed to take her rejections personally, merely gave her that blasted grin and waited for the next opportunity to provoke her anew. Damned if the man did not appear to be enjoying himself each time she invoked a previous engagement or her darling American beau.

"So, any word from David?" he queried lightly one evening, having finally chased her into a corner of the Covington ballroom.

Had she not been wearing a new pair of slippers that pinched her toes, she might have kept leading him around and around the perimeter of the room for the rest of the night. As it was, she needed a rest.

"Not recently," she replied with a longing gaze at an empty chair. "*Daniel* is, of course, busy with his own life."

"Of course. I would think, however, that he would be careful to keep his existence foremost on your mind."

"What makes you think it is not?"

St. Helier raised one dark brow. "You seemed rather entranced with young Meriton during the last set. Could it be that you are willing to exchange your American swain for a future British earl?"

She had, in fact, enjoyed her minuet with Lord Meriton. He was charming, gallant, and quite handsome. He also seemed capable of speaking to her without mentioning the weather, Beau Brummell, or Newstead's cantos. The truth of the matter was that she was basing her fictional beau rather too closely on the young viscount.

The deception had become a bit of a godsend, actually. While none of the men who spilled lemonade on her skirts or trod upon her toes seemed overly concerned with the existence of a distant competitor, it was very handy to invoke his name when attentions became too obvious.

The problem was that she could never seem to remember the name when it was most important. Lord Meriton's first name, she believed, was Damien. Very easy to confuse with Daniel.

"Tell me, my lord," she asked St. Helier, dodging his query, "why you insist on calling Lord Meriton 'young'? He is not so very much younger than yourself."

"In years, perhaps not. I assure you, though, that I have made far better use of the five or so that separate us."

"Oh, and how is that? If memory serves me, he has traveled extensively and expanded the family fortune considerably in his twenty-six years." It was true Meriton did not speak of Newstead and Brummell; he spoke most often of himself. "He has known scholars, writers, and rulers."

56

"A most accomplished man, to be sure," St. Helier agreed. "I have a distinct advantage over him in my intimate acquaintances, however."

"Yes?"

"Oh, yes. A good deal more have been women."

Noel watched as she absorbed his words and tone. The delightful flush that spread over her skin was a perfect complement to her forest-green gown. He found himself thinking of tea roses.

"Is your absent amour a favorite of the ladies, Vivian?"

"Of course not!" she shot back. "David . . . er, Daniel is endlessly devoted to me."

"Nothing is endless, my dear. The best we can hope for is long, deep, and fulfilling."

It had become something of a game, baiting Vivian with words she refused to acknowledge understanding. It was certainly far more pleasant than the constant effort of making sure she did not spy Byron at those events they attended. The man had an annoying habit of showing up at various events, with no warning and for only the briefest periods of time. Noel had all but resorted to juggling champagne glasses several nights earlier when the poet had materialized in the leafy jungle that was Mrs. Monroe's ballroom.

He had handled the matter by looming over an annoyed Vivian, thus impeding her view. The action had given him a rather decent view down the front of her bodice. He had been so enthralled by the gentle swell visible there that he had not been able to stop her from ducking around him. Fortunately, Byron had skulked elsewhere by that point.

Now, surveying the exposed skin above her deplorably modest bodice, he decided he ought to write himself a list of clever innuendos. The quick-rising blush was a pleasure to behold.

". . . teach me, my lord."

His head snapped up. "I beg your pardon?"

"I said"—she studied his avid expression with satisfaction—"I believe there is something you could teach me."

"It would be my pleasure."

This time, his grin did not set her teeth on edge. To the contrary, she was delighted. *Really, it is too easy.*

"Well, I am not certain you will be able."

"Ah, why don't you try me and see?"

She deliberately fluttered her eyelashes. "All right. I was hoping you could teach me the fine art of disappearance."

"What?"

"I think it might be most simple after all. You disappear, and I will endeavor to learn from your example."

There was a moment of silence. Then: "Insolent minx."

"Pompous lout," she shot back.

To her surprise, he threw back his head and laughed. "One of these days, Vivian, I will show you the proper use for that mouth of yours."

"I sincerely hope you have not wagered on the almanac this year, my lord."

"Why is that?"

"Because there will be snow in hell on that day."

He threw up his hands in mock defeat. "I concede, mademoiselle. A wise man knows when he has been temporarily bested." With a truly stunning grin, he offered his arm. "Will you allow the poor vanquished one to offer the spoils of victory?"

She eyed him warily. "And what might those be?"

"I thought to suggest . . . lemonade?"

They walked in nearly amiable silence toward the refreshment tables. Meriton appeared before they reached their goal, however, a puce-clad Lydia Burnham attached to his arm.

"Oh, dear." Vivian sighed.

"Bugger" was St. Helier's more succinct comment.

"Ah, returning from a dance, Miss Redmond?" Meriton asked, flashing his best future-earl's smile.

"Well, actually . . ."

"Splendid, splendid." He turned to Noel. "I have a

thought, old man. Shall we exchange our delightful partners?"

Noel was fully prepared to announce that no, they damn well would not. He was forestalled by the sudden presence of Lydia insinuating herself between Vivian and him. He glanced back at the viscount, certain that the woman had just been attached to his side. Either she moved amazingly quickly, or she had a twin. To be honest, he found the former alternative a good deal less frightening.

Meriton moved with similar speed, capturing Vivian's arm. Noel watched her face and was arrogantly pleased to note no pleasure there. "I was hoping for a respite from dancing, my lord," she said to her new escort.

"Of course. We have, after all, been seen together on the floor once already this evening. It would not do at all for us to use up our two dances so early." He did not wait for her response, but steered her efficiently toward the waiting refreshments.

At the same time, Lydia was urging Noel toward the dance floor. He had the strong urge to leave her there and plod after the other two, but decided it was not worth the bother. He did not relish the idea of a dance with this creature, but neither did he wish to appear a besotted fool in front of Meriton. He was not, after all, besotted in the least. All he wanted was a bit of fun with the girl before she sailed off across the Atlantic again.

"I wonder what Meriton's parents would say," Lydia said archly as he guided her into the Ecossaise.

"On what subject? The earl is a naturally garrulous fellow."

"Why, on their son's attachment to an American, of course."

Noel forced his face to remain impassive. "I would hardly call Meriton's relationship with Miss Redmond an attachment."

"Perhaps not yet." Lydia executed a dramatic dip which, Noel assumed, was meant to guide a gentleman's eyes to her less-than-eye-catching décolletage. "But I do believe he is considering the matter. I believe he would even be willing to overlook her connection with Byron. Money, after all, is an effective incentive to banish the past."

"What rot. Vivian has done nothing of which she needs to be ashamed, and Meriton certainly does not need her fortune." He stared over her head as she dipped again. "Really, Lydia, if you are going to be catty, you might take the trouble to do so with sagacity."

She fixed him with guileless blue eyes. "I thought you better informed. The Paiseley fortune is vastly reduced these days. It would suit the earl very well were his son to marry money."

There was a ring of truth to her words, and Noel wondered if he had, in fact, heard something to the effect that the Earl of Paiseley was in dun territory. Vivian seemed to think young Meriton had done something impressive with the family fortunes. In retrospect, it seemed decidedly odd for the man to have mentioned anything of the sort to her.

Had Meriton entered the vast ranks of fortune hunters? A man seeking an heiress was not uncommon. Snaring a wealthy wife was even considered somewhat of an art form among the ton bucks. White's betting book was ever filled with wagers on whether the Lord Qs would marry the Miss Zs for their money.

God help Meriton should Vivian's name ever appear in such a context. Noel had been involved in no wagers of late. He decided then that he had better have a look at the ledger. Soon.

"You are missing your steps, St. Helier."

He glanced down to see Lydia smiling up at him, very cattily indeed. "My apologies, madam," he drawled. "I fear my heart is not in the dance."

He had the satisfaction of seeing her eyes narrow in pique. Well, it served her right for being a sharp-tongued shrew. He wondered where she had gotten the idea that she could bait him so and not receive the cutting edge of his own tongue. It was certainly not the recommended behavior for one in search of a husband.

"I vow you are smitten," she remarked soon enough, and Noel had to commend her resilience even as he wanted to tie her jaw shut. "How quaint. Shall we all be graced with the sight of watching you and Meriton vie for her fair hand?"

Of the thoughts that slipped into his mind, *Shut up, Lydia,* was among the mildest. He counted ten, deliberately missing several steps as he did so. At last he replied, "Yes, Miss Redmond is indeed a Diamond in a sea of quartz, is she not? I must admit to seldom having encountered a lovelier pair of eyes or finer wit. Should I decide to seek out an acceptable countess, I shall certainly place her on the list of few."

Lydia was thankfully silent through the remainder of the dance. Noel, not ordinarily one for deliberate cruelty, still could not resist a rather low parting play. He delivered her back to the sidelines with all the decorum required. He even bowed politely. Then he spun quickly on his heel, presented Miss Lydia Burnham with his back, and walked away.

Vivian saw the action and quashed the instantaneous flash of pleasure. She did not, after all, care in the least with whom the earl consorted. In fact, the more time he spent with other women, the less time he would spend bedeviling her.

"Do you not agree, Miss Redmond?"

She turned her attention back to Meriton and suppressed a sigh. She had no idea what he had just said, but fully expected an affirmative was expected. "To be sure, my lord."

He nodded decisively. "Yes, I thought you would. Any native-born American with a shred of probity would feel the same way. What a shame there seems to be so little sense among your countrymen."

Deciding that perhaps she ought to find out just what she had agreed to, Vivian tilted her head and gave her best vacuous smile. "I should be very interested in hearing more of her opinions on the matter."

"Ah, I am flattered. I feared initially that my frank speech might offend, but you are, of course, a young lady of exceptional amiability." He paused to tug at the lapels of his primrose superfine coat. "My belief is quite simply that, without English rule, the Colonies will soon fall into economic despair. A fledgling nation must have trade connections, after all. It seems entirely reasonable to place a British governor in Boston. Smooth the way to better relations, so to speak."

"Why, of all the ridic—" Vivian bit her tongue and struggled to temper her words. "It is an interesting premise, sir. I feel compelled to remind you, however, that my father has been reasonably successful in recent years at effecting trade with several European nations, England among them."

"Yes, well, there will certainly be excep—"

"Furthermore," she continued, "the governing bodies have proven themselves quite talented in diplomatic measures. You must remember that Benjamin Franklin was a revered emissarial presence throughout Europe. Add to that the fact that the . . . er, Colonies are now in possession of a great deal more viable land and resources than the whole of the British Isles and I believe you have a compelling argument for continued and successful self-rule."

For the first time in memory, Meriton was speechless. Vivian could sense his confusion as to whether he had just been insulted somehow, and very much wanted to set him straight on the matter. He had, during the span of their conversation, made her doubt her earlier assertion that he was an utterly admirable sort of fellow. Perhaps it was no more than the insidiously dull atmosphere of the soiree infusing its way into his manner, but he had become something of a dead bore.

"Do you not feel a great measure of connection to your own British heritage, Miss Redmond? You *are* here for the Season."

"I am here," she said pertly, "because my mother, out of

great connection to her British heritage, decided I am in need of polish. Do you think me in need of polish, my lord? It makes one feel rather like an inferior gem." She did not wait for his response. "Besides, I am convinced I bear far more resemblance to my father's ancestors. They were all patriotic Irish. Up the rebels!" she finished with a radiant smile.

"Up the rebels, indeed!"

She turned, once again inexplicably glad to see her habitual tormentor. "I should think you would not gain friends among Parliament should you be heard saying that, Lord St. Helier."

He shrugged. "As my dear Uncle Fergus often said, 'Better one crony in Killarney than a score of mates in London.' " He nodded politely to Meriton. "Now, if you will excuse me, old man, I must deprive you of Miss Redmond's delightful company."

Even as she resented his high-handed behavior, Vivian accepted his arm. She did not object as he led her away from the crush toward the row of French doors. She was far too curious.

"Do you really have an Uncle Fergus from Killarney?"

His rich chuckle rippled down his arm to reach her own fingers. "I have, to my knowledge, one uncle—my mother's brother. His name is Baldric and he is the Duke of Sudminster. Much to my regret at the moment, I've not a drop of Irish blood in my veins."

Vivian digested this information, wondering if she ought to be miffed. Instead, she found herself laughing. "Baldric? Sudminster?"

He fixed her with a mock-severe gaze. "Those are two old family names you have just insulted, madam. I hesitate to tell you my mother's name, lest you force me to demand satisfaction."

Curiosity won out. "What is your mother's name?"

"Hibernia."

"Hibernia? But that is the old Latin name for Ireland ... Ah, you are teasing me. Very clever, my lord."

He flashed his devastating grin as they approached the balcony. "Yes, it was, wasn't it?"

"Were Baldric and Sudminster also a jest?"

"Not at all. Uncle Baldy is a rather engaging old coot . . . with a full head of hair, I feel compelled to add."

"And your mother?"

"She is a plain Jane, though she is not truly plain at all. I expect her to arrive from Bath in the next few days. I think the two of you will get along marvelously. She is a very close friend to your hostesses and, I imagine, would have fully rivaled you in her youth for sharpness and vitality."

Vivian decided she would very much like to meet the woman responsible for bringing the arrogant, irritating, and undeniably tantalizing Lord St. Helier into the world. "She must be a woman of amazing fortitude."

"To tolerate me, you mean?" He chuckled. "After my father, I assume I am a breath of tranquility." Her expression must have shown her incredulity, for he explained, "Mad Jack Windram was known by the charmingly incongruent name of St. Hell. He was a complete bounder most of the time . . ."

"But you miss him."

"Yes, I do. As does my mother. These past eight years have been quiet and lonely for her."

He could not express just how much he missed the old goat. Nor did he tell her that the goat had not been all that old at the time of his demise—riding hell-for-leather across the Devon estate on an unbroken stallion. All for a silly wager of ten pounds. But Mad Jack had been like that, and it was an unbreakable reality that both Noel and his mother had accepted.

"I'm sorry."

"Hmm?" He looked down to find Vivian staring at him, compassion glowing in her green eyes.

"I cannot imagine losing my father. I depend on him for so much."

"Does he approve of your devoted swain?"

"Wh . . . ? Oh, yes. He is tremendously fond of David. In fact, David is being trained to take over Papa's business someday."

Noel did his best not to crow aloud. "How agreeable for . . . David." Greatly emboldened by the confirmation of what had been, to date, no more than a suspicion, he steered Vivian efficiently through the doors. "And for your father, knowing his business will stay in the family."

"Oh, yes. I . . . er, *we* will see to things together."

In her obvious enthusiasm, she did not seem to notice as he guided her toward a shadowed corner. "So, you have an interest in commerce, do you?" He should have expected as much from his unconventional little American.

Her pride was evident in her reply. "There is no facet of the business with which I am not familiar. I have been handling all of Papa's correspondence with Canadian furriers for the past two years."

Noel herded her up against the balustrade and leaned in. "Whatever will he do in your absence?"

"Why, with summer approaching, the fur trade is at an ebb . . ." She peered past his shoulder. "You are blocking my view of the ballroom, my lord."

"Trust me—there is nothing there you need to see."

"Perhaps not," she shot back, "but *I* need to be seen."

Instead of answering, he moved even closer. Vivian could feel the faintest whisper of his waistcoat against her breasts. She could feel, too, her heart beating the oddest tattoo against her ribs. "You must stand away, my lord," she said, surprised to hear the breathiness in her voice.

"I have a name, Vivian. Perhaps if you use it, I will respond."

The sound of a giggle reached her ears, followed by rustling silk. She was vaguely aware of someone passing near them to reach the doors, but could not be bothered to look. She could feel the warmth of St. Helier's breath on her cheeks, smell the faint, spicy aroma that stirred her senses whenever he was near. "Noel," she whispered, and waited for him to respond.

When he did, leaning down to cover her lips with his own, she was too startled to stop him. His mouth was firm against hers, yet gentle, and the very wonder of this kept her hands still at her sides. It was not her first kiss, to be sure. More than one young man in Boston had dared a quick peck at her lips.

Not one had managed to hold her still with only the lightest touch, nor had the experiences put strange flutters in her stomach. Noel was doing both.

As if of their own will, her hands crept upward to grasp at his lapels, steadying her and bringing her closer to him at the same time. In answer, his hands circled her waist, lifting her as the warm play of his lips against hers very nearly swept her off her feet.

From a distance she heard the uneven tread of heels across the stone balcony. Some sensible corner of her brain acknowledged that the steps were far closer than they seemed and, with a reluctant burst of strength, she pushed at Noel's chest. She was surprised, and almost disappointed, when he complied, taking a single step backward.

Vivian lifted shaky fingers to her mouth. From the corner of her eye she could see the figure of a man move past them and into the ballroom, and wondered if he and his companion had been embracing too.

"Silly girl," she scolded herself. Of course they had been embracing. That was, after all, what one did on a darkened terrace.

"What did you say?"

She gazed up into Noel's face. Even in the shadows, she could see the arrogant, catlike smile. Something between anger and desperation welled within her. "I am a silly girl," she said bitterly, pushing past him.

"Vivian, wait . . ." He reached for her arm but she shrugged it off.

Gathering her skirts, she all but ran back inside. And came to an undignified halt just inside the doors. Ahead, a vaguely familiar figure vanished into the crowd, flanked now by two young women. Vivian was not watching him, however, but the faces now turned toward her.

Had she been standing on the staircase, she might have thought she was reliving her first night among the ton. As it was, she could only wonder if she had dirt—or the imprint of Noel's lips—on her face. Thinking he could very well be close behind, she lifted her chin and headed through the throng in search of the Tarrants.

The whispering did not bother her. Not, that was, until one fragmented phrase reached her ears.

". . . Vivid One . . . She was out on the balcony with Byron."

6

xxvii

I see your face illumin'd by the stars
As we with solitude could be endowed,
Surrounded, yet alone, paradise ours.
Able then to speak my plight aloud,
Into your ears I whisper heart avowed.
Across the room, you cast a radiant beam
And beckon me, though words are not allowed.
My Vivid One, 'twould be a waking dream,
To be alone with you amidst a crowd.
                    —Newstead's *Heart's Notions*, canto IV

VIVIAN DODGED YET one more encroaching parasol and wondered what could possibly have possessed Aurelie to suggest a shopping expedition on crowded Bond Street. She disliked shopping on the whole, and the crush in the shops and bazaars had the inevitable effect of setting her teeth on edge. At her side, the viscountess's sister-in-law chatted animatedly as she picked through a display of gloves, clearly not in the least discomposed by the excess of people.

"I know you do not wish to speak on the subject, Vivian, but it is no longer a matter of hushed speculation."

"Grace," she replied dryly, "it never *was* a matter of hushed speculation. People have made their opinions well and loudly known since the very first day. The only change has been the obvious conclusion that such opinions need no longer be made discreetly."

Discretion seemed to have all but flown from reach. Not only had St. Helier kissed her, but she had allowed him to do so. Even worse, she had responded. The man was an unmitigated roue, and she heartily wished him in Hades for his arrogance, but the truth of the matter was that his embrace had sparked something dangerous and glorious within her. She had been forced to flee—from his presence and from the feelings he engendered.

As had become distressingly common during her times in his company, she had flown from the proverbial pan into the fire.

Contrary to the instant expectations she had had, standing flushed and frozen in the midst of the Covington ballroom the night before, her supposed foray into the shadows with Byron had brought her not disgrace but a sort of enhanced celebrity. The consensus, as Aurelie had informed her later, was that she was leading the poet on a merry chase.

It had been duly noted that she had walked onto the balcony with St. Helier. No one seemed inclined, however, to condemn her for that breach of propriety, nor to remember that her return had not been *with* Byron but in his wake. For the moment, her behavior somehow distinguished her from the unfortunately vulgar antics of the man's past paramour, Lady Caroline Lamb, who did nothing to make her affections either discreet or difficult to attain.

"Time," Aurelie had said with wry humor, "will tell. If you continue to appear reasonably indifferent to Byron, you shall most likely be lauded. You need only be concerned should your inclinations lean toward either extreme."

"I beg your pardon?"

"It is simple, really. Should you succumb to his charms, you would be labeled fast and cut for promiscuity. Should you take no interest whatsoever in our mesmeric bard, you would be labeled overly righteous and cut for dullness."

Aurelie's words had been spoken with no small amount of blithe irony, but their truth was indisputable. Vivian's opinion of Society was dipping lower with each successive day. Stupidity, intolerance, and hypocrisy seemed the character traits of choice, and she was disgusted.

"Do you not think," she asked her companions now, "people would see the fatuousness of the whole situation? Why, Simon Hartford made an utter cake of himself this afternoon."

Aurelie and Grace had arrived at the widows' townhouse just in time to see the pièce de résistance. The young man had spent the better part of his visit with his nose buried in the cantos, sporadically startling the assembled party with a triumphant crow over some line that made the Vivid One's identity obvious. No one had paid him much attention until the fateful moment when he had sprung to his feet, crying "Thy charréd visage ever doth ignite . . . !"

Not only had the line been "Thy charméd visage ever doth incite," but Simon had also, in his enthusiastic rise, managed to overturn a small table, upsetting a towering vase of gladiolas and sending a torrent of water over the hapless visage of a young lady sitting nearby.

"Well," Grace remarked impishly, "had Elspeth Vaer been ignited, Simon would have been a hero."

Vivian snorted. The entire day thus far had been a trial. Only the appearance of her two friends had kept her from running wild through the parlor, screaming like a banshee and scattering volumes of *Heart's Notions* like a vengeant wind.

"Perhaps you ought to consider penning your memoirs. Add just a bit of Drury Lane satire and the queues would quite equal those for *Heart's Notions*." Grace grinned at Vivian's black scowl. "Oh, look—reticules!" She skipped toward the next stall. "Here, Vivian, this would be perfect for you!"

It was impossible to hold the girl in any sort of disregard. Vivian stepped forward, vowing nonetheless as she did to tromp off should the reticule be adorned with beadwork resembling either flame or emeralds. Grace's sense of humor tended to lean toward the outlandish.

To her surprise, the object in the girl's hands was subdued to an extreme. Covered with jet beads, it resembled nothing so much as an oversized lump of coal. Seeing her expression, Grace grinned. "Feel it," she instructed, dumping the thing into Vivian's palm.

The back of her hand hit the table with enough force to bruise her knuckles. "Good heavens! Is it made of lead?"

Grace's grin widened devilishly. " 'Twould be a formidable weapon, would it not? Woe to the next person who approaches you with Newstead's book proffered!"

The three laughed with abandon, drawing more than a few curious stares. "Come along," Aurelie said eventually, "I believe I have had more than enough shopping for one afternoon. I suggest repairing to Gunther's for ices."

They were making their way toward the street when Grace stopped short. "Oh, dear. Perhaps we ought to use the other door."

"Why?" her sister-in-law queried, scanning the crowd in front of them.

"I just spied Chloe Somersham. She is moving straight toward us."

Aurelie peered into the crush. "Is Annabella with her?"

"That is the problem. I could not tell." Grace gripped Vivian's elbow. "Hurry. This way."

Flanked on either side by a determined Granville, Vivian dutifully headed toward the bazaar's side entrance. "Who is Chloe Somersham and why are we avoiding her?"

"Chloe is the lesser of evils" was Grace's terse reply. "It is her cousin, Annabella, whom we must avoid. They are much together in Town."

Vivian was losing her patience. She was more than ready to be done with the bazaar, but she did not appreciate being herded like a mindless sheep. "Fine." She stopped, dragging her companions to a halt beside her. "Who, then, is Chloe's cousin?"

"Annabella Milbanke . . . now Byron," Aurelie informed her, clearly impatient herself. "It might be a bit awkward should we be forced to introduce you."

"Rubbish. It might serve perfectly well to dispel some of the ridiculous speculation."

Her protest fell on deaf ears. Aurelie pushed, Grace pulled. "Honestly, Vivian," the latter scolded, "I should think you would know better ... or worse of the ton by now. A meeting with Lady Byron will merely provide fodder for the gossip mill. Now, before we are spied ... Why, Lady Chloe!" She came to a sudden halt. "How lovely to meet you here!"

Vivian peered over Grace's blond head at the diminutive redhead there, whom she quickly recognized as one of the two women who had departed with Byron the night before. The second must have been his wife. The woman on the balcony had, quite probably, been neither.

Chloe Somersham hardly looked dangerous. In fact, she resembled nothing so much as a woodland faerie with her brilliant hair and freckled nose. "Lady Grace," she greeted the other girl, smiling cheerfully, "and Lady Tarrant. I thought I spied you a few moments ago, but it is such a terrible crush."

"To be sure, it is," Aurelie replied. From the corner of her eye, Vivian could see her listing slightly to the side, clearly looking for the sprite's companions. "Is your cousin with you? I vow I have not seen her in recent weeks."

"I fear Annabella could not accompany me today. I am here"—Chloe wrinkled her pert nose expressively—"with my maid, two footmen, and Mama's companion. As if I might take it into my head to bolt for freedom." She turned at last to Vivian. "I do not believe we have been introduced."

"How careless of me." Obviously relieved that any scene would be a mild one, Aurelie performed the introductions. "Chloe, Miss Vivian Redmond. Vivian, Lady Chloe Somersham."

If the girl was apprised of the situation—and she certainly must have been with her connection to the Byrons—she gave no indication. "It is a pleasure, Miss Redmond.

Are you enjoying your sojourn in London?" Then: "I daresay it is a far cry from Boston."

So much for deceptive innocence.

Vivian gave her best serene smile. "London thus far has been . . . lively, though not so very different from Boston. There are simply a great many more people."

Chloe nodded sagely. "It is rather barbaric, is it not, for much of England's population to crowd itself into a not large section of the city for the express purpose of crowding itself into even smaller ballrooms? I do wonder how the tradition started. It would be ever so much more efficient to gather in some field in Yorkshire. Would it not?"

"I should think . . ."

"But of course Society mamas would balk at such a concept. Heaven knows what trouble would arise from being surrounded by so much available space." She paused, ostensibly to draw breath, then wrinkled her nose again. "Oh, dear. Miss Midgely is beckoning." She sighed. "I have strayed more than the allowed five paces away. I imagine the Midge would like to see me leashed. I do hope we shall all meet again soon." Then, with a blithe wave, she skipped away, her red curls bobbing like a beacon through the crowd.

At Vivian's side, Aurelie gave a rueful laugh. "Encounters with Chloe always leave one feeling as if one has met with a light wind."

"I rather liked her," Vivian mused. "Is her husband so very possessive then?"

"Oh, Chloe is not married," Grace said.

"But the title . . ."

"Like mine, a dubious gift from her father. He is the Duke of Earith. Never lets Chloe out of the house without a veritable queen's guard."

Even Vivian had heard of the duke. A longtime advisor to the king, he had been among the more vocal in decrying self-rule of the Colonies and one of the first to advocate sending troops across the Atlantic once again. She felt heartily sorry for young Chloe without ever having met the man.

The girl's irreverence was appealing. Vivian decided then and there that an alliance might be advisable. Perhaps Chloe was her means of getting to Byron. God knew patiently waiting for him to speak to her again was not working.

"Well, I must say that was disaster averted," Aurelie remarked lightly as they once again made their way toward the door. "With luck, we shall not meet with any member of the family in the near future."

Vivian did not agree. She was past tired of the whole farce—weary most of all of the eyes that inevitably followed her every move in public. The walk to the bazaar's egress was already a torturous procedure due to the masses. The questioning gazes made it intolerable. Unless she came face to face with Byron soon and received a public proclamation, she was liable to do something rash.

They made it to the street at last. Vivian promptly ducked as a capacious parasol swept by her ear. "I am beginning," she muttered under her breath, "to dislike this town prodigiously."

Aurelie chuckled as she returned the enthusiastic waves of a group of acquaintances across the street. "Ah, but how this town adores you!"

They made their way slowly down Bond Street. Ahead, three young fops walked toward them, three abreast, blocking the pavement. "Oh, dear." Grace sighed. "Loungers."

Vivian surveyed the approaching trio. "Loungers? They seem to be rather active." As she spoke, they all but forced a grandfatherly-looking man into the gutter. "How rude!"

"Yes," Aurelie agreed, "rudeness is the dictum of loungers. At least this group does not seem to be employing their walking sticks."

"Do you mean to tell me this is common behavior?"

"Sadly, it is. Bored young men have made lounging a prime form of entertainment. Do you not have their ilk in Boston?"

"To be sure we do, but I believe the term you use here for the Boston variety is *footpad*. Their goal is crime, not amusement."

Aurelie shrugged and gestured to the opposite side of the street. "We shall simply avoid them."

"We shall do no such thing." Vivian had caught the eye of the central dandy. "I think it abominable that they are allowed to behave so." Another hapless shopper was forced into the street. "I believe I will make an admirable lounger myself."

"Now, Vivian . . ."

But she was already moving purposefully away. Grace, ever ready for a bit of adventure, skipped by her side. Within moments, they were face to face with the foppish trio.

The center lounger, blinding in his salmon waistcoat and chartreuse coat, peered through his quizzing glass. "Ah, gentlemen, I believe this lady is known to us."

Vivian watched as he rose a good two inches and surmised that he was now standing on his toes. Seconds before, they had been eye to eye. He was by no means a prepossessing character—all contrived blond curls and studied ennui. "It is a possibility, sir, though if we have met, I vow I have quite forgotten."

The petulant mouth thinned at the insult. " 'Pon my word, madam, your poet must be a chuckle-headed fellow."

"Must he?"

"Only one utterly deficient in wit could have penned such . . . er, vivid words."

Vivian tilted her head to the side and surveyed the boor carefully. After a time, she gave a brief nod. "I believe I might just be correct."

"What was that?"

"Why, the poet's identity, of course. In the wake of your eloquent address as to his character, I have decided that *you* could very well be he." The man's jaw dropped. "Now, if you would be so kind . . ."

She looked at him pointedly, but neither he nor his companions budged an inch. Rather, all three stood still, peering through their quizzing glasses like myopic statues. Vivian's grasp of science was limited, but she understood enough of Archimedes and Newton to solve the problem. "Very well, then. Come along, ladies." She removed her parasol from where it had been safely tucked under her arm and lodged the tip against the pavement behind the odious man's leg. One tiny shove with her shoulder sent him sprawling backward onto his ecru-clad rump.

As she and her companions made their leisurely way toward the carriage, she could hear the grunts and curses as the other two tried to right their fallen comrade, all to the clapping of numerous bystanders.

Grace clapped along. "Really, Vivian, that was marvelous! However did you learn such a trick?"

"Good tutors and six male cousins."

Aurelie gave a wry smile. "You certainly chose your opponent well."

"I would say that he picked us and not the other way about. But why was my choice so admirable?"

Now her friend's grin turned decidedly wicked. "That particular lounger was Noel's cousin and heir, Derwood Windram. They positively loathe each other."

"Well, then," Vivian muttered, tucking her parasol back under her arm, "I have done his lordship a great service. I hope, wherever he is, he is suitably appreciative."

Noel was furious.

"The girl will be the death of me!"

Jason peered over his shoulder. "Why? You are not mentioned anywhere."

"No, I am not, but some faint, chivalric instinct prompts me to call out more than one of these bounders and"—he scanned the page before him—"we both suspect that Fremont cheats. I do not fancy facing the business end of his pistol."

The two men were at White's, studying the infamous betting book. For his part, Noel was heartily wishing he had refrained. Thirty-seven wagers had been recorded since the beginning of the month. Eighteen of these involved Vivian, four in the past week alone.

Mr. DeB. wagers Mr. H. £50 that a certain young lady from the Colonies will appear in canto V.

£20. Mr. O.G. to Lord T. Miss V.R. will wear blue to the Covington affair.

Lord F. wagers Mr. Y. £200 that fortune will urge a certain peer to take an American viscountess.

Lord P. £100 to Mr. S. that he will persuade a young lady to accompany him onto the balcony of the Kingley ball.

Fremont's wager was enough to make Noel's blood boil. Paxton's made him want to commit an imminent and violent crime. "I will wring the toad's fat neck!"

"Really, St. Helier, there is nothing to suggest he is speaking of Miss Redmond. He has, after all, been angling after Prudence Waverley."

Noel snorted. "He would not wager £100 pounds on her. Nor, I believe, would persuasion be necessary. No, he was sniffing about Vivian last night after the balcony incident." His fingers flexed powerfully on the pages. "If he so much as tries to lead her to the refreshment table, I will have to cause him serious discomfort."

Jason slid the book from his friend's grasp and urged him back to their corner. "Careful, man, your jealousy is showing."

"Jealous? Of Paxton? Good God, Tarrant, where are your wits?" He reached for the brandy and poured himself a liberal amount. "Next you will be telling me I am making calf's-eyes at the girl."

"Nothing so innocent, I am afraid. The gazes you direct at Miss Redmond bring to mind a falcon surveying a sparrow."

"Yes, well, she is a rather delectable little morsel. I fancy that white breast would be soft as a bird's."

Jason did not respond to the deliberately lewd pronouncement. Instead, he leaned back in his seat and tented his fingers in front of his mouth. "I wonder," he said eventually, "that you would feel chivalric instincts for something as flighty as a sparrow."

Noel lifted one brow. "You should know by now that I take every sport seriously. I rather like your image of falconry. There is something extremely satisfying about the sudden, determined sweep and grab. The only difference is that I will let go more quickly, I think, than my feathered counterpart."

"Leaving the prey irrevocably damaged?"

"Going all high-in-the-instep on me, Tare? The girl is nothing to you."

"The girl," came the terse reply, "is Aurelie's friend. And I like her."

Noel grinned. "So do I, man. So do I. Why make sport with a woman one does not appreciate?"

"I do not know why I bother." Jason rolled his eyes. "I am far too well acquainted with you to even mention the sweetheart in Boston. But what of her connection to your own family? I daresay your mother would be most upset to hear you had ruined a ward of her bosom bows."

"I have no intention of ruining anything or anyone. I fully expect Vivian to leave my company nothing less than she is now, and a good deal more." He noted that Jason's expression had become a bit grim. "Leave off, Tare, I can hardly have honorable intentions toward the chit. Allow me a few dishonorable contemplations."

The truth of the matter was that he planned to do far more than contemplate. He did not, however, wish to bring the wrath of all aforementioned parties down upon his head at present. Lord Tarrant might perhaps understand; Lady Tarrant would not. In fact, Noel could quite imagine sweet-tempered Aurelie coming at him with a pistol should he compromise her friend.

That was, if Byron had not gotten to Vivian first.

He cursed silently at the thought. It appeared the ton was

78

as entranced with the girl as the poet himself and was apt to regard her behavior with a sort of salacious tolerance. No doubt any number of young bucks would be angling after her now. The only thing better than an heiress was a beautiful heiress with social appeal.

Paxton was easily ignored. Vivian, he was confident, would sooner share the company of a venomous reptile. As for the sweetheart in Boston . . . Noel caught himself smiling. Poor Daniel-David was about as much competition as old General Washington's ghost—and far less likely to appear. He had to give Vivian credit, though. Inventing a beau back home had been an inspired move on her part. Pity she could not have kept the sorry sod's name straight. Next she would be calling him Damien.

The smile faded. Meriton was a concern; the bounder could be dashedly charming when he set his mind to it. He had already wormed his way into her good graces. Nor could she be so completely averse to the concept of marrying a handsome young lord. She was, after all, female.

He was back to cursing. Byron, damn his black heart, was the very epitome of the romantic young lord. True, he was married, but Noel derived little comfort from the fact. The man was too handsome by half and seemed to draw women like moths to flame. Vivian, intelligent as she was, was already intrigued. If given the chance, she would undoubtably gravitate toward the limping, limpid-eyed poet.

Noel's insect analogy took a grim turn. Byron, like a spider, would have her mesmerized and enwrapped the second she hit the web. It had happened before.

Not this time, damn it!

He would keep the impetuous minx away from Byron if it meant wrapping her in stout rope and tying her to his own wrist. Until he was well and fully tired of her, Vivian Redmond had lived her last vivid moment in the public eye.

"I have just heard the most marvelous little tidbit!" Noel looked up to see Rafael Marlowe drop into the third seat. The debonair young marquess was an old friend of both

79

himself and Tarrant, and had returned to Town from Wiltshire just the week before. He brushed dark hair from his eyes and continued, "I was coming out of my tailor's and met with the news that the Vivid One had only just completed a stunning act in the middle of Bond Street."

Noel's fist hit the table with enough force to set the glasses jumping. "God's teeth! Can she not even shop without attracting chaos?"

Rafael looked at him curiously. "If the tale is true, she merely reacted to a disagreeable situation." Noel growled. "Careful, man, your emotions are showing." The marquess grinned at the responding curse. "Quite. But do try to restrain yourself for the moment. I believe you will enjoy this story."

He paused to fortify himself with a hearty sip of brandy. "It seems a group of loungers was cutting a swath down Bond Street when Miss Redmond, Aurelie, and Grace were there. One made the mistake of being a bit ... crass and, employing nothing more than a parasol and a bit of science, Miss Redmond sent him flying into a mud puddle."

Jason laughed aloud. "Splendid! I imagine Aurelie and Grace enjoyed the whole event immensely. Trust our little American to defeat the fine English tradition of lounging."

"Ah, but the tale gets better." Rafael turned back to Noel. "Do guess who the hapless lounger was."

"Prinny?" Noel offered sourly.

"Really, Hel, you can do better than that."

"Paxton."

Rafael grinned as he plied the bottle to all three glasses. "I say we drink a toast to the vivid Vivian for sending St. Helier's dearly beloved cousin arse-first into the mud."

"Derwood?" Noel felt his jaw dropping. "She upended Derwood?"

"Without so much as soiling her gown. Apparently the whole street cheered."

All three men raised their glasses to the absent Vivian. "I'll be damned," Noel muttered. "I suppose I owe her a good turn. Who told you this tale?"

"Chloe Somersham. She said they had all just parted at the bazaar."

This time, Noel's fist sent drops of brandy spraying over the table. "Of all the addlepated, hen-witted things to do!" He was on his way out the door seconds later, determined to purchase a length of sturdy rope.

Jason and Rafael watched him go. "Who," the former asked reluctantly, "is Chloe Somersham?"

"Really, Tare, she is a friend of Grace's."

"And?"

Rafael grinned broadly. "She is cousin and frequent companion to Annabella Byron."

Jason chuckled and called for another bottle.

7

NOEL ARRIVED HOME, sans rope, to be greeted by the sight of his front door wide open and a steady stream of footmen flowing through it. Each was burdened with some heavy object. He entered the foyer to see his own valet, Tavis, struggling under the weight of a monstrous, cloth-shrouded dome. A footman weaved behind him, trying valiantly to manage a stunted Grecian pillar.

Tavis leapt a good three inches off the floor as an ungodly shriek sounded from beneath the cloth. Yet another footman hurried forward as the valet's grip faltered, steadying the dome as it listed dangerously toward the floor. Absorbed in contemplating the circus that had once been his home, Noel did not hear the footsteps behind him and was nearly knocked off his feet when a large valise collided with his back.

"Oh! I beg your pardon, m'lord!" A pair of eyes that Noel believed to belong to one of his grooms appeared over the top. "I didn't see you there."

"It is quite all right, Hawkins," he muttered. "I understand." He deftly avoided a portmanteau with legs and sighed.

It appeared his mother had arrived.

"Noel!" On cue, a diminutive figure appeared at the head of the stairs. "Oh, do be careful, dear!" He looked about to see what hazard threatened him at present before realizing his mother was speaking to Tavis. "You nearly missed that first stair. I would not want you to do injury to yourself!"

As the valet made his awkward way up the staircase,

Noel suppressed a smile. His mother's concern for the well-being of his staff was ever admirable, but did not extend to arriving in Town without half of her possessions in tow.

"Hello, Maman." He waited for her to descend and enveloped her in a fond embrace. "I did not expect you for a few days yet. Did Bath grow wearisome?"

Gazing down at the crown of her head, which rested somewhere in the vicinity of his top waistcoat button, he marveled as always at her resilience. Marriage to Mad Jack Windram, thirty-one years of motherhood, and a schedule that made Wellington look like a sluggard had done nothing to diminish her spirit or beauty. The mahogany hair was liberally threaded with gray and there were faint lines at the corners of her blue eyes, but she had the aura of one twenty years younger.

Right now, the lines were deepened by her bright smile. "Bath is often wearisome. I was ready to be on my way after the first ten days, but your grandmother was insistent that I stay the full fortnight."

"Ah, how is Grandmama?"

"Exceedingly well. She is terrorizing the fine citizens of Bath in that phaeton you bought her. Really, Noel, dearest, do you not think it a bit much for a woman of seventy-five?"

"Shame on you, madam. You know she prefers to be thought fifty-nine. And I imagine she looks quite splendid at the reins."

Jane, Lady St. Helier, laughed aloud and stretched to kiss her son's jaw. "You are absolutely right. She looks marvelous. Last I saw her, she was careening 'round the Circle with her footman and maid hanging on for their very lives. Mother might adore you, dear, but her staff is ready to have you tarred and feathered."

It was Noel's turn to laugh. "And ridden out of town in the phaeton, I suppose. It was her seventy-fifth birthday, Maman. What would you have had me do, give her something for the solarium?"

"Of course not. You did so last year. Which serves to remind me—she wished me to inform you that the flytraps are flourishing and that she has graduated to giving them grasshoppers."

With that rather glib pronouncement, Lady St. Helier gestured hospitably toward the library. She was nothing if not supremely comfortable in her son's townhouse. Tea was ready and she settled herself in one of the chairs which, to Noel's eyes, were suited for average human occupancy, but dwarfed her nonetheless. "So, what has my beloved London spawned in my absence?"

"You detest London, Maman."

"Oh, yes. I do, do I not? Well then, what scandals have erupted of late in this tawdry town?"

"A poetic turn of phrase, that—tawdry town, and very apt. The bard is at it again."

His mother was nothing if not sharp. "I thought Byron to have married and settled down."

"So, I imagine, did his wife," Noel replied with irony.

He then proceeded to tell her about the cantos, and about Vivian. He did contrive to leave out his own pursuit of the Vivid One's fair form, concentrating instead on less personal facts. His mother sighed over the ton's cavalier intrusiveness and got a good laugh out of the tale of Derwood's public upset.

"I am sorry for the girl, becoming the focus of Society's eye in such a way, but she is obviously not the wilting sort. I expect Derwood was wearing some garish outfit. Mud could only have improved his appearance." She paused, and Noel had a very good idea of what was to come. He was not to be disappointed. "You really ought to consider marrying, dearest. I shudder at the thought of that man taking over the title. Not to mention the estates." She did actually shudder, albeit delicately. "Puce carriages, festucine livery . . ."

"Yes, it does give one pause. I am not, however, going to rush into marriage to prevent my homes from being debased by Derwood's color preferences."

"As well you should not. Do consider, though, the fact

84

that you are the last of the wild Windrams. The rest of the family is quite a watered-down lot."

Noel raised his brows. "You advocate the begetting of more wildness? I should think you would appreciate a modicum of peace in your life."

"Nonsense. Peace is severely overrated. Life is nothing without a bit of chaos. Grandchildren provide it so very charmingly."

"Buy another parrot," Noel retorted. "A pair will bring you all the chaos you desire. That is," he added, "if Tavis does not throttle Falstaff first."

"Tavis *adores* Falstaff. He simply tends to be startled by the volume of the dear bird's utterances."

That was certainly true. Everyone except Lady St. Helier tended to be startled by the noise. Tavis, for his own part, never seemed to adapt to the fact that the parrot shrieked "Off with his head!" whenever he approached the cage. Noel himself had brought the bird back from a trip to the West Indies as a birthday gift. At the time, Falstaff had spoken only a few, unidentifiable Creole words. His mother still insisted that she had no idea where some of the creature's vastly expanded vocabulary had come from.

"There must be one young woman in Town who has caught your roving eye. From what little I have heard, this Season boasts an uncommon number of Beauties."

Noel was not about to tell her that one young woman had indeed caught his fancy. She would be meeting Vivian soon enough, and he did not care for the knowledge that she would start in again on the subject of marriage when his intentions were far removed from that institution.

"Father was thirty-two when you married. You may resume your arguments next year."

She sighed, as much from memory of Mad Jack, her son knew, as frustration at his own obstinance. "You cannot fault a mother for wanting to see her only child happy." She shook her head at his expression. "Do not say it, dear. I refuse to believe your happiness depends on being unattached."

Deciding to humor his beloved parent, Noel reached over to squeeze her hand. "We will strike a bargain, then. You may identify whichever young ladies impress you as being appealing daughter-in-law material, and I shall promise to give them at least adequate perusal."

"Well," she replied with a wry smile, "if nothing else, I shall gain some amusement in hearing the excuses you will inevitably provide."

The St. Heliers attended the opera that evening. It was an insufferably dull affair, and Noel would certainly have fallen asleep if not for two inconveniences. The first was that the soprano was gratingly sharp and would have cut through even the deepest of slumbers. The second was that Vivian was not in attendance. Noel had turned his glass to the widows' box as soon as he had arrived and had been startled to see it empty.

He had looked to the Tarrant box next. Jason and Aurelie were there with Grace, and were joined eventually by Rafael. Noel wanted very much to visit at the first intermission, but was prevented by the need to escort his mother to visit various acquaintances. She was extremely well liked, and her continued absence from Town made it necessary to stop countless times.

He was not able to greet his own friends until the second intermission, by which time his ears were ringing and he was thoroughly furious with Vivian. The damn girl should have been there, and her absence set this teeth on edge. Heaven only knew what mischief she was getting herself into without him to watch over her.

"Lady St. Helier," Aurelie greeted his mother warmly. "How lovely to see you again."

The two women exchanged embraces. Noel's mother had known Jason since he was on leading strings and had been delighted with his marriage. She had informed her son in no uncertain terms that he was the worst of buffle-heads for not getting to Aurelie first. Grace too was a particular favorite, and soon the three ladies were chatting away.

Noel could not very well interrupt them to ask where Vivian was, so he did the proper thing and conversed with the men. He thought himself clever enough to get what information he could from them. "Did you get the full story of the day's escapades from Aurelie?" he asked Jason.

"Little more than Rafe did, actually" was the reply. "Apparently the lounging incident went rather quickly. Did your mother bring the parrot?"

"Of course. She goes nowhere without it. But really, I should like to hear of Derwood's humiliation."

"Pity," Jason said. "I cannot tell you much. How long is your mother staying? Her sojourns tend to have the quality of seraphic visitations, enchanting but fleeting."

"She will stay until Devon calls, I suppose. One never knows with Mother." Noel tried another tack. "She was looking forward to seeing Lady Fielding and Mrs. DeLancey this eve. It seems they are not here."

"No?" Jason directed a lazy gaze toward their box. "Ah, it seems not."

Rafael, damn his hide, took the opportunity to change the subject. "The divine Jondine is not herself tonight."

It was Grace who answered. "I have heard she was slighted by Prinny recently. It would appear she has not yet recovered."

"Do you know what he said to her, dear?" Lady St. Helier asked. She was ever ready for a good *on dit*.

"I believe he informed her that her gown made her resemble an overfed peacock." Grace's brow furrowed. "Or was it that her voice brought to mind the cry of a bilious peacock?"

"Well," Rafael said cheerfully, "either would be more than enough to send her off-key for the remainder of the Season."

The first gong sounded and Noel gritted his teeth. If he were going to unearth Vivian's whereabouts, he was going to have to do so quickly. The rest of the party, however, was now engaged in an animated discussion of La Jondine's ruffled feathers.

Just as he was ready to howl in frustration, his mother, splendid woman that she was, solved the matter. "I expected to encounter Mrs. DeLancey and Lady Fielding here tonight. Do you have any idea why they are not present, Aurelie?"

"Their ward is unfortunately indisposed and they were loath to attend without her."

"Vivian is ill?" Noel spoke louder than intended and found himself the recipient of five curious gazes.

"Not ill, precisely," Aurelie announced after a moment. "Just . . . indisposed."

Noel did not want to imagine what "just indisposed" meant. He damn well wanted to see for himself. As he would be unable to do so before the next day, however, he pressed, "Was she not with you all afternoon?"

"Most of it," Grace offered. "She was engaged to go driving in the park with Lord Meriton later."

Sheer force of will alone kept Noel from thundering out of the box and onto the street. "Of course," he muttered through clenched teeth, "that would be enough to indispose anyone."

Jason promptly chuckled. "Careful, man, your—"

A loud party passing behind the box interrupted his words and saved Noel the effort of stuffing the man's cravat down his throat. The second gong sounded and his mother rose to her feet. "I am certain we shall all meet again soon." She tucked her arm through her son's. "And I know I shall be able to count on you, Aurelie, to help me in planning my ball."

"Of course, madam," Aurelie replied.

"Ball?" Noel did not remember her having mentioned anything of the sort.

"Why, yes, dear. It has been so long since I hosted a fete in Town. I thought Tuesday after next would do quite nicely." She smiled sweetly up at him. "You told me I might."

"I did?"

"To be sure. I shall do just as you suggested and identify

an acceptable guest list. You, in turn, shall give it adequate perusal."

Trying not to grind his molars into dust, Noel led her back to their box.

"Might I suggest a book, dearest?"

"Hmm?" He glanced across the parlor late the next morning to find his mother gazing at him in amusement. "A book, madam?"

"There is no need for you to stay home on my account. But if you must, I suggest finding yourself a good book. You are wearing tracks into the carpet."

He had not been aware of his pacing and was startled to find himself near the windows. "Perhaps I will go out for a bit. I believe there is something going on at . . . Tattersall's."

In truth, he wanted only to ride over and have a look at Vivian. It was still too early to do so, however, so he might as well occupy himself in another manner. "And what are your plans?"

"I thought I might pay a visit on some friends." She looked at the clock. "It is early, but I am certain they will not mind. I would ask if you would care to play escort, but . . ."

Images of an hour spent sitting on Hepplewhite with a cup of weak tea perched on his knee were enough to make him wince. "Of course, if you wish me to do so, Maman."

"Oh, it is not necessary. I know you find such matters tedious to the extreme. I will simply pop over to Lady Fielding's . . ."

He had her out the door and into the carriage within minutes.

Vivian drummed her fingers against the windowsill. "I never thought to say it, but a day without visitors will be insufferably dull."

"Well, you'll not be receiving anybody as you are," Esther returned tartly.

"I am perfectly well."

"You are a fright."

"Really, Esther . . ."

The maid was resolute. "You will have to occupy yourself today. Go find a book and be done with the moaning and groaning."

It was an uncustomarily sunny morning, and Vivian sighed as she stared out the solarium window. "I suppose I could read in the gardens."

"There you are, a wise choice indeed."

Vivian rose to her feet and gathered her shawl. It certainly was not how she wished to spend such a glorious day, but she was resigned to it. She thought she had spied a volume of Thomas Paine's works in the library—Lady Fielding's choice, no doubt. Mrs. DeLancey's tastes leaned toward sweet, romantic novels. Vivian had nothing against Jane Austen, certainly, but was more in the mood for a bit of vibrant political discourse.

As she entered the hall, voices reached her from the parlor. She was curious as to who would be paying such an early visit but decided not to risk a peek. Instead, she tiptoed quietly past the room toward the library. She turned the corner off the main hall—and ran straight into St. Helier.

"Miss Redmond. I had heard you were unwell. Are you feeling . . ." He leaned to view her averted face. "Good God, Vivian! *What* did you do to yourself?"

She straightened her shoulders and lifted her chin. "Good day to you too, my lord."

His hand snaked out to snare her jaw. "You look as if you've gone a few rounds with Gentleman Jackson."

"Yes, well, he looks no better for our meeting. In fact, I heard he was sporting *two* black eyes this morning."

The swelling, she knew, had gone down since the previous afternoon, but her cheekbone sported a bruise the mottled color and size of a ripening plum.

His fingers were surprisingly gentle as they touched the bruise. "My God, Vivian . . ." Then, as she watched, his eyes took on a steely edge. "Is Meriton responsible for this? I will see him dead and cold . . ."

"Lord Meriton? Responsible?" She could not help but laugh. "He was present, to be sure, but it was my fault entirely."

Noel did not care if she had planted herself a facer. Meriton had been present and he was damn well going to answer for his lack of care. Whatever object had struck Vivian's face had been hard and forcefully cast. He had himself sported more than his share of blackened eyes through the years, and knew the pain involved.

Glancing about, he spied the open library door and, before she could object, hustled her inside. He did not stop until they were standing directly in front of the tall windows. Then, cupping her face in his palms, he tilted her head upward and surveyed the damage.

"Who did this?" he demanded gruffly.

"I told you, I—"

"Damn it, Vivian, you did not smack yourself in the face!"

"Well, of course I did not."

"Who did?"

She blinked at him, her eyes greener than ever against the lividity of the bruise, and he felt something twist deep inside him. "It was not a *who*, Noel. It was a *what*. I suppose the simplest explanation is that I was felled by a tree branch."

"I beg your pardon?"

She blushed so fiercely that he could almost feel the heat on his fingers. "The phaeton was moving too fast and I was not paying attention. I was hit in the face by a low-hanging branch."

He did not bother trying to restrain the lurid curse that burst from his lips. She started slightly and pulled back, but he did not release his hold on her face. "I might just have to kill him."

"Who?"

"Meriton," he ground out. "You were driving with him, were you not?"

"Well, yes, I was . . ."

"He damn well should have been watching where he was going!"

If possible, her blush deepened. "Meriton was not driving."

"No? Who was?"

This time, she did pull away and dropped her head. "I was."

The memory was every bit as humiliating as the actual event, as she felt her cheeks burning. Lord Meriton had been hesitant to let her drive, but she was a dab hand at the reins and had been driving her father's pairs since she was thirteen. She had simply badgered and cajoled until the viscount finally relented.

She had been doing splendidly until that last turn. In truth, she had managed the turn rather splendidly too, considering their speed and the horses' soft mouths. The outer wheels had left the earth for no more than a fraction of a second. Meriton's shout and lunge for the reins had diverted her attention just long enough for the tree to strike. The phaeton had veered to the edge of the road, putting her in exactly the right place to meet with the branch.

The impact had nearly sent her flying off the seat. Fortunately, her momentum had pulled the horses back, and they had come to a shuddering halt half on and half off the road. Lucky too, her encounter with the branch had distracted her companion. Whatever tirade he might have loosed had been lost in his concern for her injury.

She did not think he would be in any hurry to let her drive again, but at least he had not howled at her.

She lifted her eyes to see Noel regarding her with a mixture of marvel and exasperation. "You were driving."

"I was, and I was doing perfectly well until Lord Meriton became jittery." The more she thought about it, the more she was convinced that the man owed her an apology.

Everything would have been just fine had he not interfered. "I am perfectly capable at the reins."

"Yes," Noel said slowly, "I imagine you are." He shook his head. "You really ought to meet my grandmother."

"Your grandmother? Whatever for?"

"She is as feckless and foolish as you are, Vivian, with a prodigious liking for phaetons. You will not go driving with Meriton again."

Whether it was the word *feckless* or his high-handed behavior in general that set her off, she did not know. When the color rose this time in her cheeks, it was in high pique. "And you, my lord, are an arrogant, officious boor! I shall blessed well go driving with whomever I choose. You may take your flapping tongue and choke . . . oh!"

She suddenly found herself flat up against his chest, his hands like iron bands around her upper arms. She was forced to tilt her head back to see his face and promptly wished she had not looked. A muscle twitched in his formidable jaw, and his eyes had darkened to a stormy gray.

"I will be the judge of what I am to do with my tongue, Vivian," he announced huskily, and, just as his intention dawned on her, lowered his head.

With strength born more of pique than will, she braced her hands against his chest. "Oh, no! You are not going to kiss me, St. Helier!"

His mouth was mere inches from her own and she watched as the corners twitched into a semblance of a smile. "I am not?" The sudden softening was far more appealing than the temper of moments before but, she decided, just as perilous.

"No, you are not." She was mortified to hear the lack of conviction in her voice. Her lips, curse them, were far more interested in meeting his than in forming sharp words. "You did so before, and I did not like it."

"You did not?"

"No, I . . . don't you dare grin at me like that!"

His breath was warm on her face. "You are full of commands this morning, Vivian. I, however, am not of a mind to heed them. I will give you a choice. Either I kiss you, or I turn you across my knee and paddle you soundly for being a reckless little fool."

She opened her mouth to give him a proper dressing-down. She never had the chance.

"Wise choice," he announced, and covered her lips with his.

The kiss was nothing like the one before, except in the instant reaction it sparked within her. He was not gentle this time, but fierce and demanding. His lips were firm, unrelenting, and, as before, seemed to fit perfectly against hers. Even as she tilted her head to give him better access, she knew she was teetering on the edge of something ruinous. This was not some insipid, harmless dandy. This was St. Helier, of the decadent speculations and wicked tongue.

Then, just as she gathered sufficient wits to realize a protest might be in order and prepared to give one, his tongue swept forward. Her gasp was lost in a helpless sigh of pleasure. What began as a softly glowing ember burst into full flame within her and she leaned into him, wanting nothing more than to melt right through his coat and be wholly absorbed.

Had he been able, Noel would have consumed her. Her response, innocent though it was, had him in flames. Releasing his grip on her arms, he spread one hand over the small of her back, drawing her even closer, and cupped her face with the other. His thumb brushed over her bruised cheekbone and she whimpered softly.

The sound reminded him forcibly of the reason she was hurt, and he was struck again by the urge to put Meriton out of his own misery. This was superceded by the feel of Vivian's warm body pressed against his and the urge to keep her securely in that very spot for rather a long time. She smelled like summer, tasted like the sweetest of berries, and felt like sin itself.

"Good God," he murmured against her lips, not certain whether he was speaking in awe or in a plea for sanity. "Vivian . . ."

"Noel," she whispered in response, and he was lost.

With the blood thundering hard and hot in his ears, he barely heard the knock at the door. Vivian mush have, for suddenly she jerked away from him to face the portal.

Her obvious relief at seeing the butler enter moments later, rather than either of the widows, was far more charitable than Noel's thoughts. Stevens was a decent fellow, but he had just placed himself on the imminent-demise list, directly above Lord Meriton.

"I beg your pardon, Miss Redmond. Lady St. Helier sent me in search of his lordship."

"Well, Stevens, you have found me."

"Indeed, my lord." Message delivered, the butler disappeared, leaving the door wide open behind him.

"Cheeky bugger," Noel muttered. Vivian was too busy trying to restore some order to her tousled curls to respond. Noel carelessly ran his hands through his own hair before reaching for her hand. "Come along, Vivian. I believe it is time for you to meet my mother."

8

SHE WAS BECOMING decidedly tired of being dragged about like a recalcitrant child. In fact, she was having a difficult time remembering the last time she had walked anywhere truly of her own volition. If it was not a Granville or widow herding her someplace, it was Esther prodding and nagging. Noel too had developed a nasty habit of hauling her about by the arm whenever they met.

She did not want to meet his mother.

Well, that was not precisely true. She wanted very much to meet Lady St. Helier, but just not then. She could only imagine the state of her hair, and she knew she looked as if someone had smashed a piece of overripe fruit on her cheek. In short, she was quite the wreck Esther had so charmingly pronounced her to be.

She tried literally digging in her heels, but they were moving across the slick, marble floor and she only succeeded in skidding along for a few feet.

"St. Helier," she protested. "*Noel,* stop!" To her astonishment, he did. "I cannot meet your mother!"

He frowned. "Whyever not? I assure you she will not bite."

"Do not be a goose. I cannot meet anyone looking as I do."

"You look fine. Come along."

She got both hands on his sleeve, holding him in place. "I do not look fine! My hair is in a state and, as you said, I resemble a loser in Gentleman Jackson's ring."

He sighed. "Vivian, your hair is always in a state. That

96

is its charm. And my mother will applaud when she hears how your eye was blackened. Now lift your feet, please. I do not fancy having to drag you all the way."

She did not doubt he would do just that. There was nothing she could do about the bruise and little she could do about her hair, especially with the use of only one hand. She did her best, however, to smooth some order into the rioting curls as Noel led her toward the salon.

Her first view of Jane, Lady St. Helier, was enough to make her wish she had not risen from bed that morning. The petite woman positively exuded elegance, from her neatly coiled hair to her pristine lavender skirts. In truth, she resembled an exquisite porcelain doll Vivian's father had once brought her from France. The doll, after a few days of being dragged in the little girl's wake, had come to look very much as Vivian did right then—wild hair, mussed skirts, and smudged face.

"Mother," she heard Noel saying, "may I present Miss Vivian Redmond of Boston. Vivian, my mother, Lady St. Helier."

Unnecessarily, and with enviable grace, the woman rose from her seat. Vivian's hand went up instinctively to cover her cheek. "My lady," she mumbled miserably, cursing Noel with all her heart. She had thought him careless but never truly heartless. Introducing her to his perfect little mother while she looked as she did was unforgivable.

To her dismay, the countess glided toward her and reached for her hand. Vivian briefly thought of putting up a struggle, certain she would vanquish, but abandoned the notion. She looked silly enough as it was.

"It is a pleasure, Miss Redmond," the lady said warmly. If she sensed that Vivian had, less than five minutes earlier, been engaged in the most improper embrace with her son, she gave no indication. Instead, she offered, "My son has spoken of your loveliness and vitality. I daresay he underestimates you."

"I—I beg your pardon?"

"Your hostesses were just telling me that you sustained an unfortunate injury while driving in the park. What they did not say was that *you* were driving. You were, were you not?"

Vivian's jaw dropped and it took her a full minute to regain use of her tongue. "How did you know?"

"Oh, merely an educated guess, my dear. Why, my son and I were only recently discussing a woman's skills at the reins. He is ever glad to put a woman in the driver's seat."

"He is?" Vivian asked, forgetting her discomfiture.

"I am?" Noel muttered, clearly in disagreement.

"To be sure, dearest. You said so yourself." Lady St. Helier retrieved Vivian's arm from Noel's grasp and led her over to the settee. "How do you find London, my dear?"

The familiar and hated question brought equally familiar, tart responses to Vivian's lips. She bit them back, however, and replied diplomatically, "I have enjoyed my sojourn with my kind hostesses immensely."

Lady St. Helier's eyes sparkled. "Very prettily spoken, indeed. One would think your time here in England has been dull. If I am not mistaken, it has been anything but."

Vivian groaned inwardly. She could not have truly expected her hostesses—or Noel, for that matter—to keep the lady in ignorance as to the situation. Still, she would rather not have spoken of the matter. "It has been an . . . unusual welcome, certainly, but I imagine the novelty has all but worn off. I expect the remainder of the Season to be pleasantly uneventful."

"Do you really? You seem the sort to appreciate a bit of chaos." Vivian was wondering if she had just been insulted, albeit charmingly, when Noel's mother continued. "You remind me of myself at your age, my dear, and there was nothing I loathed more than being bored."

Vivian was lost. She could sooner have walked on the ceiling than disliked this vibrant, lovely woman. Silently speculating that Noel had been far more strongly influenced by his feckless sire than his delightful mother, she gave a warm smile.

"I too loathe boredom, my lady, though I am not averse to a bit of peace and quiet on occasion."

"Well, I wish you all the peace you desire. I am afraid, however, it is to be delayed."

"My lady?"

There was as much mischief in the countess's smile as sympathy. "Word has it that Newstead's Canto V has been rushed through the presses and is being prepared for sale even as we speak."

"You must be mistaken, madam. It is much too soon."

"I fear Jane is quite right," Mrs. DeLancey said with a sigh. "I heard rumors of a new canto yesterday, but did not mention the matter in hope that it was mere speculation."

Vivian cursed silently but tried to smile. "Well, then, perhaps it will be the end to all this nonsense. Newstead will undoubtably have turned his attentions to a new subject, and the Vivid One will be forgotten."

"Not likely" was Lady Fielding's gruff pronouncement. "The man is like a bulldog—never releases anything until he has shaken every last vestige of life out of it. He will earn a few pounds yet with the Vivid One."

Her sister nodded sadly. "I imagine the lines at Hatchard's are already filling Piccadilly. Everyone will want to have had a glimpse before the Tate ball tomorrow night."

This time, Vivian groaned aloud and slumped in her seat. Lady St. Helier patted her hand kindly.

"You will be up to the challenge, my dear." Then, with the dexterity of a Vauxhall fire juggler, she changed the subject. "Now, we were just discussing a ball my son is to give and your input would be most welcome. I favor costumes, perhaps with a theme, but Felicity suggests that perhaps a smaller fete would be better. A musical evening, was it not?"

"Oh, yes," Mrs. DeLancey announced with a rapturous smile, vivid woes already forgotten. "A string quartet would be so lovely, perhaps playing Bach . . ."

"Rubbish," her sister growled. "That would be insufferably dull. I vow I have slept through more of those noxious little soirees than Prinny himself. It should be a masqued ball without question. I believe a medieval theme would do, or Greek mythological . . ."

Not wanting to give any thought at all to the appearance of a new canto, Vivian did her best to stimulate unvivid contemplations. As the conversation whirled around her, she took the opportunity to covertly study Noel. Not wise. Deep in contemplating something, he looked almost impossibly handsome. His mouth, which had, not so very long ago, stirred feelings in parts of her far removed from her own lips, was curved in an ironic smile. He looked more than a little satyric, and she would have given nearly anything to know what was behind the smile.

Noel, for his own part, was deliberately avoiding looking at Vivian. He was instead considering what the ramifications would be were he to toss her over his shoulder, carry her out to his carriage, and head for the coast of Devon. His estate there covered several hundred acres, including a stretch of towering cliffs and the beach below. He doubted anyone within fifty miles of the estate had heard of Newstead. The sea wind would lift and tumble Vivian's ebony curls, and scatter any thoughts she might have of Byron and his blasted poems.

He could imagine her standing atop a windswept cliff, proud and glorious, as wild and irresistible as Nimuë herself, eyes flashing with vitality. He could imagine her hair rippling behind her, then later, spread like black silk over pristine white sheets.

He blinked to banish the vision. And opened his eyes to meet the very gaze he was trying to forget—so alluring that a man could drown as easily as in the sea.

"Witch," he murmured unconsciously.

"Which would you prefer, dear?" His mother's voice did not quite break the spell of Vivian's gaze. "It is, after all, your affair too."

His affair.

Vivian blinked. Noel shook his head. "I beg your pardon, madam?"

"You must have an opinion as to which sort of ball we are to have. Though I myself am in favor of a masquerade."

"A masquerade." He detested masquerades. He never bothered with a costume, of course, but even the masks were distressingly uncomfortable. "Would it not perhaps be simpler to avoid anything that requires wigs and paste?"

"And tails," Mrs. DeLancey added decisively. "Lord Higgenbotham attended the Clarke masquerade last year as a dragon. He managed to upset three ladies and the Duke of Kent before someone thought to secure his tail to his sleeve."

Dragons, of course, brought to mind knights in shining armor, fair damsels, and wizards. Noel had the sudden and disconcerting image of himself rigged out as Merlin, complete with looming boulder. No, a masquerade would not do at all. "I have decided . . ." he began.

"Splendid!" His mother clapped her hands. "I very much hope Higgenbotham arrives in dragon garb again. We shall sic him on Derwood."

Lady Fielding chuckled, Mrs. DeLancey sniffed, and Vivian, her bruise partially obscured by the bright color suffusing her cheeks, quietly groaned.

She was quite certain she was leaving a cloud behind her as she walked. Esther had assured her that the powder would stay where she had put it, but Vivian doubted anything applied to one's face with a trowel would stay put. She reached up to gingerly touch her cheek and promptly had her hand swatted for the effort.

"Do not touch," Lady Fielding admonished, readying her fan for another swipe at the girl's fingers. "You will leave smudges."

"I will leave craters."

"Honestly, Vivian, I am beginning to wonder why you came at all."

Vivian refrained from reminding the older woman that

she had all but begged on her knees to be left at home. Her hostesses had been resolute. She must attend, head held high. No one in the household had as yet obtained the newest canto, due primarily to the fact that all copies had been sold within twelve hours of its release. The presses, rumor had it, were running round the clock to print more.

The trio headed up the stairs toward the ballroom, Vivian trailing grumpily behind the sisters. It was bad enough that she had been bullied into attending the Tate bash, far worse that she had been forced to wear white. Mrs. DeLancey clearly did not share Esther's faith in her cosmetics application. It would not do at all, she had declared emphatically, for Vivian to have the shoulders of her gown blemished by fallen powder.

Had she not already felt clownlike, her garb would have decided the matter. A splash of color had been called for—by Lady Fielding, of course. The splash had been provided by a brilliant blue sash purloined from Vivian's lemon-yellow gown and a collection of sapphires taken from Lady Fielding's jewel box. They sparkled in her ears and hair, and circled her throat. They were heavy, cold, and quite blinding.

"Nothing better than good jewels to draw the eye from an imperfection," the older woman had announced.

Now, darting a surreptitious glance down at the sapphire and diamond pendant resting above her bodice, Vivian silently mused that the eye would certainly be drawn from the disguised bruise. In fact, she was reasonably sure that more than one male eye would be drawn improperly south of her cheek.

"The Dowager Baroness Fielding," the butler intoned from his position at the entrance. "Mrs. DeLancey. Miss Vivian Redmond."

With a unity that Wellington himself would have admired, nearly every head in the ballroom swung toward them.

Is it not amazing what mere weeks can do? Vivian speculated dryly. Well used to the scrutiny by now, she automatically lifted her chin, squared her shoulders, and forged ahead. To its credit, the ton was above cordial. In fact, had she not already been half blinded by her own fripperies, she would have winced at the myriad of bright smiles she received as she passed.

"I do believe you are on your way to being labeled an Incomparable," Mrs. DeLancey commented, her own smile no less bright. Apparently her earlier displeasure at the poet's prolificity had been supplanted. "Brava, dearest."

"You would do better to salute Newstead." was her sister's tart rejoinder. "No offense meant, of course, Vivian."

"None taken, madam."

Mention of the poet brought her task to the forefront of her mind. Not, she reflected silently, that he was ever far from her thoughts; she simply relegated him to the nether regions of her brain. But she did have a crusade. She was going to find Byron and, if she had to knock him flat on his impeccably attired rump and sit on him, she would do so. It was time to end the farce once and for all.

First things first, of course. There was the requisite and tedious wait in the receiving line. Mrs. Tate thanked her for attending with rather more gratitude than Vivian thought necessary, and the woman's son stared rather longer than was appropriate at the sapphires. Then, when she would have begun a discreet circuit of the room, the swains arrived.

"I must say," young Lord Yarrow gushed as he led her into a minuet, "you look especially fine this evening, Miss Redmond."

"Thank you, my lord," she replied, willing the orchestra to quicken the tempo to double time.

"You bring to mind visions of alabaster goddesses on the Aegean coast." He nodded decisively at the end of the phrase and promptly trod upon her toe, clearly awed by his own eloquence.

"Again, my lord, thank you." As absurd as the compliment was, it was far better than devious Arthurian sorceresses. So much better, in fact, that she added a gracious "I cannot help but be touched by your kindness."

She regretted the impulse soon enough. The remainder of the dance was liberally peppered with compliments far more absurd and far less articulate than the first. By the time Yarrow returned her to Lady Fielding, Vivian's jaw was stiff from maintaining a fixed smile and her toes throbbed in her scuffed slippers. When the young lord announced his intention of visiting the following day, she could manage no more than a weak nod.

She made it through the next few sets with adequate aplomb. She sensed a good deal of not-disapproving buzzing about her but, much to her relief, no one mentioned the newest canto. She was curious about its contents, to be sure, but not overly so. Someone was bound to mention the matter eventually. For the moment, she was more than content to avoid the topic and was grateful for her partners' forbearance. There were solicitous questions about the state of her health—despite the fact that she had only been out of commission, per se, for one day, and the requisite compliments on her appearance. As always, the men were charming, gallant, and deadly dull.

Two men were notable in their absence. Vivian periodically scanned the crowd for Byron's dark curls, annoyed each time they were not in evidence. She looked for Noel too, but for a far different reason. She did *not* want to encounter him and decided that forewarned was forearmed. As he stood above most of his peers, she should have ample opportunity to flee should he appear. It did not countenance in the least that her heart did a strange flutter at the sight of an ash-brown head. Nor did it matter that the flutter transformed into a sinking when the man turned out to be a stranger.

Back with Lady Fielding, and ready to embark on her search for Byron, she did spy Lord Meriton, resplendent in ruby kerseymere. She promptly decided she did not want to dance with him. There was, of course, the possibility that he would be entertaining, but she was loath to take the chance. Five minutes of potential boredom was five more minutes than she could stomach at the moment.

She had spied Aurelie and Jason some time past, and concluded that now would be a very good time indeed to greet them. She would be able to avoid Meriton politely and, even better, could more easily slip from their side than Lady Fielding's. Announcing her intention to that lady, she took a step away and collided with a silk waistcoat.

The instant rise of her pulse waned when she recognized Mr. Burroughs, a widowed acquaintance of her hostesses. It was not that she did not like the kindly man—she had found him quite warm and charming at their earlier meetings, but she was looking for . . . someone else.

"Good evening, Miss Redmond," Burroughs greeted her cheerfully. "It has been some weeks since I last saw you. How are you finding London?"

"Good evening, sir." She managed a smile, wondering why he could not have asked *anything* else. He was, without question, a highly intelligent fellow. "London has been vastly entertaining."

"Good, good." His responding smile lifted bushy gray brows and lit his kind blue eyes. "I do not suppose you would grace an old man with a dance."

"I would be delighted, sir."

Despite his age, and Vivian decided he was well past fifty, Burroughs had a lively step and took genuine pleasure in the music. She found herself soon enjoying the dance far more than any other of the evening.

"Have you remained in Cambridgeshire these past weeks, sir?" she queried.

"I passed a brief time here soon after your own arrival, my dear. A splendid season of grouse called me home, however, and I have only just returned these eight days past."

"It was good hunting, then?" Vivian was not herself an enthusiast of the hunt, but she recalled the older man's devotion to all aspects of the sport.

"Quite exceptional. Quite." Burroughs executed a dramatic series of turns, making Vivian laugh and catch her breath. "Although, if I have heard correctly, the Season here has been decidedly lively. Rumor has it you have taken the Town by storm, my dear."

Vivian shook her head wryly. "I fear it is not me at all, but the foolish cantos."

"There are two things you must not underestimate," the older man announced sagely, eyes twinkling. "The first is the power of a lovely face and vivid nature."

"And the second?"

"Poetry, my dear. You must never underestimate the power of poetry. It can bring awed speechlessness to the articulate and inspired eloquence to the quiescent."

"*That,* sir, was poetry," Vivian announced. "I venture to say there is the soul of the bard within you."

Burroughs smiled, then winked. "I have dabbled a bit in the art, Miss Vivian Redmond. What man has not? Mind you, I fancy myself a far greater reader than writer."

As the last chords of the dance resounded, Vivian recalled a bit of the information the widows had provided about their old friend. "Yes, Mrs. DeLancey told me you have one of the country's finest collections in your library. What was the subject?"

"Legend," was the reply as Burroughs escorted her from the floor. He deposited her back at Lady Fielding's side and bowed elegantly over her hand. "I have the great fortune, my dear, to possess one of England's better collections of Arthurian legend." Before she could speak, he was off, vanishing into the crowd.

"No," she whispered. "Not possible."

"What was that, girl?" Lady Fielding turned to regard her placidly. "Good of you to dance with Carlton. He is a marvelous fellow, and he has lived such a subdued life since his dear wife passed away."

Subdued was not a word Vivian might have chosen for the charming widower. Still, she asked, "Was he so very active before?"

"It is not to say that he was unfaithful to Penelope. On

the contrary, they adored each other. But in his younger days, he was quite the rake, albeit a delightful one. Oh, yes, always a great one with the ladies was Carlton. I remember . . . oh, thirty-some years back, he had this huge black brute of a horse on which he used to charge about. Always put one in mind of some knight errant with his destrier. He set all our hearts a-flutter, I must say . . ."

Vivian had stopped listening. It was altogether too possible. Burroughs had been a frequent visitor to the widows' home during their sojourn in Cambridge, giving him ample opportunity to view her own impetuous character, not to mention a constant view of her person. He had, too, been in London at precisely the right times to have given a manuscript to a publisher.

To be honest, the concept was quite viable, and rather amusing. She began to laugh quietly. There was no doubt in her mind that Mr. Burroughs, if he were in fact Newstead, was nothing less than grandfatherly in his regard for her. There was nothing remotely lascivious in his expression or demeanor. He would not, however, be averse to reliving some of his wild younger days through poetry.

". . . ever so adroit of speech," Lady Fielding continued.

"And pen, perhaps," Vivian added quietly.

"What was that, my dear?"

"Oh, nothing of import, madam." Over the lady's shoulder, Vivian spied Meriton making his way toward them again. His bright coat worked rather like a beacon. Still not ready for an encounter with him, she once again expressed her desire to find the Tarrants.

"Of course, dear." Lady Fielding nodded her approval. "I shall accompany you. I believe I spied Jane with them. Her visits to Town are so rare. One must grab one's time with her before she flits off again."

Lady St. Helier was, indeed, with the Tarrants. Her son was not. Vivian stifled the flare of disappointment. She would, she informed herself firmly, have plenty of time to gloat over the Newstead matter as soon as she was certain. She did not particularly care that she did not feel like crowing at Noel. There could be no other reasonable explanation for her feelings. Yes, she wanted to gloat, but it would wait.

It was not until Lord Tarrant turned to greet her that Vivian saw the rest of the party. Grace was there, and Lord Holcombe. Vivian had met the young marquess several times and could not help but like him. There was a natural charm and appealing irreverence that quite suited his distinctly diabolic beauty.

He greeted her as warmly as the rest of the party. "Good evening, Miss Redmond. Your presence was sorely missed at the opera. I trust you are . . . er . . . feeling well."

His eyes flashed briefly over her cheek, and she silently berated Aurelie for having passed on the sorry tale to her husband who, in turn, had obviously passed it on to Rafael. She could not maintain any degree of pique, however. She had grown far too fond of the group.

She grinned. "I am feeling much more the thing, thank you, my lord. It is truly amazing what a bit of . . . rest can achieve."

The marquess chuckled, the Tarrants with him. It was Jason who spoke next, saying cheerfully "It is a relief too, Miss Redmond, to see that you managed to arrive without an unfortunate encounter with any blueing."

"Jason!" Aurelie scolded affectionately. "You are becoming bold in your dotage."

"Was I not always a bold fellow, sweetheart?"

"You were anything but when we met. In fact, the word stodgy comes to mind."

The viscount silenced his wife with a melting smile. "May I not at least compliment Miss Redmond on her gown? It is so rare, after all, to find white a divergence."

Vivian, realizing that she had never felt so much at home, so comfortable, as she did with these people, found herself saddened even as she smiled. She would be leaving before too long, returning to Boston and her life there. She was unlikely to ever wear white and even more unlikely to ever meet with her friends again.

"Vivian, is something the matter?"

She turned to find Aurelie studying her with concern, and pushed her melancholy thoughts aside. "Not at all. I was merely thinking of the violet gown that has yet to make its way out of my wardrobe."

Aurelie did not appear convinced, but any comment she might have made was forestalled by a trilling laugh. A tumble of bright red curls appeared briefly over the edge of Rafael's shoulder, then vanished again.

"I detest white!" Chloe Somersham declared, bouncing once more into view, this time behind Grace. "Oh, dear, hide me please! I have just spied George and he looked not in the least pleased. He does so hate it when Bella sends him in search of me."

Vivian turned and craned her neck, searching for Lord Byron. Her view of the ballroom was immediately impeded by yet one more waistcoat, this one a muted bronze. The waistcoat in itself was not familiar, but there was something about the form it covered. Yes, there was no doubt about it.

Noel had arrived.

9

H E WAS NOT in a cheerful frame of mind. In the half
hour he had spent navigating the packed ballroom in
search of Vivian, he had encountered Byron. Twice. And
now it appeared the number was about to rise to three times
if Chloe were correct. As far as Noel was concerned,
George could damn well have the bouncing little chit. He
could not, however, have Vivian.

"Good evening all," he said as evenly as he could.
"Maman, I apologize again for not being able to escort
you ..."

"Nonsense, dearest. Jason served quite nicely in your
stead. I trust your business has been completed to your
satisfaction?"

His business had, in fact, not been completed at all. He
had visited White's, Waiter's, and several other clubs in
search of the men whose entries in the betting book had involved Vivian. All wagers, he was avowed, would be called
off with discretion and speed. The matter could be solved
most efficiently with his fists, to be sure, but he had decided to try simple words first. Unfortunately, Paxton, Fremont, and the others had managed to be everywhere he was
not.

He wondered if Byron could be taught that particular
trick.

"Come along, Vivian," he commanded. "You have promised me this set."

"I have done no—"

He hauled her away from the group before she could

complete her dismissal, sweeping her into the dance. He allowed himself a small smile. At least it was a waltz. She would very likely snipe at him throughout, but he would have his hands on her slender form while she did so.

"Really, St. Helier, that was not well done of you."

He maneuvered her through several sweeping couples. "On the contrary, my dear. It was very well done, indeed. Should I pause to consider my dexterity, I should very likely swell my own head."

Her indelicate snort made her opinion on that matter abundantly clear. "I did not wish to dance with you."

"Ah, Vivian, you wound me." He allowed his fingers to spread more intimately over her back. She felt warm and pliant under his hand. "I fancy I shall recover, however. You usually melt somewhat after a time." He looked down at her face then. From the flashing of her eyes and set of her mouth, he imagined her skin would have been well flushed with familiar pique. Instead, it was a rather dramatic white. "What have you done to your face now?"

"It is powder, St. Helier," she snapped. "I could not very well leave the house with a mottled face, and my hostesses would not let me stay home."

He leaned closer for a better look. "Not bad," he mused, "though it looks a bit like flour. We shall have to make certain you do not overly exert yourself."

"And why is that?"

"Because, my love, a few good dances and you would be wearing dough. Then, if I were to kiss you thoroughly, you might create cake."

Vivian felt her jaw dropping. "Good heavens, Noel, that was *crude!*" Then, before she could stop herself, she was grinning. The grin soon turned into a giggle, and before long, she was laughing heartily. "Cake! What a thought. Though I find it highly unlikely. I am not feeling particularly sweet this evening."

"Vivian," he replied, his own grin lighting his already comely face, "your sweetness might not always be of temperament, but it is never absent."

"You, sir, are outrageous." *And rather marvelous.* The words formed themselves in Vivian's head with a speed and puissance that startled her.

The simple truth of the matter was that she was pleased to see him and no less content to be swaying in his arms. His hand felt very large splayed across her back, wicked in its intimacy, and very nice.

"And your smile warms me to the very core of my outrageous being. It is a far cry from your frequent glares."

"Do I glare at you so very often, then?"

"It would seem so, at the beginning of each of our encounters."

"Have you stopped to consider that it might perchance be your behavior, my lord?" She caught her breath as he pulled her closer.

"My behavior is nothing but that to which you drive me, my love."

Speech had become difficult. "You are a rogue through and through." Needing a respite from the force of his silver eyes, she scanned the crowd. And received a decidedly quelling stare from Lady Fielding, who had by then been joined by a rather imperious-looking woman in livid green. "I believe you shall come to an unsavory end as well, if you do not loosen your grip."

"Why? Are you concealing a knife inside your bodice?" He looked down. "Or perhaps you mean to cosh me with that gem. It might work." He did not lift his gaze.

"Noel," she hissed, battling yet another smile, "stop it! Lady Fielding is watching, and as much as she admires you, she looks quite ready to have your head."

He stopped ogling her bodice and followed her gaze. "Ah, yes. She does seem a bit tight of lip, does she not?" He did not, however, relax his grip.

And she did not particularly wish for him to do so. Perhaps, she mused wryly, life in the midst of gossip had finally turned her into the hoyden her mother so often accused her of being. "Who is that lady with her? She seems a bit tight in the lips herself."

112

"That," Noel informed her as he swept her into a daring turn, "is no one of great import. Merely Sally Jersey."

"*Lady Jersey?* Good grief, you might have told me sooner!"

She nearly upset his balance when she stopped moving her feet. Vivian had a habit, he decided, of stopping dead in her tracks on an altogether too-frequent basis. He seemed to drag her about as often as she moved on her own accord. "You might have asked me sooner. One, two, three . . . one, two, three, Vivian. It is a waltz, you know."

"Yes, it is, and you are holding me indecently close in full view of one of the patronesses of Almack's. Release me at once."

"No." He did release her to nearly arm's length, albeit reluctantly. "Count with me now. One, two . . ."

"Oh, shut up, Noel." She resumed the dance. "Just when I was beginning to like you a little, you behave so."

"Are you not being overly dramatic about this?"

"Perhaps I am." She gave a tight smile. "But matters are feverous enough without adding more fuel to the fire." She met his gaze. "The newest canto was released today."

Noel was more than aware of the fact, but his intent search for Paxton and company had precluded securing a copy. In fact, he had hoped to take advantage of Vivian's aversion to the entire subject and avoid it. He certainly had no desire to hear that she had figured again into the miserable work.

"I take it you are not pleased with Newstead's latest?"

"I have no idea of what is mentioned in Newstead's latest," she shot back, her eyes once again on her estimable hostess. "But I have no wish to draw further attention to myself this evening, especially not from Sally Jersey. We are due to attend the Assembly this week."

"How unfortunate," Noel drawled. He detested Almack's. "Perhaps we ought to see to it that your approval is revoked." He tightened his grip on her waist.

"Oh, no." She braced her hand firmly against his shoulder. "Mrs. DeLancey is looking forward to the evening, and I will not have her disappointed."

"Again, how unfortunate." Noel made a mental note to have Tavis dig about for his knee breeches. He believed he had tossed them into the deepest recesses of his wardrobe some year past. Or perhaps he had chucked them out . . .

"Ah!"

He looked up at Vivian's soft exclamation. *Well, bloody hell.* With a talent born, he was certain, of utter perversity, Byron had reappeared and was standing on the edge of the dance floor not twenty feet from the Ladies Jersey and Fielding. He was conversing with, of all people, old Carlton Burroughs. "Damn," he muttered aloud, and deliberately missed a step. Then another.

It was to no avail. With a final flare, the music ended and Vivian was all but dragging him from the floor by his coatsleeve. He had little choice but to follow, hoping as he did that a bit of maneuvering might get her off in another direction. He should have known better. With a blithe smile and sketched curtsy, she was past Lady Fielding and heading hell-bent toward Byron.

Noel decided it was time to stop her—immediately. He set his feet. And watched as she scooted away. The chit had released her hold on his sleeve and he had not even noticed.

"Damn," he said again, and followed.

Vivian had Lord Byron in her sights. As an unexpected bonus, he appeared deep in conversation with Mr. Burroughs. Splendid. She could not have planned the scenario better herself. She would simply walk up to them, raise her chin, and announce, "Gentlemen, I must insist that you . . ."

"Help me!"

She blinked. And again as a fiery head bounced into view. "Please, Miss Redmond, you must!"

Before she could object, Chloe Somersham had grasped her arm and was dragging her in nearly the opposite direction with a strength that should not really have been sur-

114

prising. The girl might be small, but she was possessed of enough energy to move mountains.

"Lady Chloe . . ." Vivian cast a harried glance over her shoulder. Neither Byron nor Burroughs appeared to have noticed her at all. "Lady Chloe!" Using her own not-insignificant will, she pulled the other girl to a halt. "I am afraid I must insist that—"

"You are an angel!" Chloe's own smile would have been positively beatific had it not been bracketed by a pair of utterly devilish dimples. Vivian's annoyance vanished without a trace. "I am ever so grateful for your aid!"

"I have done nothing," Vivian began.

"Poppycock! You have quite rescued me." Apparently the rescue was not complete, however, as she got an even firmer grip on Vivian's arm and turned away. There was an ominous tearing sound. "Oh!" The girl looked down in dismay. "I have trodden upon my hem. Well, hell and damnation!"

Vivian was ready to offer her condolences when Chloe glanced up again. Her smile, if possible, was wider than before. "I take that back. What providence! Now we have an excuse to visit the retiring room. I daresay it will take some time for a maid to make the necessary repairs."

With that, they were off again.

Some minutes later, seated on one chair while Chloe was perched on another with a maid probing at a rather impressive tear in the flounces of her skirt, Vivian was reminded of Aurelie's comment the first time the girl had crossed their path. Chloe was not, she decided, a light wind. She was a tornado, of the sort that swept over the Western Territories, blithely scattering all but the most solid of edifices in its path.

Well, if she were not to face Byron at the moment, his wife's cousin was an acceptable alternative. "I take it you were fleeing from your family."

Chloe gave a theatrical sigh. "As always, it seems. I do hate being hauled about like some lapdog, allowed only as far as the lead will stretch."

"Are you not perhaps overstating matters, my lady? You are not a dog, after all."

The girl's response was to stomp a delicate foot with vigor, startling the maid into dropping her needle and nearly toppling herself from the chair. There was a moment of high drama as she flailed her arms about, trying to regain her balance. A second maid rushed forward, and Chloe got a grip on her hair. The maid, to her credit, merely winced as the girl regained her equilibrium.

"Thank you," Chloe said politely, sending the poor woman's hair into greater disarray as she tried to pat it back into place. Then, on the same breath, "No, I am not a dog, but upon reconsideration, I vow 'twould not be such a very bad life. Papa's dogs are allowed the run of the estate. When he wishes them back, a groom rushes out with a pan of chopped steak. If my freedom were temporarily curtailed with *my* favorite treat, I suppose I would not mind so much. But instead, the Midge or George come lumbering after me, and I am given a tongue-lashing rather than steak."

Chloe jumped from the chair to assist in the search for the dropped needle. "What is your steak, Miss Redmond? I am especially fond of Milton."

"Milton?"

"Yes, you know, *Paradise Lost*. Ah! Found it!" She crawled under the chair to retrieve the needle. By the time Vivian had made sense of things, Chloe was back atop the cushion. "I find myself feeling decidedly sorry for poor Lucifer. How hard it must have been to be an angel. No fun at all."

Vivian could not help but smile. "And your fun is reading poetry?"

"Reading anything," was the prompt reply. "Except guides for the proper deportment of young ladies. Papa is exceedingly fond of giving me those. He claims I am unmannered and reckless."

"How sad." The sentiment was altogether too familiar. Vivian's own mother had been saying much the same thing for years. "And Milton is your chosen alternative?"

116

"Well, I must profess a certain partiality to some modern poetry, of course."

"Your cousin's, perhaps?"

This time, Chloe's smile was far more wistful than blithe. "I find George's words glorious—expansive and effusive. Not at all like George." She shook her bright curls. "Papa will not allow them in the house. George or his words. He calls both of them profligate and iniquitous."

"Does Lord Byron supply you with his books?"

"Goodness, no! He notices me only when Annabella has sent him off on a retrieval mission, and then hardly with warm regard. No, I must steal the books from the Midge. She hides them in her wardrobe. I fancy she is in love with him."

I fancy you are, too. Vivian felt a rush of sympathy for the girl. Rather like Lucifer in heaven, young Chloe must have a terribly hard time of it, being so close and yet denied what she desired as it belonged to another.

All of her plans to press for clues regarding Newstead's identity vanished. "Chloe," she asked gently, "if you could do anything you wished, what would it be?"

The girl's eyes brightened, as Vivian had suspected they would. She was certain no one had bothered to ask any such question recently, if ever. "If I could do anything," Chloe replied immediately, "I would travel, as George has, to the Continent and beyond. And I would write of it, as he has."

"You will have the opportunity."

"Perhaps." The girl shrugged. "If Papa marries me off to an adventurous sort of man."

"You think he will not?"

Chloe laughed, though it was not with her customary gaiety. "I suppose it will depend on how I stand in his eyes when he makes his choice. At the moment, he seems to be considering the sort of suitors who might actually take me to the Continent."

"Well, that is good."

"Not at all. What I mean to say is, considering his present frame of mind, Papa might choose one who would eventually be forced to flee to the Continent after fighting a duel."

Vivian blinked. "Over you?"

"Over another man's wife, most likely." This inspired a startled gasp from the maid. Chloe patted her head consolingly as she hopped from the chair. "Thank you," she said brightly, bending over to check her mended hem. "It looks just like new." Then, to Vivian, "Shall we go? I do not fancy having to face George and Bella, but I am ever so grateful for the respite. It has been fun, Miss Redmond, has it not?"

"Chloe . . ." Vivian put out her hand, unsure of what she could possibly say.

She received a brilliant smile. "Pay it no mind, please. I knew from the moment we met that you would be an angel. I cannot tell you how much I appreciate your great kindness, but I assure you, I am very good at seeing to myself."

Yes, I am certain you are, Vivian thought sadly as Chloe skipped past her. *And it should not be so.* She had not been so very kind, after all, merely sympathetic. And she was hardly an angel. How sad it was that this vibrant young woman had seen so little sympathy that she would be so grateful.

She followed in Chloe's wake, hurrying to keep up. If the girl was going to hand herself over to Byron, Vivian was determined to be behind her. All thoughts of the cantos had been pushed from her mind, replaced by an equally righteous resolution to take the man to task for causing his wife's cousin such distress. The least he could do, she thought heatedly, was provide copies of his blasted books.

As it turned out, she did not have the opportunity. Chloe had just cut a rather daring path through a gaggle of matrons when Vivian, trying to follow with a bit more decorum, found her path blocked by perhaps the one person she least wanted to encounter.

"Good evening, Miss Redmond. I thought I spied you

earlier, but I could not be certain. Your face did not seem familiar, somehow. Are you unwell?"

Vivian sighed and suppressed the urge to send a blast of powder onto the leaf-green satin before her. "Good evening, Miss Burnham."

Lydia Burnham, thin smile in place, leaned forward. "Ah, I see now that it is powder on your face. I really had thought you ill."

"How gracious of you to be concerned. I assure you, I am quite well." Really, the woman was an unpleasant piece of work. "Are you enjoying yourself this evening? I daresay I would have expected you to be dancing." She could not help herself. "I myself had a lovely waltz with Lord St. Helier. He is a splendid partner, so attentive." She vowed to scratch a cushion or two on returning home. If she were going to be a cat, she might as well do so properly.

Lydia's eyes narrowed but she managed another semblance of a smile. "I have had the pleasure of being partnered by St. Helier on many occasions, and I do agree he is charming company. Flighty, though, I am afraid. He seldom retains his interest for long. So few of us have been blessed with his regard past a Season at most."

"How gratifying for you. I fancy as such a close acquaintance, you have seen him at his very worst." Vivian had a few choice comments to add, but was ready to be done with the encounter. "If you will excuse me, Mrs. DeLancey is beckoning . . ."

She moved to step around the other woman but was brought up short by a sweeping hand. "I cannot let you go, Miss Redmond, without congratulating you on your own continued favor."

"With St. Helier? Goodness, we have known each other such a short time. It is perfectly understandable that we find each other intriguing. I fancy we shall grow bored soon enough."

"Undoubtably," Lydia replied. "Though I was not referring to St. Helier, but to Mr. Newstead."

Oh, bother. "Oh?"

"Why, yes. You are the first subject to last past one canto. Really, Miss Redmond, you must tell me how you have managed it. Byr ... er ... Newstead was not nearly so smitten with his Lady of August Charms, and she did grant him her ... favors."

Vivian had quite had enough. "I expect is it the element of the chase," she said pointedly. "Whoever the young lady is, she has likely led the poet on a merry chase. Men do so hate women who make their sentiments too obvious. Rather like monkeys, you know, attaching themselves to the gentlemen's arms and gazing upward with soulful eyes. Now"—she all but shouldered her way past the speechless Lydia—"I really must go to Mrs. DeLancey. Good evening to you, Miss Burnham."

She did eventually make her way to that lady's side. Much to her relief, the widow was settled comfortably in the shadows of a large potted tree, chatting with her friends. Vivian slipped into the seat beside her, grateful for the concealing leaves.

She had just encountered two women who were very much in love with two impossible men. Yes, she mused, Byron and Noel were much alike in many ways: sinfully handsome, too clever by half, and blessed with enviable social presence. Chloe and Lydia, however, could not have been more different. Chloe's heart was true—expansive and effusive, as she had called Byron's words. Vivian thought it would be a long time, if ever, before Chloe abandoned her affections for the mesmeric poet. She sent a heartfelt prayer heavenward that the girl might have the speediest and most painless of resolutions.

Lydia, on the other hand, was as cold and selfish of heart as possible. It was not Noel she cherished, but his looks, wealth, and status. Vivian was startled to realize that she thought he deserved far better, despite his irreverence and occasional crudeness. He deserved a woman who would appreciate his wit and cherish his spirit, at the same time taming his rashness and invoking the tenderness he so fully possessed.

Several possibilities popped into her mind. Chloe might bring out the very best in Noel, if he did not throttle her first. Then there was Grace. The two of them seemed to share a teasing yet genuine affection. Both families would certainly be overjoyed at such a match.

Vivian was not so pleased with the prospect.

No, she liked Grace far too well to wish her the burden of someone like Noel Windram. The girl deserved far better than a careless, officious, Casanova of a man. The Marquess of Holcombe was far more suitable. He was a rake, to be sure, but there was a sensitivity under his satyrlike exterior. And he too seemed genuinely fond of his friend's younger sister. There was no doubt that Grace admired him. She could do far worse—and Rafael could find none better.

"Your thoughts are amusing, dearest?"

Vivian surfaced from her contemplations to find Mrs. DeLancey regarding her benevolently. "Not amusing precisely, madam. Satisfying, though I was thinking of a perfect match for a friend."

"Well, that is certainly an agreeable occupation. But what of you, my dear? Have you no desire to find such a perfect match for yourself?" The older woman tilted her head, birdlike, to the side and remarked thoughtfully, "The young man in Boston of whom you have spoken is perhaps not truly the one for you."

"Why would you say that?"

"He has been less in your conversation, of late. Less in your thoughts, I assume. And he is, after all, in Boston. Distance is one of the greatest detractors from a man's consequence."

Vivian smiled. "That might well be true, madam, but he has his usefulness."

"Does he? I rather think he might get in the way of your happiness, when all is said and done. Convenience so often supplants real suitability."

"Dav ... er ... Daniel's existence suits me perfectly, madam. He makes no unreasonable demands, does not expect me to change in accordance to popular whims, and he never, ever bores me. What more could I wish for?"

The kindly widow's eyes sharpened with a shrewdness that was more than a bit disconcerting. Then she blinked, gave a bright smile, and patted Vivian's hand. "Then you have found your match in this distant ... Daniel. I am merely a silly, romantical old lady to suggest that you could find such a one here."

Vivian could not say why, but the words and affectionate touch brought a prickle to the backs of her eyes. No, she would be far better off at home in Boston. Where everyone seemed to make unreasonable demands, expected her to change the very essence of herself, and bored her past tears.

10

There lies a truth that through our fleeting days,
We live to love and do through loving gain
Such grandeur as sets heart and soul ablaze—
A fire coursing fast within the vein,
Inspiring us to rise above the pain
Of solitude. What magic do you weave?
What vivid, restless bond doth oe'r me reign?
Enlighten me! Is love the force to lead
Me to perform each unexpected deed?
                    —Newstead's *Heart's Notions*, canto V

"HELL," LORD TARRANT muttered, "would be a vast improvement."

His wife elbowed him in the ribs. "Really, Jason, you say those exact words each time we are here."

"Consider it a sort of incantation, my love. Each time we are here, I hope for a miracle."

"You have yet to receive your miracle, and I would advise you not to expect it in the foreseeable future." Aurelie smiled teasingly. "Do you continue to come in order to test your Faith? I vow no martyr has suffered more than you."

"I come," her husband replied softly, "because it is important to several of the women I love that I do so." There was a moment of eloquent silence as the two regarded each other. Then Jason grinned. "The agony I endure at Almack's is nothing compared to what I would suffer should I refuse to attend. Grace must have her time in the public eye, after all."

His sister sniffed aloud. "I assure you I would be more than pleased to spend my Wednesdays at home with a book! I derive no pleasure from this, either." Her tawny eyes took on a wicked gleam. "Do you see Lord Manning leaning against that column? I vow he expired Wednesday last, but no one has thought to ascertain whether his stillness is due to his demise, or merely another deathly dull evening at Almack's."

Vivian laughed with the rest of the party but, for her own part, she had to admit she was highly intrigued by the scene around her. Almack's, the bastion of the London elite, was hardly what she had expected. She had been warned, certainly, but nothing had prepared her for the warped floors, excessive heat, and appalling refreshments. Her mouth was still puckered from the single sip of lemonade she had taken some time earlier.

As decreed, all of the men wore knee breeches, white cravats, and tail coats. With the impressive number of rotund figures and bright colors, Vivian was reminded of a flock of complacent budgies, strutting and bobbing. It was a decidedly amusing sight.

She was, much to her continued disgust, garbed yet again in white. Her hostesses would hear of nothing else. Apparently it was one matter to buck tradition at private affairs, quite another to do so at the Assembly rooms. Grace, too, was in requisite white, but her golden hair and charmingly flushed face were far better suited to the color.

Vivian had noted of late that the younger girl's cheeks, ever a lovely pink, deepened to rose in a certain gentleman's presence. No matter how fluently she professed her boredom, her face belied her words. Wherever Rafael Marlowe happened to be was where Grace was happiest.

Vivian wondered why she seemed to be the only one who could see it. Without a doubt, Aurelie, Jason, and Rafe were among the more intelligent persons she had ever met.

They appeared utterly benighted, however, on the matter of Grace.

Love is blind—the Shakespeare line flitted into her mind—*and lovers cannot see the pretty follies that commit.*

She pondered the older trio's inability to comprehend the girl's heart. There was no doubt that the Tarrants adored Grace. Aurelie treated her as a sister by birth rather than simply by marriage, and Jason, as he so firmly voiced, was willing to endure the torments of Almack's for her sake. Rafe, too, was openly fond of her, ever teasing and provoking her to laughing retorts. Perhaps it was their affection that blinded them.

What a terrible shame, Vivian thought, that Rafe apparently could not see how very lovely—and in love his friend's little sister was.

Jason yawned, then coughed as Aurelie's elbow once again made contact with his ribs. "I am sorry, sweetheart, but if something interesting does not happen soon, you shall have to carry me out on a board along with Manning." He turned to Grace. "You might consider doing us all a favor and falling in love with one of the poor sods who are always fawning at your feet. I do not fancy another year of passing my Wednesday evenings here. It is your second Season, sprite. Are you aiming to have a third?"

"Yes" was the tart reply. "And a fourth, fifth, and sixth if necessary!"

Jason groaned.

"You will be back again soon enough," Rafe announced blithely, "once you have daughters to be brought out. Will you be so quick to throw them to the lads?"

"Any man who thinks to sniff about my daughters shall meet posthaste with the business end of my pistol!"

"Admit it," Aurelie teased. "You would do the same for Grace. In fact, you very nearly have done so on more than one occasion."

"Yes, well, it would not be necessary if she were not so resistant and our parents not so determined to see her wed.

Their eagerness makes them careless in whom they consider an acceptable match."

"Like Fremont?" Grace offered with a grimace.

Noel, who had been standing quietly off to the side, made a choked sound. "Fremont offered for Grace?"

"And was accepted," the girl replied, "until Jason took matters into his hands."

"It was nearly a dueling pistol that I took into hand," her brother muttered. "Fortunately, Father was not willing to let that happen. Rickey has no interest in inheriting the title or managing the estates."

Vivian was finding this all vastly entertaining. "He was afraid you would actually challenge the man to a duel?"

"The challenge was a forgone conclusion should the match not have been called off," Jason replied. "He was afraid I would die. I am a proficient enough marksman to put a bullet in an opponent's arm, but the consensus is that Fremont is the sort who would cheat."

The orchestra struck up a Scottish reel then, and Grace grinned up at her brother. "It is ever so gratifying to know you would risk a bullet for me, Jason. Dare I ask you for something much more dire?"

"What would that be, sprite?"

"I should very much like to dance."

"I would prefer a bullet," was the instant retort. "Go find one of your fawning admirers and dance with him." Jason glanced about. "I see Brighton and Havers skulking by the windows. It is a wonder they have not come to sweep you off as yet."

Grace pouted good-naturedly. "They fear your wrath, of course. And I cannot very well go ask them for a dance. It would be beyond forward."

"Ah, but when has that stopped you in the past?"

She promptly stuck her tongue out at him. "You are truly impossible this evening."

Noel stepped forward. "In the interest of maintaining good family relations, I feel I must intervene." He gave an elegant bow. "I would be honored, my lady, if you would deign to share this set with me."

Grace smiled happily. "I should be delighted, my lord. Thank you." Then, with a last sneer at her brother, she allowed Noel to lead her onto the floor.

As they entered the set, a rather energetic young man collided with Noel. The fellow's flailing arm connected solidly with his shoulder, causing him to wince. As he and Grace took their places, he rotated his shoulder. If his expression were any indication, it was not a comfortable act.

"Looks like Dillingham has brought his flask with him again," Rafe announced cheerfully. "Really, the fool ought to be more careful. A few more drunken escapades and he will be barred from the Assembly Rooms for good."

Vivian was more concerned with Noel's response than Dillingham's imminent social demise. "Has Lord St. Helier injured himself recently?"

It was Aurelie who replied. "A war wound. It still pains him at times."

Vivian remembered Noel mentioning something of the sort. She turned to Jason. "Ah, yes. He said you saved his life on that occasion."

"Did he?" Jason shook his head and gave a wry smile. "How gracious of him."

"Then it is not true?"

"In a manner of speaking, it is quite true, I suppose. I did manage to get him out of the fray and to a field hospital. Did he happen to mention that he should not have been anywhere near that particular place at the time?"

"No, he did not. Are you saying he foolishly put himself in jeopardy?"

At this, Jason gave a startled laugh. "Well, that is certainly one way of looking at it." He gazed at her for a moment. "I suppose I shall have to tell you the whole tale."

"Please do, my lord. I confess I am most interested."

"My own company had been engaged for several days in a hopeless battle. I had lost far too many men, and the ones who remained, though steadfast to the core, were too battered to continue. I would have called a retreat, but we were surrounded. I was convinced that I had seen my last day." His eyes clouded. "Though it was far harder to accept that the young men under my command, who had seen so much less of life than I, were to be denied their chance."

"I am sorry," Vivian said softly, and Aurelie reached out to clasp her husband's hand.

Jason managed a smile. "I lost more men that day, but providence stepped in and saved those of us who were left. Apparently St. Helier got news of the battle where his own regiment was resting some ten miles away. He roused his men, rode hell-for-leather in our direction, and, though we were still outnumbered, managed to divert the enemy long enough to allow for our escape. He was wounded protecting my back."

He shook his head at the memory. "His men were as weary and battered as mine. I think he was even more so. But he deliberately disobeyed Wellington's orders to stay put and came to our aid. He could very well have been court-martialed for doing so. Not to mention killed in the effort. Damned foolish bugger," he cursed, but there was a wealth of emotion in his voice.

"Oh." Vivian found herself suddenly speechless.

This was not the tale Noel had told her. She had conjured up images of Jason riding to the rescue, pulling his friend from the jaws of death. Apparently, it had been the other way about. She found herself awed, albeit reluctantly, by the humility and devotion she perceived. When Jason had first mentioned that Noel should not have been at the battlesite, she had assumed it had been a matter of recklessness, perhaps even a wild grab at heroism.

The heroism had been the result, not the intent. He had ridden into the worst of situations, ignoring the odds in order to make even the most desperate of attempts to save his friend.

Love is blind, and Noel had closed his eyes to his own quite probable death. All out of love for a friend.

Suddenly her own eyes were clouded by tears. Needing

a moment alone, she whispered to Aurelie, "I believe I will visit the retiring room."

The other woman regarded her shrewdly for a moment as if deciding whether she ought to offer her company. At last she nodded. "We shall be here when you care to rejoin us."

Vivian dampened her handkerchief in the retiring room basin and pressed it to her face. She had not wanted to hear Jason's tale, had not wanted to consider the fact that Noel was not as feckless, as much without concern as she had believed. He was, without even trying, insinuating his way into her affections. It would be altogether too easy to fall in love with such a man, and she could not allow that to happen.

Noel Windram, Earl St. Helier, was all she wished to avoid. He was arrogant, loose of tongue, and an unmitigated rogue—honor or no. He was also British to the very center of his being. His place was among the blithe, intricately regulated English aristocracy. Hers was in common, simple Boston.

"Miss?" A maid appeared at her side. "Are you unwell? Can I fetch you something to drink?"

Vivian blinked to clear her eyes and her thoughts. "Thank you," she replied, "but I am . . . fine."

She made her way slowly back into the ballroom, uncertain that she could face Noel at the moment, certain she did not wish to. Perhaps if she found her hostesses and claimed a headache, they would take her home.

She was so absorbed in contemplating the best course of action that she did not see the figure in her path until she was nearly upon it. She skidded to a stop just short of a collision. "I beg your pardon," she murmured, taking a step to the side.

"It is I who beg pardon, Miss Redmond. I seem to have made a habit of getting in your way."

Her eyes flew up to meet a sardonic blue gaze. Byron looked, if possible, more handsome than he had in the past, and every bit as raffish. "My lord," she managed after a moment.

He gave her an enigmatic smile. "Are you enjoying your evening, Miss Redmond? I imagine Almack's would be an odd experience for an American."

Her mind whirled, searching for the words she needed to say to him. It was no great surprise that she was left with a veritable blank. His reputation for mesmerizing his audiences was not undeserved. "I find people much the same everywhere," she said eventually. "Though their choice of entertainment varies, the motivations are much the same."

She had finally been worn down by Esther's prodding and had read the latest Newstead canto only that morning. It was considerably shorter than the last. True, the Vivid One had been the subject, but there had been a palpable change in the tone. It had confused her. Where the earlier theme had been one of lurid fascination and conquest, there was now a sense of soul-searching. She knew the vast majority of readers would disagree heartily, but she had the strong sense that the woman was not really the core of the work, but love itself, and the quest for inner fulfillment.

It no longer mattered, at least to herself, whether she was the Vivid One. The poet, be he Byron, Burroughs, or another, was no longer writing of base gratification. She was certain the piece had been written for the purpose of making money, but it had been conceived out of something far different.

Byron continued to regard her through unfathomable eyes. "Perhaps you would care to enlighten me on what that motivation is."

Suddenly she saw not a charismatic, unprincipled rake but a man like any other, in need of the same sustenance. "I believe we are all motivated by a need for basic affection, my lord. No person exists in a void, after all. We all must feel we are valued by and of value to those around us."

There was a lengthy silence as they stood, gazes locked. Vivian realized that she did not really know this man at all. She only knew what others said of him, and what she sensed. She had no idea what to expect from him in the

130

wake of her words—assent, derision, no response at all. When he at last nodded and opened his mouth to reply, she found she was holding her breath.

"It is always a novelty . . ."

Whatever he was going to say was lost in a cry from behind him. "Miss Redmond!"

Lord Meriton strode forward, the perfect picture of the ton buck. For the occasion, he was garbed in emerald green and gold. There was no questioning the fact that he was an exceedingly handsome man. At the moment, however, he was about as welcome a sight as a hobgoblin. "I am delighted to see you here," he announced, bowing over Vivian's hand. "Byron," he greeted her companion coolly.

"Meriton." The poet gave an equally cool smile. Then, even as Vivian willed him to stay, he nodded and said, "It has been a pleasure, Miss Redmond. Enjoy the remainder of the evening." His gait, she noticed as he walked away, was almost determinedly even.

"How fortunate that I spied you." Meriton too was watching Byron's departure. "He has no call, speaking to you in the midst of polite society. Yes, good thing I was here to see to the matter."

She turned, wondering how she could possibly tell him just how unwelcome his intervention had been. She decided it would not be worth the effort. "If you would be so kind as to escort me back to my hostesses, my lord. I must speak with Lady Fielding."

And she did. It was high time to leave. She needed to think.

"With pleasure." Meriton offered an impeccably clothed arm and they made their way toward the corner where the widows were seated.

It was slow going in the crush, and there was no haste in Meriton's pace. Vivian, lost in her own thoughts, payed scant attention to his comments, giving an occasional nod of agreement. It was very important that she not encounter Noel as she left. If she did happen to get too close, she might not want to leave at all.

". . . this dance, Miss Redmond?"

She realized the viscount had stopped. He was looking at her expectantly, and she tried to recall what he had said. It had sounded like an invitation to dance. "I beg leave to demur, my lord. I am not feeling quite the thing, and think it would be best if I were to make an early end to the evening."

His handsome features shifted in concern. "I am certain that would be very wise. We cannot have you taking ill just when the very best round of the Season is commencing."

"Thank you, sir, for your consideration." At least he seemed to be moving slightly more quickly now.

". . . tomorrow, to ascertain you are well?"

Again, she took a stab at responding. "I am not certain I shall be receiving, my lord, but you are always a welcome visitor."

He seemed satisfied with the answer. "Perhaps it is for the best. I must pay an unfortunate visit to my Shropshire estate."

"Nothing serious, I hope." She had only the sketchiest idea of where Shropshire was—somewhere to the northwest, she thought—and wondered just how long such a trip could be counted upon to take.

"Nothing you need concern yourself with. I expect to be back within a sennight. If it is agreeable, I shall call upon you then."

"Of course, my lord," Vivian replied vaguely, back in her own musings again.

Lady Fielding was more than happy to leave. She made no secret of the fact that she found Almack's a smashing bore. Mrs. DeLancey, however, was quite content in the Assembly Rooms. She responded immediately to Vivian's mention of a headache, though, and was actually the one who had them out the door in minutes.

"It would not do at all for you to miss the St. Helier affair. I vow it will be quite the event of the Season. Dear Jane always manages to organize the most lively evenings."

As the carriage rolled away, Vivian silently debated

whether she could possibly extend a headache for a week. It was improbable. Neither sister was likely to be fooled, and both would expect an explanation.

She did not think she was up to explaining that she was in imminent danger of losing her heart to the dashing Lord St. Helier, or that if she hoped to avoid such a catastrophe, she would have to remain indisposed for every event at which she might meet him. No, she did not think she was up to explaining at all.

Noel strode into his club the following afternoon, still miffed from the night before. Vivian, damn her eyes, had vanished like a puff of smoke after her encounter with the bloody ubiquitous poet, leaving behind a brief message for Aurelie that she was feeling unwell and would be departing. He had been looking forward to having time with her. The waltz was still considered indecent at Almack's, but there would have been other dances. He had been set on taking his limit of two. Then, too, there would have been time for the lively banter that had become so pleasant a part of his evenings. Few women of his acquaintance, if any, could hold a candle to Vivian when it came to verbal sparring.

He mentally ticked off the weeks remaining in the Season. There were not nearly enough. Then she would be returning to Boston. He was going to have to double his efforts if he were to have her charms well and truly expended by the end of June.

Jason and Rafael were waiting for him at Tattersall's even as he passed through the club's hallway. He had a small matter to attend to first. Paxton always engaged in a game of whist on Thursday afternoons, and Noel was determined to have the matter of the wagering settled once and for all.

Paxton was in the White's game room, all right, lounging in his chair and looking for all the world like a dissipated pasha. The man favored colors on much the same scheme as Derwood, and usually wrapped his portly frame in a her alarming combination. On th...

use waistcoat and purple coat.

Noel did not bother with greeti...

ouchy to bother with any of the

aned over the table, scattering ca...

handful of the man's surprisi...

rowled, "You will remove any

Redmond from the book, Paxto...

make no others." He accented

shake.

Paxton merely gave a small s...

green in his florid face, and N...

minded of a ginger tomcat he h...

beast had a habit of eviscerati...

leaving the entrails on the mano...

gift. Grimacing with disgust, No...

and straightened.

"Really, St. Helier," Paxton

twitch to the mangled neckcl...

went out with the advent of the

equally unpleasant lot, chuckle...

not my wagers that ought to c...

that are far more interesting."

"And which might those be...

The group at the table la...

pounding the lot of them, but

two or three before he found h...

a fist or walking stick. His sh...

and he did not relish having

"Ah, that would be too eas...

with unsuppressed amuseme...

dig for yourself. I will tell

is all but won. Or lost, of c...

sition in the matter."

Noel cursed silently and

again. "Let me make my p...

you are so much as think...

alone wagering on her, I w...

time before you are able to lift a pen again. Do you comprehend what I am saying?"

"I expect I can extract your meaning from in between the grunts and growls." Paxton turned his eyes back to his cards. "Happy reading, St. Helier."

Still fuming, Noel spun on his heel and headed for the betting book. A quarter hour later, he was still reading.

There were twenty-four new wagers either naming Vivian or hinting at her identity. He was enraged by every single one of them.

11

NEWS OF THE duel spread through Polite Society like wildfire.

"It is too much to bear!" Mrs. DeLancey gasped, waving her limp handkerchief in front of her flushed cheeks. "I vow I have not been so discomposed in eons. My poor nerves are quite overset!"

Her sister, uncustomarily subdued, nodded her assent. "It is unfortunate, to be sure. We always knew the young man was wild, but it is distressing nonetheless to be proven all too correct in our assessment."

Vivian, for her own part, was mute with sick horror.

The three were gathered in Aurelie's parlor, only one of many such groupings in Town that day. The viscountess, restrained as her guests, nonetheless managed to take some control over the situation. Summoning the butler, she gave him a quiet order. The man returned some minutes later, bearing a decanter and four glasses.

"I believe something a bit stronger than tea is required," she said matter-of-factly as she poured the brandy. She handed the glasses around. Even the decorous Mrs. DeLancey accepted hers with alacrity.

"Shocking," that lady murmured as she took a hearty sip. "Absolutely shocking."

"A bloody disgrace" was Lady Fielding's more apt contribution. She downed the contents of her glass and held her hand out. "Ply that bottle, Aurelie."

The four fell silent after that, the only sound in the room coming from the ticking of the mantel clock. Each absorbed in her own thoughts, none heard the sound of boot heels in the hall. Vivian nearly spilled her brandy when the parlor door flew open.

Aurelie jumped to her feet and rushed to greet her husband. "Is it true then?"

Jason nodded a terse greeting to the others. "I am afraid it is quite true. Reports are sketchy, but it looks as if he will be forced to flee to the Continent, at least for the time being."

"Well." His wife sat down heavily on the nearest chair and absently handed him her full glass.

"I hope there is one of those for me." Noel strode across the room, deftly plucked Vivian's glass from her fingers, and downed the brandy in a single swallow. "It is still damnably cold out there."

Vivian moved her skirts as he dropped onto the settee beside her and peered out the window. It was, to her, as much like England as ever, damp and chilly. Still, she had become accustomed to the inclement spring weather and thought the present atmosphere well suited to the day. "I take it then that Idlesby died."

Noel refilled the glass and handed it back to her. "You look as if you could use this. But no, the man is still alive at latest report, though it is uncertain whether he shall remain so. Apparently Fremont's bullet is lodged somewhere high in his chest."

"Well, at least the poor man can afford the best of surgeons," Mrs. DeLancey murmured. "My heart goes out to his family. No one deserves to suffer such pain . . . and scandal."

Her sister snorted. "The poor man should have known better than to challenge Fremont! Anyone with any sense would have considered the fact that the bounder might cheat."

"Vivian?" Noel gently touched her arm. "Are you all right? This foolishness is hardly liable to start a shooting frenzy across the country."

Vivian had not seen much of Noel in the past few days,

and she looked her fill now. His hair was misted and wind-blown, his eyes bright from his time out of doors. He looked wild, careless, and utterly beautiful. And it was just such beauty from which she knew she must keep her distance.

"I am fine," she replied, glancing away. "I am merely feeling for Miss Idlesby. She is a good sort of girl and does not merit such torment."

Lady Fielding snorted again. "A good sort of girl would not have been caught half dressed in a gazebo with a man like Fremont!"

"I would venture to say, madam," Vivian replied with far less fervor than she was feeling, "that the fault is less hers than Society's. She is not stupid, nor is she deaf. The ton has made no secret of the fact that she is determined terribly plain and that any attention she receives is due to her fortune alone. I expect she was merely showing a bit of the spirit to which, I feel compelled to believe, she is well entitled."

There was a moment of heavy silence. Then Aurelie added, "Nor is it true that she was discovered in a state of undress. Even Lady Cowper, who was among the group who found them, will attest to that. She and Fremont were engaged in an improperly close embrace, to be sure, but nothing more than that."

"It would seem her father disagreed," Mrs. DeLancey said sadly.

"Idlesby is a fool," Noel replied, ableit without rancor. "He is so determined to see the chit married off that he pushed Fremont too far."

"Fremont fired before the count was finished!" was Lady Fielding's tart comment on the matter.

Noel flashed a sardonic smile. "So did Idlesby."

"Did he?" Aurelie shook her head. "What a tale. I take it that *his* shot went wide."

Her husband nodded. "It was bound to. Fremont's bullet struck first."

"Scandal," Mrs. DeLancey repeated. "I do so hate duels.

They make everyone so giddy and bloodthirsty. I daresay we will be talking of nothing else for months. Well, I suppose the family brought it on itself. Nothing good ever comes of toying with the Marriage Mart."

"Everyone toys with the Marriage Mart, Felicity!" her sister snapped. "It is the nature of the beast."

"I still feel heartily sorry for Regina." Vivian stared into the depths of the brandy. "She has done nothing a hundred other debutantes have not done, and yet she will probably end up in complete disgrace, relegated to a quiet life on some distant country estate. All for falling into a bit of excitement." She scowled. "I do not like the ton at all."

"Ah, Vivian." Noel patted her hand. "Do not fret. Should her father live, they will undoubtably retire to the country until next Season. He will be a bit of a hero. And should he die, Regina will be an obscenely wealthy young woman. Money erases most scandals. Either way, rest assured that she will be back in Town next year."

There were several muffled chuckles from the group. Vivian, for her own part, thought the entire situation cruel and horrible, but Noel's charm was impossible to ignore. "It is still a terrible thing to have happen."

"True." Again the wry smile. "But it could not have happened at a better time, at least as far as my mother is concerned. I daresay my home will be filled to bursting." He sighed. "I suppose I will have to order more champagne."

True to his prediction, there was not a space left unfilled in the ballroom the following evening. Polite Society had come out in force despite the continued poor weather. Most would have attended regardless, Vivian thought. There did not seem to be a person present who was not fond of Lady St. Helier. Then too, there were those who simply could not resist joining the gossip mill. The Idlesby-Fremont duel was quite the most scandalous event of the Season thus far, and could be counted upon to provide salacious conversational fodder for months to come.

The tale had wiped all thought of Mr. Newstead from the

ton's mind, and Vivian was grateful. Not that she was pleased to hear Regina Idlesby's name falling from forked tongues, but she was vastly relieved that she had not once heard the word "vivid." Horace Idlesby had survived the night, and wagers were leaning toward his favor.

"They will all be leaving soon enough," Vivian had heard one smug matron say. "The women shall not be able to show their faces in public until they are able to leave. The question, of course, is whether Idlesby shall be accompanying them in the carriage—or in a box!"

As far as Vivian was concerned, the entire sordid event was indicative of Society's inherent disinterest in anything genuine or meaningful. No one had been hurt by Regina's foray into the gazebo, and nothing had been solved by her father's dawn meeting. Idlesby was gravely wounded, Regina was in disgrace, and Fremont was on his way to the Continent to kick up his heels until such time as he could return.

Vivian speculated that Fremont's absence from Town could well be considered a benefit. She had no liking for the man. The fact remained, however, that none of the Drury Lane melodrama had been inspired by anything worthy. Fremont had not compromised Miss Idlesby out of any true affection, nor, she believed, had the girl's father been motivated by love. No, if all was to be believed, he had acted more out of outrage that he would never be rid of her.

"Dismal affair," she muttered under her breath.

"How can you say such a thing?" the fair maiden at her side asked. "It is perhaps the most smashing success of the Season!"

"I beg your pardon, madam," Vivian replied. It was, in fact, Mrs. DeLancey to whom she spoke. The long blond wig and conical headpiece were a bit incongruous for the plump matron, but she was obviously having a splendid time. She had dropped her spangled handkerchief no less than a dozen times for passing gentlemen to retrieve. "I was referring to the duel, not the ball."

"Oh, pooh." Mrs. DeLancey waved the handkerchief in

Vivian's direction but managed to keep a grip on it. " 'Tis a shame to even think of the matter in the midst of such fun." She peered through her painted half-mask. "Does not Jane look marvelous?"

Lady St. Helier, resplendent as Marie Antoinette, did indeed look exceedingly well. The gown, Lady Fielding had informed her, was one of Jane's own, from her younger days. Vivian caught herself sighing, wondering if she would age half so well.

She had yet to spy Noel and wondered how he was garbed. Images of a dashing buccaneer sprang to mind. She could well envision him in billowing shirt and tight pantaloons, brandishing a wicked-looking sword. Yes, such a costume would suit him admirably.

She had herself refused to don a costume, much to her hostesses' dismay. She had contrived to divert them by suggesting that she attend the masquerade as a Colonial soldier. Uncle Thomas's gear was buried in a trunk in Boston, but she had assured the ladies that she could make due with items purloined from their own attics. The late Lord Fielding's collection of weapons, she announced, included a perfectly ideal musket. The widows had capitulated with amusing speed, allowing that a beaded domino would serve, indeed. The domino had been duly procured, covered with a dazzling array of beads, all in shades of silver and purple.

Vivian had decided to wear the violet gown.

Now, standing amid what appeared to be much of London, she was glad of her decision. The profusion of absurd costumes was enough to make her swear off masquerades for good. There was an ungainly dragon, complete with hideous snout and scales—Lord Higgenbotham, she assumed. Lady Jersey was in attendance, garbed as Cleopatra. Vivian thought the breast plates and silk asp a bit excessive. A rotund Bacchus reeled throughout the crowd, sandals flapping, grape-leaf coronet askew, spilling wine on all and sundry from his basin-size chalice. Rafe, regal as King Richard the Lion Heart, whispered that Dillingham's drinking would soon relegate him to the role of mythical clown.

Vivian scanned the crowd, searching for Noel. She was concerned, of course, that the cup-shot Dillingham might plow into him again, causing further injury to his shoulder. That thought lasted only through one circuit of the ballroom. She wanted to see him because she wanted to see him. After all, there was no harm in a brief glance now and again. As long as they did not speak, dance, or meet gazes, she would be quite safe.

He was nowhere to be seen.

It was his ball—or at least it was taking place in his home, and she could not find him anywhere. Perhaps he was fully costumed, and she was looking right past him. But no, she would know him even if he were cloaked from the top of his head to the tip of his toes. As the minutes passed, her mood took a decidedly downward turn.

Her spirits soon lightened, however, at the appearance of the Tarrants. She studied Aurelie's flowing gold gown and Jason's ornate tunic with confusion. Both were embroidered with unfamiliar scrollwork, and neither rang any bells. Aurelie, catching her furrowed brow, laughed and explained, "We are Emer and Cuchullain, from an ancient Celtic folktale."

Vivian had not heard of them. "I assume it was a love story of epic proportions," she said cheerfully.

"As epic as can be," was Jason's reply. He gave his wife a melting grin and offered his arm. "Would you grace a poor warrior with this dance, fair Emer?"

"With pleasure!" They disappeared onto the floor.

Vivian turned to greet Grace. "Now you I recognize."

The younger girl sighed as she looked down at her gauzy white gown. "Mother would not let me wear my first choice."

"And that was . . . ?

"Salome. I thought to create a platter to place about Rickey's shoulders, paint a bit of rouge around his neck, and drag him about by his hair. *I* thought it a decidedly clever idea, but neither he nor Mama would cooperate."

Vivian laughed. "What a shame!" She thought Grace

looked quite lovely, actually. The filigree halo sat in artless glory in the golden curls, and the papier-mâché wings seemed a natural extension from her slender shoulders. Yes, Grace made a very fetching angel. The irony of her impish character only made the costume all the more delightful.

Rafe apparently agreed. "I vow I did not recognize you at first, Gracie. You have never precisely been the seraphic type." When she shot him a murderous glance, he flashed his own devilish grin. "Careful, my celestial creature. You will have your wings revoked."

"Good! They are ever so uncomfortable." Her eyes took on a wistfulness that tugged at Vivian's heart but appeared to have no impact whatsoever on Rafael. "I should gladly exchange them for a bit of earthy paradise."

See her, you dolt! Vivian shouted silently. *Why do you not see this wonderful gift that is yours but for the taking?*

Rafe was gazing off somewhere over Grace's head. "I must say, Elspeth Vaer is looking splendid tonight. I fancy I could play an admirable Romeo to her Juliet." Vivian wanted to smack him. "But she is presently occupied." He glanced down. "Dance with me, Gracie?"

For a moment, Vivian thought Grace was going to cosh him over the head with her harp, and silently cheered her on. But the girl shrugged instead. "Of course."

Vivian understood. One took one's heaven however one could.

Young Lord Yarrow arrived moments later to request her hand for the set. He was a pleasant enough fellow and she went gladly. He managed to stay off her toes, and Vivian managed to chat blithely on the merits of stream fishing versus lake. She was hardly an authority on either, but Yarrow certainly did not appear to care. He was far too pleased with her interest to be bothered by trivialities.

He released her with some reluctance into the hands of the next young man. This time Vivian discussed the theoretical approach to Whig politics. With the next it was the Peninsular Campaign, followed by Walter Scott's latest.

Anything to keep from thinking about love, and its perversity.

The supper dance arrived too soon. Charles Addington escorted her off the floor, all the while berating himself rather comically for being such a bufflehead as to not engage her for supper. She was decidedly relieved he had not. His topic of choice had been the vast success to be had in raising pigs on one's estate, and she had run through her porcine knowledge within the first two minutes. She spied Lord Yarrow hovering about the sidelines and thought he would be as good company as any. He certainly appeared more than willing. True, the concept of waltzing with him brought no quiver to her heart, but then, it hardly mattered.

"I believe this one is mine, Miss Redmond. Surely you have not forgotten promising it to me."

Her heart did a mighty leap. She had certainly not promised Noel anything of the sort. But she went into his arms without a murmur.

"You look very beautiful tonight, Vivian," he said softly as he swept her into the waltz.

As do you. "Thank you." He was not wearing a costume at all. His only concession to the event was a black silk mask, which did little more than circle his eyes. Eyes that flashed silver in appreciation. Vivian cleared her throat. "Your ball is a smashing success. Your mother must be pleased."

"I imagine so."

She waited, but he said nothing further on the matter. "You have a lovely home, Noel."

"Thank you."

"How pleasant it must be to be directly on the Square, no curious neighbors to peer across into your windows."

"Quite."

Again she waited. And again, nothing. " 'Tis fortunate the weather has not worsened. People are taking great pleasure in the balcony." No response. "Have you seen Lord Higgenbotham? He did come as a dragon, after all. At first

144

I thought Mr. Smythe-Barrows was Higgenbotham, but he was a crocodile, not a dragon. It was the tail, you see . . ."

"Vivian."

She blinked. "Yes?"

"You are prattling."

"Yes, I suppose I am, but you are not helping matters."

"Perhaps I am content to stare."

And stare he did. She felt suddenly as if he could see past the vibrant silk, past her skin even, into her heart. It was not a comfortable sensation. "And perhaps *I* would prefer to chat." She gazed past his shoulder. "I do believe that is Lady Cowper over there. Do you suppose she is Diana or Helen of Troy?"

"Vivian."

"Yes, Noel?"

"Look at me."

She forced her gaze past the broad shoulders to his eyes. And shivered, yet not with cold. "Yes, Noel?"

He stared at her intently for a moment, before saying thoughtfully, "There is a change about you."

"A change?"

"Yes. There is a vagueness to your gaze, Vivian, more softness to your mouth. You seem as if you are . . . expecting something."

She wondered if she had become so transparent, then. No, not transparent, she amended. Just somewhat short of opaque. She could not very well tell him that she was expecting to have her heart shattered in the near future. Nor that she was beginning to understand that it would never repair itself, no matter how many seas she crossed nor how many pleasant Boston men she encountered. She could not tell him anything close to the truth.

"June is not so very far away. I will be returning home—to Daniel, before I know it."

"Ah, yes. Daniel. I rather thought you had forgotten him."

She raised her eyebrows in eloquent incredulity. "Forgotten him? Hardly." She allowed herself a moment of truth.

"One cannot ever get feelings of the heart from one's head."

"True, perhaps, but one can always push them into some dark recess."

"Really, Noel." She sighed, with more unhappiness than the faint sound revealed. "You have no romance in you."

"On the contrary, my dear, I am a firm believer in romance. Have I not made that abundantly clear to you?" With that, he spread his fingers across her back and pulled her closer.

He watched as her eyes took on a shadowed aspect. "Your idea of romance, Noel, does not quite meet with mine."

"Pity. We shall have to change that." He bent his head and whispered, "Come for a drive with me tomorrow."

"I do not think so."

"Why not? I will even let you take the reins."

She gazed up at him suspiciously. "Oh?"

"Of course. At a certain point I will be more than happy to have you in the driver's seat. Once properly readied, I am certain you will set an appropriate pace. You are well suited to such endeavors. The only concern, Vivian, is whether you would ever want to stop."

There was a long pause before she replied, "Do you think me totally lacking in wits, my lord?"

"Not at all. Whyever would you ask such a thing?"

She tilted her head and gazed up at him with more weariness than reproach. "I do not believe you are speaking of driving at all, and it will not countenance, Noel. I am not a toy to be played with, then discarded. I have pride and purpose, and will not end up like Regina Idlesby, all for want of sense and a need for excitement."

He felt himself scowling. "What does the Idlesby chit have to do with anything?"

She smiled then, a smile that tugged, not pleasantly, at his emotions. "You should know, my lord. Of late, Regina Idlesby seems to have everything to do with everything."

They finished the dance in silence. Noel, for perhaps the

first time in recent memory, found himself without anything to say. The girl really made no sense. He was far more discreet than Fremont, and she was certainly no Regina Idlesby. There was an undeniable attraction between them, and she had talked of a desire for excitement, had she not?

Yes, well, he would simply ply her with wine at supper and have another go at her resistance.

The problem, he decided with no small amount of discomfiture as he led her into the supper room, was that he understood. And he did not particularly like himself at the moment.

He glanced around bemusedly, wondering if Grace and her ludicrous costume were nearby. Something was affecting his brain. He did not want to develop a conscience just then. It was dashedly inconvenient, and not in the least comfortable. Either he was going to have to get his scruples well and truly under wraps, or he was going to lose his chance with Vivian and her temporary charms entirely.

"Oh, bother!" he heard her say.

I quite agree. Then he looked up. "Oh, hell."

Derwood had been in attendance all evening, his presence bringing to mind an absurdly colored storm cloud. This time, it was a garish red velvet surcoat over peacock pantaloons and chartreuse stockings. With his pursed lips and surly expression, he made a very good Henry VIII, indeed. Noel heartily wished him an appropriate case of gout.

"Cousin," Derwood drawled.

"Hullo, Derwood. Enjoying my hospitality?"

The man gave an unpleasant laugh. "You were ever the gracious chap, St. Helier. Very much the lord of the manor." His eyes swung to Vivian. "Do you not agree, Miss Redmond?"

"Lord St. Helier seems well suited to his position, Mr. Windram. It is fortunate, is it not, that it fell to him? There is such chance attached to progeniture, after all. He could have been given a responsibility to which he was not fitted."

147

Noel wanted to kiss her soundly. Derwood's lips compressed for a moment, then curved into a smug arc. "Quite. Some aspects of a title require such . . . nobility. *Droit du seigneur,* for example. But I imagine you are familiar with that one, my dear."

That did it. Noel's hands clenched into fists, and he took an aggressive step forward. Vivian's hand on his arm stopped him. When he looked down at her, he saw that her face was taut but composed. She and Derwood regarded each other tensely for a moment before, with the faintest curl of her lip, Vivian lifted her head and walked past him.

"Vivian," Noel said as they continued across the room, "I am sorry. He had no call . . ."

She stopped in her tracks and faced him. "It is jealousy, my lord, of your wealth and title that makes him speak so."

"But he insulted you with his implication that we had . . . that I had . . . exercised some right over your person! Why did you not let me deal with the matter?"

Again, that sad, slightly pitying smile. "Why? Because he implied nothing more than what you yourself have contemplated. If you were to pound every man who spoke some version of the truth of you, Noel, you would have no strength left to deal with those who really deserve it."

"Vivian . . ."

A sudden buzzing rose above his voice—a good thing, actually, for he was speechless again. Whatever news was sweeping the gathering seemed to have reached the far wall in seconds, and even the orchestra was drowned out by excited whispers.

". . . Newstead," he heard.

". . . Vivid One . . ."

". . . identity . . ."

He felt Vivian stiffen at his side. "Good heavens," she whispered.

She was gazing past his shoulder, and he turned slowly. The sight which met his eyes was enough to make him lose whatever slight powers of speech he still possessed.

There, standing regally at the top of the stairs, swathed from head to foot in star-spangled purple velvet, was Merlin.

12

"DEAR GOD," VIVIAN whispered.

"Well, I'll be damned," Noel muttered.

If his eyes and common sense were to be believed, Newstead had made his appearance. And it seemed he was ready to disclose his identity. Noel scanned the crowd. He had not seen Byron, but then it was dashedly hard to identify half the guests behind the masks, paints, and false whiskers. True, Merlin looked rather rotund to be the bard, but padding was easily enough applied. Byron had played out the farce thus long; he would certainly not want to end with anything less than a grand performance.

Vivian stood stiffly at his side, one small hand gripping his arm with impressive force. He doubted she was aware of the gesture, but he took no small pleasure from the fact that she had reached for him at all. He glanced down quickly, deciding her hand looked rather well there, pale and delicate against the midnight blue of his coatsleeve. He lifted his free arm and covered her fingers with his own. If she were to meet her starry-eyed admirer, she was damn well going to do it with him by her side.

He peered intently at the figure descending the stairs. They were too far away for a clear view, and the man's identity was well and truly hidden by the voluminous robes and flowing whiskers. As much as he hated the concept, a much closer look was necessary.

"Come along, Vivian," he commanded. "Let us meet Mr. Newstead."

She did not budge. "I cannot."

"I beg your pardon?"

The emerald eyes that lifted to his were full of despair. "After all this time, I find I cannot face him."

"You have faced him several times already."

"Yes, I suppose I have, but it was without any certainty."

"Vivian, he is merely a man. A devious, scoundrelly one, to be sure, but a man nonetheless."

"He is not scoundrelly. He is merely an old man reliving a bit of his wild youth."

Noel frowned. "Old? He is younger than I am!"

"Burroughs? He is above fifty."

"Burroughs? Why on earth would you think it that old coot? 'Tis Byron."

This time, she frowned. "Byron? That is not Byron! He is far too portly."

Noel said something that Vivian thought was about padding, but his mutterings were lost in a new wave of whispering. Merlin had reached the floor by then, the tip of his towering hat visible above the crush. If her eyes were not mistaken, he was heading directly toward them. The crowd seemed to part before him like so much wheat, and she had the sudden and almost overpowering urge to snatch up her skirts and run.

Not like this, not with everyone watching. Not with Noel here!

Truth be told, she could not have fled had her life depended upon it. Her knees were locked in place.

She felt Noel's fingers tighten over hers. "Steady on," he said gruffly.

Then, suddenly, Merlin was before them. Vivian peered weakly into the bearded face but saw only a pair of twinkling blue eyes. "You are looking particularly vivid this evening, my dear!" he boomed. "My compliments!"

She could not respond but merely stared, mute, as he turned to Noel. "Splendid do, St. Helier! Appears I have arrived just in time for supper. What exceptional timing!" Then, in the next second, he had turned away and was heading for the dining room. He paused after a dozen steps and, looking back over his shoulder, gave a guffaw of laughter. "Alvanley said this costume would quite outdo all others. Damme if he wasn't correct!" Then he was gone, his chuckles trailing in his wake.

Then there was a lengthy and utter silence.

"Noel," Vivian's voice came back at last in a breathy rush, "who *was* that?"

"That, my love," came the laughter-filled reply, "was the one man in England who most certainly did *not* pen any eloquent verses—to you or any other fair maid. That was our dear Prince George."

Vivian had a headache. It was not the worst she had ever had, to be sure, but it was quite bad enough. Perhaps, she thought, if Mrs. DeLancey would cease prattling for a time, it would recede, but the good lady had been going on since breakfast and showed no inclination toward stopping anytime soon.

"Did you see it, Jane? The man very nearly kissed the dear girl's cheek! She is quite set in her success now. One might even dare to call her an Incomparable."

Lady St. Helier smiled patiently. "Yes, Felicity, it was indeed the most fortuitous event."

Vivian thought the kind woman must be half mad by now. Noel's house had undoubtably been flooded with visitors from the very second it became appropriate to call, and she was certain Prinny's appearance had been the choice topic of conversation. Despite the relative disfavor in which many of his subjects held him, it was still considered the greatest of coups to have him attend a fete, and his little caper had made his appearance all the more noteworthy.

He had certainly not come anywhere near to kissing her. In fact, with the exception of his few words, he had not so much as glanced her way. She thought it rather poor form indeed for Mrs. DeLancey to be embroidering the tale so, but the lady was so warm and approving in her chattering that Vivian did not have the heart to gainsay her.

"Why, the dear man knew Vivian's name and they have

not been introduced." She reached out to pat Vivian's hand. "How clever of you to make such an impression, dearest!"

Vivian suppressed a sigh. "I am afraid he was prompted, madam. It was Lord Alvanley and not the Prince who thought of the costume, and I have met his lordship on several occasions."

It seemed Mrs. DeLancey would never quite be able to make up her mind on the matter of Mr. Newstead. She alternated with dizzying frequency from resigned disapproval to giddy delight. It was, Vivian decided, just a bit unsettling. That morning, the persuasion seemed to be leaning well toward complete approval, jubilation even. She was unsure how Mrs. DeLancey had procured the information, but the lady had announced, more than a bit triumphantly, over luncheon that every last copy of canto V had flown from the shelves. If she were to be believed, there was not a copy to be found in all of London.

Vivian was delighted. For all she cared, the blasted cantos could rot into dust in the recesses of the ton's bookshelves.

"I wonder," Mrs. DeLancey mused, absently accepting a glazed cake from the tray Lady St. Helier proferred, "if we ought to hold a masquerade. Not that it would be able to equal yours, Jane, dear. Why, you threw quite the Event of the Season!" Lady St. Helier smiled graciously. "But perhaps Prinny would attend . . ."

"Felicity, really!" Lady Fielding groaned. "Fill your mouth with that pastry you are clutching and leave off!" She ignored her sister's offended sniff and inquired of their hostess, "Has there been any word of Idlesby?"

"I cannot see," Mrs. DeLancey muttered, "that the subject of Idlesby is any better. Miserable affair. All blood and scandal. Dearest Vivian's success, on the other hand . . . and that of your fete, of course, Jane . . . Yes, we should be quite the hostesses of the hour. The crush will be utterly horrific. How delightful!"

Lady St. Helier hid her smile behind her teacup. After a moment, she said, "I do believe Idlesby is much improved,

Constance. His wife engaged the Duchess of York's physician, and he removed the ball."

Lady Fielding nodded. "Well, Idlesby is a tough old coot. He shall rally, I daresay."

"Perhaps an evening of Bach," Mrs. DeLancey said dreamily. "Or Purcell. I do not expect we could secure La Jondine, despite the vast appeal of the event. Well, I suppose that is no great tragedy, especially if Prinny is in attendance. One soprano is rather like the next, I always say . . ."

Lady St. Helier smiled behind her cup again, Lady Fielding rolled her eyes, and Vivian sighed. At the moment, she would have given nearly anything to be safely home in Boston.

"I believe I will make my permanent home in England," she muttered several hours later. "Boston would hardly be an improvement at present."

"Your mother does not send pleasant news of home?" Lady Fielding looked up over her copy of the *Weekly Political Register*.

"I have no idea what the general news is, madam. The addresses, however, are not pleasant in the least." She grimaced as she scanned her mother's letter.

Daughter,

The most Distressing report has reached me—not through your hostesses, as one might expect, but through Mrs. Lovell. It was all over town within hours, an event which I assure you did no good to my poor Nerves. Rumor has it that some poet or other is composing Verse to you, and that he is not *a Good man. Could you not have contrived to acquit yourself with even a Modicum of Restraint? I tell you, Daughter, you* delight *in distressing me, even from across the sea and it is* not *to be borne. A child's filial Duty is to her Mother's Comfort and Tranquility . . .*

154

Vivian skipped over the list of filial duties, which took up a full two pages. There was nothing mentioned, after all, with which she was not already fully familiar. Her mother wrote in haste and at length, much as she spoke, and never bothered to repent at all.

Her father's greeting was a good deal more brief, and a great deal more congenial.

Vivvy, my dear,

    So you have got your mother in a tizzy again. I must say, I admire your gumption. I am quite terrified to strain her poor nerves even one time a year, yet you dare to do so even when you are not present. Noble girl!

Vivian smiled, as she imagined her father had done as he wrote. His response to his wife's tantrums was to hide out for the duration on one of his ships. And he usually arrived home with a fur or jeweled bauble just in case the separation had not diffused her temper.

    Keep this poet fellow at bay, my dear. Writers and artists are an ungainly lot, always expecting one to sponsor or inspire them, and usually the latter by the former. Awkward to have them dropping about all the time. If you must have a husband, find a good sporting man, with half a brain in his head and a bit of business sense.

Your fond Papa

Vivian knew he missed her, even if he did not say so. But she also knew he pottered along perfectly well in her absence. In fact, he had probably dropped his pen after his farewell and gone out to his favorite pub for an afternoon constitutional. Her mother, on the other hand, was never quite herself without someone on whose head she could heap dissatisfaction.

So, word of Newstead had reached Boston, had it? She

was not surprised. Matrons like Mrs. Lovell, who was her mother's dearest friend and deadliest adversary, could always be counted upon to gather the most livid *on dits*. Something so insignificant as the Atlantic Ocean would not be more than a bit of an inconvenience.

Still, it was not a heartening thought that if word of the cantos had reached Boston, the volumes themselves were sure to follow. She did not fancy having to explain the matter, and certainly not without friends like the Tarrants to support her version of the tale. Even worse was the image of having countless volumes of the wretched thing thrust into her face with spuriously honeyed requests for her inscription on the flyleaf.

"Oh, bother," she muttered, shoving the letter into the depths of the *Odyssey*. Her mother and Penelope could despair together.

The butler appeared in the doorway. "Lord St. Helier is here, my lady. He has arrived to collect Miss Redmond for their drive."

Lady Fielding smiled. "Well, show him in, Stevens." She turned to Vivian. "How pleasant—a drive with St. Helier. The dear boy is known to have such splendid hands on the reins."

"Oh, hell." Vivian groaned, and dumped Odysseus, Penelope, and her mother onto the table.

Noel decided, on entering the room, that Vivian looked quite lovely with her sky-blue gown and customarily tousled curls. Rather celestial, actually. She also looked more than a bit put out, her flashing eyes bringing to mind thoroughly celestial storm clouds. God, but she was a smashing creature.

"My lady," he greeted Lady Fielding, temporarily forcing his eyes away from the girl, and bent over her hand.

"You have come for Vivian. How nice. A drive in the park?"

"A drive anywhere with Miss Redmond will be the greatest of pleasures. Mother Nature has graciously lifted her bleak mood for us this afternoon. We shall have the full benefit of a splendid turn in the fresh air." He watched as Vivian's determined little chin lifted. She really did have a splendid supercilious look. "Good afternoon, Vivian. I trust you are ready to go."

"Ready, my lord? I do not remember agreeing to drive with you."

"Do you not? How embarrassing." He flashed his best smile and watched as her jaw went up another notch. "I daresay it is due to all of last night's excitement. We had been discussing a . . . drive just before Prinny's entrance."

"I did not . . ."

"But as I am here and you are here, with seemingly little else to do, I would say all is well." Then, before she could refuse, he grasped her hand, hauled her from her chair, and hustled her toward the door. "My lady." He nodded politely to Lady Fielding, who gave him a strange smile before turning back to her *Weekly*. "Now, Vivian, though the weather is markedly improved, I would suggest a wrap. We would not want you to take cold." He had already requested that Stevens see to the matter, and a maid waited at the bottom of the stairs with a blue-and-white striped spencer in her hands.

"Really, my lord, can you not tell that I am thoroughly displeased with you and have no intention of going anywhere in your company? This manipulation of yours is becoming most tedious!"

"Quite right, my dear." He managed to get her arms into the sleeves of the spencer. "I am aware that I have a tendency toward high-handedness." He would leave the buttons to her despite the temptation to handle those over her breasts himself. "My mother tells me so all the time."

She was not to be appeased. "You do not listen, Noel! I said I was not going driving . . ."

"Yes, yes. You are thoroughly displeased." He took the high-crowned bonnet from the maid and shoved it onto the ebony curls. He had much experience with undoing bows, but little with tying them. He managed, however, to fashion a reasonably serviceable knot. "Good, you are ready!"

Stevens opened the door with a flourish. Noel got a firm but gentle grip on Vivian's arm and propelled her down the stairs to where his curricle waited.

"You really must stop hauling me about." She waved her free arm in a dramatic arc and nodded decisively, sending her bonnet slightly askew. "In and out of rooms, on and off the dance floor . . ." She climbed up and took her seat without seeming to know she was doing so. "David never manhandles me so. *He* is the perfect gentleman!"

Noel grinned as he set the matched grays in motion. "*He* sounds a weak-spirited fellow, indeed—all pretense and no substance whatsoever."

Vivian promptly lapsed into sulky silence at his side, stirring only when they reached the Strand. "Where are we going? Hyde Park is in the opposite direction."

"So it is. Brava, my dear. Your grasp of London geography is quite impressive for not being a resident. As for where we are going, I thought a drive by the river might be a nice change. You must be weary of the Park by now."

He was telling the truth, in a manner of speaking. He fully intended to drive along the river—all the way out of Town. There was some glorious countryside not too far away, along with some charming inns, and he thought it a rather marvelous plan to take Vivian there. An inn was by no means a forgone conclusion, certainly. He thought he might persuade her to take tea in one of the drawing rooms, but a journey upstairs was, regretfully, not assured.

This time, Vivian's silence lasted all the way past the Tower of London. He was impressed. She usually lost her pique far earlier. Pouting was not, after all, in her character. She was a take-action sort of chit. And she did not disappoint him once she did deign to speak.

Glancing about, she announced, "I do not believe this is right, Noel. I suggest you turn this contraption about and take me home."

"This contraption," he replied mildly, "was only yesterday referred to by Pierrepont as the most smashing set of wheels he had seen in London. In fact, he offered me a rather obscene amount of money for it. Apparently he'd had a run of exceptional luck at the Watier's tables."

"Hmph." Vivian did not think highly of Henry Pierrepont, nor of the other three men who made up the Unique Four: Brummell, Alvanley, and Sir Henry Mildmay. They were an arrogant lot who ruled the ton by sharp dress and sharper tongues. "You should have taken his money."

Noel laughed. "Insulting my rig, Vivian? Ah"—he clasped a hand to his chest—"you have found the surest way to wound me!"

Vivian could not help but smile as well. "What rot. You do not care a whit about such things. I would wager you purchased this *smashing contraption* on a whim." She checked to see that the horses were set straight on the road, then covered Noel's eyes with her hand. "Now, what color is the upholstery?"

"Vivian, really—I must be able to see!"

She ignored him. "The upholstery, if you please?"

She felt his brow crease under her fingers. "Brown," he said decisively.

"Is it?" She moved her hand and he looked down.

"Brown," he muttered.

"I believe," she replied cheerfully, "the color is called midnight blue. You see, Noel, you do not really notice the details of things."

There was a lengthy silence as he turned his eyes back to the road and stared ahead. "Oh, but I do notice, Vivian. I noticed that you are not wearing flour matter on your face today and that the bruise is now the faint shape of a heart. I noticed that there are silk violets on your bonnet. I noticed that your gown is exactly the color of a Devon summer sky, and I noticed that the *cobalt* blue stripes in your spencer make your eyes very, very green."

"Oh," she whispered. "Oh, Noel."

Well, that had done it, done her in completely and irreversibly. She could no more deny the fact that she had fallen in love with him than she could deny the phases of the moon.

159

The city had opened into fields, bright with scattered flowers, and she caught her breath—half at the sight of gentle wildness and half at the sensations roiling within her. She had not noticed quite how far they had come, and suddenly London, with its tight streets and constricting dictates, seemed years and thousands of miles away. A winding path drifted from the road down along the banks of the Thames.

"Noel," she said quietly, but he was already guiding the pair to the right.

They drove for some minutes in silence, sunlight filtering down through the branches of the willows lining the bank. Then, as they reached a clearing, Noel pulled the horses to a stop. He secured the reins to the board and jumped down.

"M'lady?" He reached for her.

The curricle, as was the style, was relatively low to the ground. There was no need for him to wrap his hands about her waist to lift her down, but he did, and she let him. *What will I do*, she wondered, *when I am home again and will no longer know the feeling of his hands spread across my back?* It was a question with no answer.

He did not set her on her feet immediately, but lowered her slowly, so her body slid along his. She had never felt anything quite as sinful as the brush of her thighs over his, and felt her face coloring—only in part due to embarrassment. For a moment, they were eye to eye. His smoldered like molten silver, burning into her as surely as if she had been branded.

And she had. No matter how many oceans she crossed, nor how many years intervened, her heart would never belong to another. It was perhaps the saddest, most beautiful notion she had ever known as truth.

"Shall we walk or sit?" Noel asked at last, setting her on the ground. He did not release her entirely but slid his arm down to thread his fingers through hers.

"Sit," Vivian answered hazily. She did not think her legs would support her for long.

He drew a lap rug from under the curricle seat and, tossing it over his free arm, led the way. They found an ancient willow next to the river, and he spread the rug beneath it. Vivian sat down as gracefully as she could. Noel promptly dropped beside her and settled his head in her lap. She thought to make him move, but instead found herself burying her fingers in his rich, thick hair. He had removed his hat sometime back, and the ash-brown locks were tousled by the wind and warmed by the sun.

Vivian closed her eyes. She would remember—the feel of rumpled silk beneath her fingers, the feeling of tumbled emotions under her skin.

"Would I be doing something awful if I were to ask for your thoughts, Vivian?"

She looked down. He looked so young, and almost tender. No angel, this, she reminded herself. This was Lord St. Helier. "Not at all," she replied, forcing a smile. "I am merely thinking that perhaps I shall miss you just a bit after all."

"Only a bit?"

"Well, you are wild and unmannered, and hopelessly officious."

"You do not mince words, my dear." It was one of the things he liked best about her. Though at the moment, gazing up into her vivid features, with her thighs soft and welcoming beneath his head, he could not find anything about her that he did not like excessively. "And I suppose I risk your disapprobation by being officious now."

"Oh? Have you a command for me, my lord?"

"As a matter of fact, I do."

She sighed, a soft, amused sound. "I do not usually like your commands, you know."

"I know. But I hope above anything you will not balk at this one." She waited. "I think it would be a very good idea, Vivian, if you would kiss me now."

For a moment, he thought she was going to refuse. Then she slowly lowered her head, the brim of her bonnet blocking out the light, and touched her lips to his. Light burst behind his eyes.

He reached up to cup her face, drawing her even closer. Her breasts brushed against his cheek and she gasped softly. He took the opportunity to slide his tongue along her parted lips, then deeper when she did not pull away. She was impossibly sweet and warm, and when her tongue darted out to meet his, he thought he tasted heaven.

"God, *Vivian*," he groaned, then captured her mouth fully.

The kiss seemed to go on forever, fathomless and endless. Then, just when he thought he would surely go mad with one more second of glorious contact, she drew away with a ragged sigh.

"You have bewitched me, St. Helier," she said huskily.

"And I believe you have stolen the very words from my lips, Miss Redmond."

She was stealing a good deal more, he decided. His wits, for instance. And his low designs. If he were not careful, did not stay full on his guard, she might very well steal a little piece of his heart.

"Vivian," he murmured.

"Yes, Noel?"

Forgive me. "Come with me ..."

Something kindled in the emerald eyes. "Where?"

"A few more miles ... there is an inn ..."

Her hand descended to cover his mouth. "Don't." She neither looked nor sounded offended, nor even shocked. Instead, she merely looked sad and perhaps a bit regretful. "Please don't spoil this. We have so little time, really. I would not have it made less than it is."

Yes, their time was limited. All the more reason to make the most of it. The inn was no more than a quarter hour's drive at most. He would persuade her—soft words and more kisses like the last one. He could see her beneath him, her hair spread like ebony satin across the pillow ....

He nodded, once, and she removed her hand. "All right, Vivian. We will stay quietly here for a time, and then I will take you home."

Their time was limited, but not yet at an end.

"Thank you, Noel."

She lifted her eyes from his and stared out over the rippling waters of the Thames as it rushed toward the Channel and beyond.

13

NOEL WATCHED IN amusement as Felicity DeLancey divested herself of a good three yards of gauzy wrap. His butler, to his credit, managed to accept the growing mass with relative grace. Noel himself had only just returned from his bootmakers and waited until she was completely unwrapped before handing over his own hat and gloves.

"What marvelous timing!" Mrs. DeLancey beamed as she took his arm. "Now you can have luncheon with your dear mother and me."

"It would be my pleasure, madam."

In truth, he did not think himself up to an hour of the lady's prattling, but she was a sweet old hen, and he had nothing else planned. Besides, he had not seen Vivian in several days, and there was every chance that some news of her would flow out amid the inane chatter. He smiled gallantly and led the older woman toward the drawing room.

His mother put aside her embroidery as they entered and rose to greet them. "Will you be joining us, dearest? I had assumed you would stop at your club." Noel caught her tolerant smile as he promptly headed for the claret decanter. "Ring for Hobbs while you are standing, dear, and have him set another place."

Mrs. DeLancey bent over to observe the embroidery frame. "What a cunning design, Jane. Did you do it yourself? Well, of course you did. You have always been so clever. I, myself, must rely on the designs of others, but I did see the most lovely silks on Upper Bond Street only yesterday. Constance said the colors were much too drab, but I informed her . . ."

Noel sighed as she recounted the great embroidery silk debate in detail and considered sneaking off to have his luncheon at White's after all. He took one look at his mother's cautioning expression and went instead to the bell-pull. Hobbs would set another place.

Some minutes later, as they waited for luncheon to be announced, Mrs. DeLancey completed her tale with a plaintive sigh. Noel leaned against the mantel and tried to look as if he had been paying attention. He was not certain, but he thought Lady Fielding had won the debate. If any silks had been purchased, they had been of the brightly colored variety.

"How is Miss Redmond getting on?" his mother asked pleasantly. "She seemed a bit beleaguered when I last saw her."

Noel snapped to attention.

"Oh, the dear girl is quite well. I believe she was a bit blue-deviled for a brief time, what with the cantos and her eventual return to Boston, but I expect she is feeling far better now."

"About the Newstead business?" Noel queried, far more interested in Vivian's imminent return to Boston.

Mrs. DeLancey giggled. "Oh, she considers all that to be so much rubbish. No, I was referring to her planned departure. She does have that beau at home, you know."

"David," Noel muttered.

"I believe it is Daniel, dear. But I do not suppose his name means much of anything, really. You see, the splendid girl might not be returning to Boston after all. I could be mistaken, of course, but I have always said that when the right man calls, a woman's heart replies. Yes, I do believe Vivian might be staying past the Season."

Noel could not prevent a satisfied smile from spreading across his lips. So she was considering extending her stay, was she? That boded very well for his designs. Very well, indeed.

The grin faded slightly as he considered the fact that she might be expecting a proposal of marriage. Women did, after all, seem to make a habit of such expectations. But no, Vivian was not at all a foolish sort of girl, nor had she ever shown any such notion. She understood him perfectly. And it appeared she was perhaps beginning to see things as he did.

He realized he was grinning like an idiot when Hobbs entered the room and gazed at him curiously. "Er . . . luncheon is served, my lord."

Noel composed his features. "Thank you, Hobbs. Ladies . . . ?" He gestured toward the door and followed as they quitted the room.

Yes, he would have another go at the glorious Miss Redmond. Soon. Another drive seemed the appropriate action. It might be tactical to take another direction this time, of course. Predictability was the curse of the very dull or very stupid. He was neither. And there were charming inns whichever road one chose.

". . . Meriton as I was leaving."

He caught only the end of Mrs. DeLancey's statement—and her giggle. She and his mother were approaching the dining room and he caught up with them in a few strides. "What was that you said, madam?"

"Oh, I was discussing Vivian's plans. As I said, the right man makes all the difference. Young Lord Meriton was arriving at the house just as I was leaving. We passed in the hallway." She giggled again. "I imagine he is down on one knee even as we speak, making his offer. He is a charming boy, and so very handsome . . ."

Noel did not bother with excusing himself. Nor did he stop for his hat and gloves. He was out the door and flagging a passing hack before Mrs. DeLancey had finished her sentence.

"Do get up, my lord!" Vivian knew she was twisting pleats into her skirts, but she needed to keep her hands occupied. Otherwise, she might very well cosh the man

166

soundly, and pounding a prospective spouse was hardly appropriate, no matter how guaranteed one was of declining the proposal. "Please, my lord."

Meriton remained where he was, one knee on the widows' parlor carpet. "I shall not, my dear, until you have given me the answer I so crave."

"Really, my lord, I must . . ."

"I am resolute in this, Miss Redmond. Make me the happiest of men, and I shall be able to stand proud."

"I am truly sorry, sir, but as I have told you, I cannot marry you!"

This had been going on for some minutes now. Vivian was beginning to quite despair of ever getting the man off of the floor and out of the house. She did not want to cause him any undue pain or embarrassment, but if he did not desist soon, she would be forced to resort to complete candor on the matter of his character, not to mention the garishly striped waistcoat he had apparently thought appropriate to the occasion.

Meriton was clearly not accustomed to being on his knees, for he shifted his weight with a small grimace before saying "You are peeved with me for delaying my return so long. I assure you, 'twas business which prevented me from flying back to your side. And I know these feminine wiles, my dear. It is expected that a young lady shall pretend pique with her intended and make him plead his troth."

He smirked. "I am wise to such ploys. I am also determined to waste no time. I shall simply remain here while you demur several times, then we shall be done with the matter. You see, Miss Redmond, I know you could not refuse me."

"I could not?"

"You are an intelligent creature, and what reason could there have been for your visit to England but to capture a mate?" He flecked a speck of dirt from his champagne-polished Hessians. "I am certain you did not anticipate receiving the attentions of a future earl, my darling, but you have one well and truly captured!" With this, he clasped his hands over his heart. "Have no fear; I shall never be so callous as to throw your past into your lovely face once we are wed."

"My *past?*"

He pursed his lips and shook his head. "Speak not of it. Your father's position in trade shall not matter, nor the unfortunate little matter of that horrendous poetry . . ."

Vivian had had quite enough. Good grief, the man could not even propose properly! "My lord," she replied, struggling to keep her voice even, "I am fully aware of the value you place on your intent. Honored as I know I should be, my answer is no, though a bit of politeness on your part might have brought about a twinge of regret at declining. As it is, my only wish is for you to remove yourself—"

"Miss Redmond!" He raised his hand peremptorily. "I feel compelled to instruct you here. You have little experience with these matters, and cannot be expected to comprehend the nuances of our society." Then, contrary to his fervent assertion, he rose to his feet, still unbetrothed. He took a moment to brush invisible carpet strands from his fawn breeches and check the placement of his pristine cravat. "A bit of feminine reluctance is perfectly acceptable, even charming. Inadvertently insulting your future husband is not. In fact, such behavior might provoke a man to withdraw his suit. Now"—he reached out and snared her hand—"will you do me the honor of becoming my wife?"

Vivian was momentarily speechless. As he gazed down at her, anticipating her response, she was subjected to the indignity of feeling her mouth open and close like a netted fish. In truth, her eyes felt rather as if they were protruding as well. She drew a rallying breath.

"Inadvertent?" The word burst from her lips. "You believe the insult was inadvertent?" Past any semblance of decorum, she snatched her hand back and snapped, "I assure you, my lord, all offense was quite deliberate! You say I am intelligent and yes, I am. I would be the veriest of buffleheads were I to accept a pompous, overdressed, fatuous . . . *jackass!*"

The ensuing silence was broken by a choked laugh from the doorway. Both Vivian and Meriton spun about to find Noel leaning against the frame, his eyes bright with laughter.

"Overdressed, Vivian? Of all the adjectives to choose from, you unerringly fix on the one most guaranteed to tear a man's ego to shreds."

"St. Helier." Meriton's handsome face was dark with anger. "This is a private meeting between Miss Redmond and myself. You have no right to intrude."

Noel merely raised a black brow. "Is this rotter bothering you, Vivian? If so, I shall dispatch him posthaste."

Vivian, torn between furied raging and hysterical laughter, could do no more than blink. Meriton, however, was fully capable of speech. "Dispatch me, St. Helier? You think too highly of yourself. Now begone. Your presence is unwelcome."

"Unwelcome? How unfortunate." Noel sighed expressively. "And unnecessary too, it seems. It appears Vivian was doing quite well at dispatching you on her own."

"Now see here . . ."

"No." Noel stepped into the room. "You see here. The lady does not want you. I believe she made that abundantly clear, but should it not be enough for you, you may consider this: *She belongs to me.* Did you get that, Meriton? To *me.*"

This time, the silence lasted far longer. Too long. Then, with a snarl, Meriton turned on Vivian. "You may consider my offer rescinded, madam. It appears too many have come before me!" With that, he shoved past Noel and stormed out of the room, sending the door crashing shut behind him.

Noel allowed himself a satisfied smile and turned back to Vivian in time to see her sink into the nearest chair. Her vivid features were taut, her skin pale. "Vivian?" He took a step forward, but she threw up a hand to stop him.

"I cannot believe you did that."

"Put the rat in his place?"

"What would you know of his place, Noel? You seem

incapable of knowing your own. My God, your presumption astounds me!"

"Really, sweetheart . . ."

"Do not call me that!" A bright flush rose into her cheeks as she rallied and sprang to her feet. "I do *not* belong to you, Lord St. Helier! I belong to no one but myself!"

"Now, Vivian . . ." He took another step forward.

"Stop! Don't you dare try to cajole me! My God, you all but told him I was your . . . your . . . doxy!"

She whirled around the settee and gripped the carved back. Noel had the distinct feeling that if he were to move an inch, she would pick the thing up and hurl it at his head, cushions and all. She looked angry enough to be able to flatten Goliath. "Now, Vivian, I said no such thing."

"Do you remember when Derwood implied much the same? You very nearly pounded him into the ballroom floor." Her eyes glittered with fury. "No one may speak of your improper designs . . . except you. Is that it? Oh, that I were a man! I would plant you a facer you would feel for weeks!"

Her grip tightened on the wood until he could see her knuckles whiten with the strain. He tried flippancy. "If you were a man, my dear, we would certainly not be having this absurd discussion."

"Ooh!" And she did hurl something at him. He ducked before realizing it was merely one of the cushions. It landed a good five feet from his boots. "You may take your levity and choke on it! How could you, Noel? Is it not enough that you behave shamelessly when we are alone? Must you shame me in front of others as well?"

"Vivian, you are overreacting." Another cushion flew at him. This time, it hit his knee. "Damn it, Vivian, you will cease this childish behavior!" He caught the third cushion midair and thrust it aside as he stalked toward her. "We are going to sit down and discuss this like reasonable adults."

"I have no desire to talk to you at all!"

He came around the settee and growled as she scurried

behind the far arm. He knew he would catch her eventually, but when she darted a furious glance toward the door, he decided the appeal of the chase came second to expedience. As she took her first step, he vaulted over the back of the settee and threw his weight forward.

He shifted at the last moment to take the brunt of the fall, and they hit the floor in a tangle of muslin and limbs. She was sprawled full against him and he tightened his arms around her before she could move. Then, deciding it best to be well protected, he secured her legs with his own. He could not have her flailing about indiscriminately.

Vivian struggled for a full minute before realizing she was well and truly trapped. Her exertions had done no more than tangle her skirts tightly between her legs and his, and a cool draft on her calves informed her that the fabric had ridden up to expose her stockings. Even as the mortified blush rose in her cheeks, she tried for bluster.

"Release me at one, you—"

"If you say overdressed jackass, Vivian, I shall be forced to seal your lips in whatever way possible."

His own lips were far too close to hers. She tried to turn her face, but he promptly tightened one arm across her back and buried his freed hand in her loosened hair.

"And," he continued, "considering the fact that both hands are occupied . . ."

It did not take much pressure to lower her mouth to his. She did not really fight him. She could not. Instead, she allowed him to kiss her. Truth be told, she even kissed him back.

There had been little sunshine since their drive, and the weather was only part of the problem. She had found earlier brightness on gray English days—in Noel's company. Even now, light burst behind her eyes.

Mirage. The word flashed into her mind, displacing dreams of countless nights spent waltzing in Noel's arms. One of her father's ship captains had told her of mirages, of the glorious, wavering images that stayed just out of reach until they disappeared altogether. Any future with this man was just such an illusion.

Using all the strength she possessed, she pushed at his chest and succeeded in freeing herself. Knowing she must work fast before her arms reached again for him of their own accord, she scrambled away. Her anger was gone, leaving in its place a wrenching irony.

"I would that you were nothing more than a figment of my imagination, Noel," she said sadly, knowing full well that he would exist as something very similar soon enough. "That way, I could simply close my eyes, count ten, and you would be gone." The lie weighed heavily on her heart.

"One cannot kiss a figment," was his throaty reply.

I suppose I will have to find a way. "Precisely," she said sharply, and fumbled her way to her feet. Her knees were not quite steady, and she resisted the urge to sink down again. "You do terrible things to me, Lord St. Helier."

"I am sorry for what I said to Meriton, Vivian, but the wretch was—"

"I am not referring to Meriton, you clod!" It was no good. She needed to sit down. "I am referring to the fact that I allow you to make me do things I would not ordinarily do. I like kissing you, damn it, and I do not like liking it!"

Dismayed by her own traitorous tongue, she dropped her head back against the chair and groaned.

Noel slowly raised himself up onto his elbows, not quite believing his ears. Damned if the girl didn't flummox him at every turn. He had never met anyone so singularly capable of expressing whichever sentiment came to mind, and he had no idea what to say in response. In truth, he wanted very much to jump to his feet, give a barbaric victory cry, and carry her out over his shoulder.

Instead, he said the first words which came to mind. "Do not go back to Boston, Vivian."

She did not look at him. "Why?"

"Why?" *Why? Because if you do, I am very much afraid*

172

I shall have to come after you. "Because I was quite serious in what I told Meriton."

"You told Lord Meriton several things."

"I told him that you belong to me, Vivian."

This time, she turned her head to regard him, but he could read nothing in the emerald eyes. "For how long, Noel?" She gestured wearily toward his boots. "Those look new. The ones they replaced belonged to you too. Did they wear out, or did you merely tire of them? Perhaps you kept them, and you have a wardrobe full of boots, choosing each pair depending on your mood."

"Now, Vivian . . ." He cut himself off, realizing he was beginning to sound like a tedious echo.

"I am not footwear, my lord." Suddenly she looked harder than he had ever seen her, and infinitely more determined. "I will not be trod upon, and I will not be discarded at will." With that, she rose gracefully to her feet and swept toward the door. Speechless, Noel tilted his head back and watched. An upside-down butler appeared in the doorway. "Ah, Stevens, how fortuitous that you have arrived. I fear Lord St. Helier has fallen, and he cannot seem to rise."

Aurelie, arriving some time later for tea, found her sitting in the morning room, staring moodily out the window. "Vivian? Has something happened?"

"Oh, nothing I cannot manage," was the tight response.

"Tell me."

Vivian turned to regard her friend. Her first impulse was to hold her thoughts silent, but Aurelie's concern was too powerful. "I think I must go home. Soon."

"Oh, dear. Is something amiss with your family?"

"It is not that." She sighed. "Something is terribly amiss with *me*."

Aurelie promptly sat down beside her and placed a cool hand on her forehead. "You are flushed, but not overly warm. Are you in love?"

Vivian was not surprised. "Someone ought to give you a

173

headscarf and crystal ball. With your mind, you would make a fortune."

"I shall bear that in mind should Jason take to gambling. Do you care to discuss the matter?"

"Jason's gambling?" Aurelie shot her a look and she sighed. "I do not know if I care to discuss the matter. I have been talking to myself all afternoon and have achieved nothing except a hideous headache."

"Trying to talk oneself out of love can do that. It is futile, you know."

"Love? Yes, I am beginning to realize that."

"Vivian, please," Aurelie scolded. "Be serious. I do not like seeing you like this. Does Noel have any idea how you feel?"

Well, she could not have expected the identity of her tormentor to be a secret either. "*I* am not certain how I feel. One moment I want nothing more than to attach myself to his side and never move, and the next I want to cosh him over the head with the nearest marble object."

"Yes, well, that is Noel." Aurelie smiled. "He is a good man, though, fecklessness notwithstanding."

Impulsively Vivian reached over and grasped her friend's hand. "Have you ever tried to imagine what your life would be like without Jason?"

"I vow I cannot."

"No, I expect you cannot. But then, you have no reason to do so. It is obvious that he cherishes you more than life."

Aurelie squeezed her hand reassuringly. "It was not always so, you know. Until he actually declared himself, I was not at all sure of his intentions."

"Well, there you have it. I am fully cognizant of Noel's intentions, and they are not at all what one might desire."

"Perhaps you are underestimating him. Men are not known for their ability to express their true feelings."

Vivian smiled humorlessly. "Noel expresses himself quite well. You have been present to hear him do so." She turned once again to stare out over the quiet gardens. "Do you know, I used to be certain of exactly the sort of man I

174

would one day marry. Calm, pleasant, with wire-rimmed spectacles and carefully pressed, white pocket handkerchiefs. He would be solid, steady, just what I need to keep me from getting into one scrape after another." She shook her head at the image. "White pocket handkerchiefs. Good grief. Whatever was I thinking?"

"You were guarding your heart, dearest. We have all done it." Aurelie gazed, too, out the window. "Little do we know that one man will come along and breach our best defenses."

Vivian sighed. "What good are defenses then?"

Apparently her friend, loving and loved by her mate, had no answer for that one.

Noel stared moodily into his third glass of port. "How many did you say?"

"Eight," Rafael replied, "and I only went back to the beginning of the week. Really, Hel, it was a dashedly unpleasant business, wading through all sorts of rot involving mills and the Newmarket races. The next time you wish to peruse the betting book, you will just have do it yourself."

"I was afraid I would do something rash," Noel muttered, "like toss the bloody thing out Brummell's window."

Jason, to his credit, did not chuckle quite as loudly as Rafe. "Amazing isn't it—what love can do to a man's capacities? I fear, old man, that marriage is the only cure."

"I never said anything about love. I am being consumed by good, old-fashioned lust. And I know a few too many stalwart chaps who were brought low when they tried to slake their lust for some sweet young thing by marrying her."

"And there are those of us who have improved considerably with marriage."

"Had your brains rattled is more like it," Noel muttered.

"I believe I will not tell Aurelie you said so." Jason smiled. "She might take offense, and she rather likes you."

"Yes, well, I like her too. She is already married."

"Really, Hel. You do have your title to consider. Yes,

175

yes, I know you've mentioned some rot about marrying next year, but you could be struck by a carriage between now and then, and Derwood would inherit."

Noel ignored him and turned back to Rafe. "Was there anything in the book I ought to know about?"

"Perhaps, but I think you do not *want* to know. I will say, however, that a few hundreds pounds in all will have been lost now that she has refused Meriton. Paxton included." Noel allowed himself a small smile. "I myself," Rafe continued, "have placed my matrimonial wager on you."

Wine spattered as Noel's fist hit the table. "Why, you traitorous sod—"

"Relax, man. I was only pulling your leg! I bet on young Yarrow." Rafe grinned as Noel's fingers tightened around his glass. "I sincerely hope you do not intend to heave that at me. I am dining with my Great-aunt Myrtle this evening and do not wish to appear with port spots on my cravat."

"As if you have ever paid any attention to such things," Jason offered genially, gesturing to a stain on Rafe's cuff. "You clearly did not pay attention to your own port."

"That is tea, which is an utterly different matter altogether."

"Damn it," Noel snapped. "The wagers!"

Rafe chuckled. "None of them are mine, Hel. Though perhaps I shall place one now. Derwood might just be the next Lord St. Helier. Judging from the color of your face, I say a stroke might be imminent."

"May I venture to offer a bit of advice, St. Helier?" Jason asked. "From an old and devoted friend, of course."

"If I say no, will you keep it to yourself?"

Jason ignored him. "It appears to me that you have three choices First, you marry the girl."

"I think not. Second?"

"Second, you risk the disapprobation of the ton and your mother, and the loss of several friends, and bed her."

Noel sighed. "Better. And third?"

"Third"—Jason topped off his own glass—"you go dig up one of those wicked dueling pistols your father collected and put yourself out of your misery."

14

INVALUABLE BEYOND WORDS, Stevens guarded the door with the implacability of a bull mastiff. Several young men had tried to sneak their way in with various vendors, but he had firmly hustled them right back out. Miss Vivian, he informed one and all, was not receiving.

Miss Vivian was, at present, taking refuge in the gardens. There was no peace to be found inside. Between the flower vendors, champagne purveyors, and the chattering, whirling Mrs. DeLancey, an aura of chaos had reigned since morning. Vivian supposed the parlor was safe enough, but she was not about to venture into that chamber for some time. It held recent and unpleasant memories.

"Five?" Grace queried, her eyes sparkling with unsuppressed amusement. "Five in three days? I vow you have set a new record, Vivian."

"Five." Vivian sighed and ticked the names off on her fingers. "Yarrow, Maberley, Paxton"—she shivered,— "Meriton, of course, and Thaddeus Campton whom, I am embarrassed to say, I would swear I had not met before!"

"How marvelous! Really, you have quite surpassed Geraldine Dunnington, and she received four proposals in one week last Season."

Vivian was in no mood to be mocked. "I suppose I could say six, but as Lord Holcombe proposed in the midst of last night's supper with a champagne glass in one hand and a fork in the other, I do not suppose I can count him."

"Yes, well, Rafe does so hate to be left out of the action," Grace replied cheerfully, not in the least cowed. "And I must say he declared himself very prettily indeed."

"Hmph." It had been all Vivian could do not to dump her own wine into his lap. Rafe, finding the entire situation tremendously amusing, had managed to include every trite sentiment of the five serious proposals—without having actually been present for any of them.

Meriton's offer had been enough of an experience to suit her for quite some time. Yarrow's had not been a surprise, but she would gladly have passed on the moment. The following three had taken on the semblance of a Drury Lane farce. Paxton, the last, had not even received a polite refusal. She had laughed, a bit hysterically, and left the room.

"You truly find nothing romantic in the matter?" the younger girl teased. "Really, Vivian, it is rather as if they were all hovering in the shadows, waiting for their chance to come and sweep you off your feet."

"Just like vultures," Vivian muttered.

"What I would like to know," Aurelie said thoughtfully after a moment, "is how everyone knew Meriton had offered and been refused. You certainly did not speak of the matter in public."

"Nor did he" was Grace's cheerful comment. "Although he did look a bit as if his best hunter had died last night."

"Grace!"

"Oh, Aurelie, leave off! Vivian needs a bit of levity in her life."

Vivian, for her own part, thought she needed a swift passage to the Orient. If she were to be completely and consistently fuddled, it might as well be in a truly foreign locale. "Actually, he behaved rather well."

"He refused to speak to you!" Aurelie snorted.

"And that was a relief. I believe Miss Courtland was very glad of his attentions."

"Her money is her dubious appeal," Grace muttered. "And I daresay he finds her fortune very appealing indeed. No offense, Vivian. *I* think you are splendid on your own merit."

"None taken." Vivian smiled. "And thank you."

She had come to the conclusion some time back that her fortune had been her greatest appeal to the young earl. His regular discussions of his own financial prowess had begun to ring false.

She imagined the rest of her erstwhile suitors had had much the same motive. Not that any of them were empty of pocket, but the general consensus among the men of the ton, as she understood it, was that if a man were to marry, he might as well look for golden leg shackles. Money, after all, appeared to be the greatest motivator.

Except perhaps for love. And lust.

There was a blessed irony in the fact that the one man she was certain admired her for attributes other than her money was the one least likely to propose. Noel had no need of her fortune, nor any designs on it. But he did have unmistakable designs on her person.

It had been harder than ever avoiding him during the past several days. No, she amended silently—it had not been hard; it had been agonizing. And, to be truthful, she had to admit that it had not really been avoidance at all. Had he made any effort to engage her, she would have tried to avoid him. As it was, he had not so much as teased or taunted her once. Nor had there been a repeat of his licentious propositions. In fact, he had scarcely spoken to her at all. When he had, it had been with excessive politeness, deference even, and it had made her want to scream.

She had become too accustomed to Noel at his exquisite worst—satyric and utterly brazen in his desire. Somehow, his wanting her had become one of the greatest gifts she had ever received, for it was not contingent on her being anything she was not, nor on her changing to suit his desires. No, he wanted her just as she was. The problem, of course, was that he was not willing to take what she had to give—her heart.

The damned arrogant, beautiful, clod-pated man had no idea what he was declining.

"Well, hell," she muttered.

"Yes," Grace announced cheerily, "isn't it just?"

She nodded decisively, Aurelie patted her hand, and Vivian sighed. Then she smiled. If she could not keep anything from her friends, she might as well be grateful for their empathy.

"Now," Aurelie said after a time, "I suggest we all go elsewhere."

"I cannot leave," Vivian replied sadly. "There is far too much to do in preparing for tonight's fete."

"Rubbish," was Grace's instant retort. "What will you do? Arrange begonias? You are coming with us." She turned to her sister-in-law. "Where are we going?"

"I had thought a nice jaunt up Oxford Street."

Vivian groaned. "Not more shopping!"

"Of course not." Aurelie stood and pulled on her gloves. "It is simply the most expedient way of getting to Great Russell Street."

"What is there?"

Her friend's eyes glittered. "The British Museum, of course. I hear there is an absolutely marvelous exhibit of weaponry on display."

Vivian skipped inside to fetch her hat.

Much later that evening, she found herself remembering a particularly lethal-looking Venetian dagger. It had belonged, the placard read, to one of the Medicis, and had undoubtedly been responsible for the untimely demise of a good number of unfortunate persons over the years. At the moment, she was considering how well the intricately jeweled hilt would look protruding from Lydia Burnham's back.

The wretched woman had attached herself to Noel's sleeve moments after his arrival and was even now leaning indecently close, whispering something into his ear. To Vivian's utter chagrin, he nodded and smiled, paying no heed whatsoever to the entertainment.

In all honesty, the chamber orchestra Mrs. DeLancey had hired for the event was less than impressive. For all its lofty reputation and, she imagined, loftier price, Vivian had heard far better in Boston. The majority of the audience seemed reasonably diverted, however, and she could not begin to fathom why. Bach's "Brandenburg Concertos" were among her favorite Baroque works, especially the Fifth, which, at present, the harpsichordist was taking to as-yet-unexperienced lows. The poor man seemed to be having a very hard time keeping track of both hands at the same time.

Nearby, Mrs. DeLancey was smiling happily, her foot tapping an odd rhythm. Well, Vivian mused as she did her best not to look at Noel, there was no accounting for taste. At least her hostess had not engaged an overblown soprano. She wondered if Lady St. Helier was having similar thoughts. The faintest curve of that lady's lips made it seem entirely possible. Vivian wondered if she would ever be able to master such elegant restraint in the midst of torture. She decided it was highly unlikely.

Grace twitched at her side and she darted a glance at the younger girl. She was not paying attention to the music either. Her gaze was directed at a pair of seats several yards away. Miss Elspeth Vaer was gazing at Rafael Marlowe who was, to his credit and Vivian's surprise, gazing intently at the musicians, nodding his head with the music. Either that, she amended after watching him for a moment, or he had fallen asleep some time past and was in danger of falling forward into the matron sitting in front of him. Vivian considered his character and decided she would have placed her money on the latter had a wager been offered. The odds were in her favor.

She could tell that Grace was miserable. For all the girl's blithe commentary on love and marriage, she was possessed of a tender and hopeful heart. Rafe seemed set, albeit without intention, on bruising and dashing it with stunning constancy.

Aurelie had been right. A woman's heart could be fortified with the best defenses sensibility could erect, but they

182

were only as strong as paper walls against that one certain man.

She attempted to divert her thoughts by gazing around the room. At least sixty members of the Haute Monde were seated in various states of uprightness; a good many more would arrive later for supper and dancing. To her surprise, Lord Meriton was present. Mrs. DeLancey had been a bit overset on hearing Vivian had refused his offer—not about the refusal, but by the fact that it might be a bit awkward to have him in attendance. Unfortunately for her peace of mind, invitations had been sent out some time past, and she could not very well retract one mere days before the event. Lady Fielding, soon tiring of her sister's agonizing over the matter, had snorted and declared that the boy would be an utter sapscull to attend.

The sapscull was, at the moment, gazing off into space. He did not look uncomfortable. On the contrary, there was a faint smile playing about the corners of his mouth. Feeling more waspish than was characteristic, Vivian imagined he was calculating pounds in his head. Miss Courtland was seated smugly by his side, her hand resting on his arm and looking for all the world like a child with a whale on a hook. Vivian wondered if she ought to pity the girl and promptly chided herself for cattiness. If Delia Courtland wanted Meriton, Vivian wished her the dubious joy of him.

A muffled grunt came from Grace's right. It seemed Jason had nodded off again. Either Aurelie or Grace had employed her elbow to his ribs. From the grumbling that followed, Vivian surmised it had been both. She offered the viscount her silent empathy. Dozing seemed a perfectly reasonable way of getting through the concert.

Several seats away, Carlton Burroughs was listing slightly to the side, his eyes closed. The only indication that he was not asleep was the gentle motion of his hands. He was conducting the orchestra, and seemed to be enjoying himself immensely. As if sensing her gaze, he opened his eyes, looked straight at her, and winked.

Bother, Vivian thought a bit peevishly. *He is not helping in the least.*

She had been watching him over the past days for any sign that he was, in fact, her nemesis, Mr. Newstead. She had perceived nothing but the charming and slightly roguish demeanor of an older man. He had certainly given her no clues one way or another.

Deciding her mood was verging on decidedly unpleasant, she forced her attention back to the music and did her best to clear her mind of all else. She succeeded admirably throughout the final movement and was even smiling when the harpsichordist lifted his fingers from the keys.

Before the applause could begin, a shrill laugh broke the silence. Whatever Noel had said must have been supremely amusing for, as the startled guests began to clap, Miss Burnham was still chortling.

Oh . . . bother.

She silently congratulated herself for maintaining acceptably ladylike thoughts.

"Shrew," Grace murmured as they rose from their seats.

Vivian did not reply. She was determined to be sweetness personified for the remainder of the evening. As the guests began to thread their way through the chairs, however, her resolve dropped a notch. Noel, on passing, merely nodded his head politely. Miss Burnham smiled. It was not a pretty sight.

"Viper," Grace declared under her breath.

Vivian counted ten, bared her own teeth in what she hoped was a reasonable facsimile of a polite smile, and waited for all the guests to move into the hall. Nothing, she resolved, was going to upset her perfect calm.

Mrs. DeLancey swept toward her, resplendent in mauve silk. "I have such marvelous news for you, my dear!"

The chandelier just fell on Lydia Burnham? "And what is that, madam?"

"He is coming!"

The remark was made with such glee that Vivian half expected to see Christ himself strolling through the

184

doors. Now, that, she mused in slightly blasphemous humor, would quite seal Mrs. DeLancey's reputation as a hostess.

She chose the negligibly secondary option. "Prinny?"

"Oh, I have no idea about *him*." The older woman dismissed the prince with a sweep of her fan. "No, this is ever so much better!" She all but rubbed her hands together in delight. "Mr. Newstead has promised to attend!"

"I beg your pardon?"

"I sent an invitation to his publisher's offices. Clever of me, was it not?"

"Extremely." Vivian certainly hoped Mrs. DeLancey had not wagered the family jewels on a reply. If Newstead, whoever he was, decided to make an appearance, it would most certainly not be with trumpets blaring. She remembered her resolve to be the image of graciousness and maintained a serene smile. The old dear was in for a severe disappointment.

The old dear positively beamed. "And the lovely man sent a response. It only just arrived by messenger. He is coming!"

"Smashing!" said Grace from behind.

"Absolutely splendid," Mrs. DeLancey agreed.

"What damnable rubbish!" Vivian snapped, and stalked into the hall.

Noel almost reached out to stop her as she stomped past, but quashed the impulse immediately. He had been doing dashedly well in the past few days at pretending cool detachment and was not about to ruin it with one instinctive act. Besides, she looked downright sour, and he was in no shape for a blast of her temper. Considering the fact that he had just spent the past hour trapped in the Concerto from Hell—with Lydia pawing at him and blathering, no less—it would take precious little to set him off.

Had his mother not given him a tart and emphatic lecture on the consequences of utter boorishness, he would not have been in attendance at all. He was sick and tired of pretending that Vivian had not dealt him a stunning blow, sicker still of his friends' obnoxious attempts to play Cupid over the past several days. On each occasion when he thought he had successfully avoided the vixen for the evening, Jason or Rafe had somehow contrived to herd him right back into her presence.

Rafe, clearly possessed of some sixth sense, materialized at his side. "Join me for a glass of champagne?" he invited, gesturing in the direction Vivian had just taken.

"Go away," Noel growled.

The rat, curse his soul, merely grinned. "Certainly." He bowed to Lydia. "Would you care for champagne, Miss Burnham?"

Lydia promptly released Noel's sleeve and attached herself to the grander title. Noel was in the process of making slight amendments to his current assessment of his friend's character when Tarrant appeared in his place. "Go away," he snarled.

The bounder, damn his eyes, merely grinned. "I will credit that to the effects of lo . . . er, lust and ignore it."

"Bloody gracious of you."

"Isn't it just? But then, that is what friends are for."

"Lord, give me enemies," Noel muttered.

Jason surveyed an immaculate cuff, studying the emerald stud before turning it to just the right angle. "Really, Hel, you are becoming quite the curmudgeon in your . . . lustful state. Perhaps you ought to get yourself a mistress."

"I do not want a mistress! I want—" He cut himself off with a growl. "I believe I hear your wife calling you, Tarrant."

"Unlikely. She is at present discussing Celtic mythology with old Burroughs. Nothing short of a military attack will divert her attention until they are done."

The image of Prinny as Merlin flashed into Noel's mind. He had quite forgotten Vivian's assertion that it was not Byron behind the disguise. His annoyance vanished into contemplation. "Do you suppose," he mused aloud, "that it could be Burroughs after all?"

"That what could be Burroughs?"

"Do not be daft, man. Newstead."

Jason's brows rose. "Good Lord, the thought would never have occurred to me."

"The man is a walking encyclopedia of all things Arthurian."

"Yes, he is. But to compose . . ."

"And he met Vivian in Cambridge before she arrived in London."

"Did he? How cur—"

"Mrs. DeLancey was babbling something about having sent Newstead an invitation. And about his acceptance." Noel was warming to the subject. "Of course, she would have invited Burroughs anyway. They are old friends and cross paths constantly in Town. He would have had ample time to observe Vivian."

Jason held up a hand. "Vivian aside, why would Burroughs write poetry that imitates Byron? He has no need of the money, and does not impress me as a man to court scandal. As far as I know, he leads an expressly quiet life with his hunting and his books."

"Precisely!" Noel pounded one fist into the other for emphasis. "He and my father were chums for years and, if my mother's stories are to be believed, were constantly trying to outdo one another in sheer outrageousness. Who is to say he is not having a bit of a lark now? Adventure," he added with a wry smile, "need not be the province of the young alone."

"Well, I still find it a bit off that he would write of Vivian . . ."

"It is not about Vivian! It is about reaching for something remembered and precious. Really, Tare, you are quite a noddy sometimes. A man should never let go of those things that have brought him the most pleasure. What sort of life would one have to look back on then?"

He left his friend staring, open-mouthed, and took off in search of Burroughs. In truth, he had no idea what he would say, but it would be of the man-to-man variety. He empathized with the motivation, but the Vivid One must not appear in future installments.

The rest of the guests had begun to arrive by then, and there was a bit of a crush in the hallway. He did not mind in the least, even when Dillingham trod upon his toes. No, he was far too impressed with his own cleverness to be upset by such trivial matters.

He was still grinning when he came face to face with Byron.

"In a rush, St. Helier?" the man queried as Noel nearly bowled him over. "I daresay the Gentlemen's is in the other direction."

"Good evening, Byron." Noel tried to get past him.

"I say, have you seen Miss Redmond this evening? She and I are past due for a chat."

"A chat?" Noel's thoughts made a sluggish turn, followed by his feet. "You wish to . . . inform Miss Redmond of something?"

The poet's infamous eyes twinkled. "I suppose that is an accurate assessment of the matter, yes. If you should see her . . ."

"Now, listen here . . ."

"Ah, it seems I am being summoned." Byron was now gazing somewhere past Noel's shoulder. "If you will excuse me, St. Helier, I must hasten to my dear wife's side. Should you see Miss Redmond, be so kind as to mention me." With that, he was off into the crowd.

"Well, hell," Noel cursed, and stalked off in search of a drink.

Vivian, after being chased from several rooms by garrulous and intrusive guests, finally sought refuge in the solarium. Apparently Mrs. DeLancey had not been shy in spreading the news of Mr. Newstead's acceptance. No less than a dozen people had oh-so-helpfully informed Vivian of Byron's arrival. None had neglected to mention that Annabella was with him. She had quickly expended her repertoire of guileless replies.

So Lord Byron was present. As far as she was concerned, he could revel in the attention without her.

Even the opportunity of talking with Mr. Burroughs had lost its appeal. She had always considered herself to be possessed of adequate self-assurance; her mother called it presumption, but she suddenly found herself beyond weary of the whole matter. At the moment, should some heavenly intervention provide her with a trail of arrows leading straight to the poet, she would be hard put to do more than peer in the direction it pointed.

If Mr. Newstead—old or young, devil or angel—wanted to find her, he was just going to have to come looking.

She held far weightier matters to consider. She did not think she could stand one more evening of keeping her distance from Noel, let alone weeks. No, she was certain that something inside her would soon grow brittle and shatter. Unfortunately, no acceptable course of action came to mind. Her last, inner defenses had turned from steel to paper, and she dared not chance letting him through them.

With a heartfelt sight, she leaned her forehead against the window. The glass was cool against her skin, and she found herself fervently wishing that she could absorb some of the coolness into her thought processes. Of course, the surface soon warmed with her touch, leaving her no better off than she had been moments before.

Wearily she lifted her head. And nearly jumped right through the glass when a reflection loomed up beside hers. Heart pounding, she spun about. And came face to face with Lord Byron.

15

I blink and each successive day is gone,
Flying past with speed no man can beat.
Through deepest hours of darkness before dawn,
So vague of soul, of body incomplete,
I yearn and burn and suffer my deceit.
Those fleeting moment of our doomed affair
Taste bitter even as they are so sweet,
For you will go—of this I am aware—
Leaving me with nothing but despair.
                    —Newstead's *Heart's Notions*, canto V

VIVIAN LEANED BACK against the window frame and clasped her hand over her pounding heart. Byron watched her for a moment, then smiled.

"I am sorry, Miss Redmond. I did not mean to frighten you."

"It is quite all right, my lord. I was merely . . . startled for a moment." The truth, she realized, was that her elevated pulse was due only in part to the fright. The rest had come from the instant and fleeting belief that it was Noel who had entered her sanctuary. "Were you looking for . . . someone?"

Byron flashed her a slow, utterly libertine grin. "Two someones, actually, Miss Redmond, and you were one. Not the one, however, I expected to find here."

"I see." It was on the tip of her tongue to ask him if, in

fact, the second was his wife. And to offer her help in locating that lady. She rather thought he would decline. So, instead, she merely asked, "Is there something I can do for you, my lord?"

"I imagine there are a great many things. Shall I list the options?" He took a step closer.

Vivian was in no mood to be intimidated, nor was she awed any longer by the man's reputation or potent presence. She sighed. "Really, sir, unless you plan on giving a dastardly laugh and chaining me in some dank dungeon, I suggest you speak to me as you would a peer. I confess I am weary of the games that seem to characterize every encounter in this blasted town."

This time, his smile was rife with genuine amusement and even a bit of admiration. "Miss Redmond, I vow you are quite the most unique female I have met in some time."

"That," she shot back, "is not necessarily a compliment."

"Perhaps not from another's lips, but most certainly from mine."

"Then I suppose the appropriate response would be to thank you."

She managed to hold her ground as Byron moved to lean against the sill beside her. She noticed he did not step and turn as most would have done, but swiveled on his hip almost like a mechanical figure. "Your injury is bothering you again?" she said, unwittingly reminded of their first encounter when she had all but barreled over him.

"My injury? Ah, yes. If I remember correctly, you were once most concerned for my well-being." His mouth twisted into a wry grimace. "Your naïveté is really quite refreshing."

"Now that was *not* a compliment!"

"It was not meant as an insult, my dear. I was merely speculating on which aspects of my flawed being the ton apparently terms fit to discuss. The truth is that I have not been injured at all. My affliction is one of birth, you see, a foot that has always served to keep me more a Haphestos than an Adonis."

191

Vivian, knowing his reference to Aphrodite's malformed brute of a husband, was suffused with a burst of sympathy which, she was certain, he would not welcome. Byron was a proud man and, honored as she was by his quiet revelation, she knew to hold her commiseration to herself.

"I confess, my lord, to finding Haphestos a far more interesting character. Better to forge a legacy of steel than one of something so transitive as flesh."

She blinked when Byron let out a resonant laugh. "Miss Redmond," he announced, "I amend my earlier assessment of your character. You are not merely unique; you are quite awe-inspiring!" He glanced into her face and raised both hands in a semblance of submission. "Do not glower at me, if you please. *That* was a compliment of the highest order. It is one thing, my dear, to inspire art, altogether another to inspire awe."

"Really, sir . . ."

"No, fair Nimuë—I am now thoroughly convinced that the term Vivid does not even begin to do you justice. What a shame that alliteration so often falls so short of what needs to be said."

He had made the reference with no encouragement. Vivian felt her hands grow cold even as her cheeks warmed, and she struggled to put her raging thoughts to words. "You . . . you said you had been searching for me earlier. Did you wish to discuss . . . poetry?"

It appeared forthrightness was going to evade her.

"Poetry?" Byron's eyes narrowed and he gave a strange smile. "I think, my dear, that I do not wish to discuss . . . poetry at all."

"No? Then . . ."

He glanced around the shadowed solarium, then stretched out an arm to touch a trailing wisteria branch. "Have you ever been to the Mediterranean, Miss Redmond?"

"Much to my regret, I have not."

"It is, I think, perhaps the last place on earth where magic still lives. There are places, ruins of temples, that feel much as this chamber does now. The walls crumbled so many hundreds of years ago that no one knows precisely when they stood erect, and nature has reclaimed the land. Trees have sprung up amid the stones; vines crawl through the crevices."

He released the branch and turned to face her again. "One knows that society was once very much there and is at present not so far away, yet one can feel utterly alone in the midst of a wilderness. Do you understand what I am saying?"

"Yes. I do." And she did.

"When we last met, at Almack's I believe, you said something that has been much on my mind since. You said that all people are motivated by an intrinsic need for connection and that no man exists in true isolation. Do you remember saying these things?"

Vivian was suddenly consumed with sad irony. "Yes, I remember. Pure naïveté, my lord?"

"I did not think so then and do not now. I believe it was impressive insight."

"Insight?" She could not prevent the hollow laugh. "Well, my insight has been altered considerably since then."

"You no longer believe in the motivating power of connection?"

I believe in the power of money and social stringency. And fierce human needs. But a need for affection? She sighed. "I am no longer certain of just what I believe."

"Interesting." There was a lengthy silence. Then Byron slapped his hands against his thighs. "Well, I have enjoyed our conversation immensely, but I fear I must depart to continue my search. I have another . . . person to locate." He rose to his feet with a grace that belied his attested impediment. "May you find those things for which *you* search, Vivian." He looked down at her. "Ah, I forgot the other statement you made. You said we all must feel we are valued by and a value to those closest to us. *That,* my dear, is something I expect you still believe with all your romantic little heart."

She almost let him go, so busy was she in trying to decide what, in fact, her value was to Noel—if she even had a value to him. Her romantic little heart certainly knew his. By the time she realized she might be losing her last chance for another revelation, Byron had nearly reached the door.

"My lord," she called out wildly, "please stop!"

He did, the brighter light from the hallway framing him like a wavering aura. "Yes?"

She curled her fingers into her palms, feeling the bite of her nails. "I must know, sir. Are you . . ." She drew a breath and tried again. "Are you . . . ?"

His single, short laugh resonated through the glass-encased room. "I am a good many things, Miss Redmond," he replied. "Some of them are quite surprising, others exactly as expected."

Then he was gone.

"Well, hell," she whispered, and walked a few feet to sink onto a wrought-iron bench.

She had realized, in a flashing moment, that she really did desire to know Newstead's identity. In fact, it had suddenly become of almost too much importance. And she knew why. Her chest ached with an emptiness. She had given her heart completely to a feckless knave and had no great hope of receiving his in replacement. Boston loomed on her horizon, its only clear promise being chaos and continued emptiness.

With so much unsteady ground beneath her, she needed to be certain of something.

Idly she wondered what strange quirk of fate had destined her to have so little control over her own life. Was it simply that she had been born female? Or that she had been born to a mother who prized control over all else and a father who seemed innately capable of bending with whatever wind should be blowing at the moment? She had money of her own. Her father had seen to that. By all rights, that should have made her mistress of her own destiny.

What a shame, she thought, that she did not truly believe happiness could be bought.

194

A faint noise pulled her attention from her disquieting thought. Behind her, leaves rustled. She spun about and, for the second time that evening, nearly jumped from her skin when a head popped into view.

"Is he really gone?" The rest of Chloe Somersham followed the bright curls as she emerged from behind a potted azalea bush. "I vow I thought I was quite done for when he stopped but inches away!"

Vivian smiled wryly. "Hullo, Chloe. Fleeing the leash again?"

The girl let out a dramatic sigh as she plopped down beside her on the bench. "Always! Annabella is most cross this evening. She and George had been quarreling and I had no wish to spend a moment more than necessary in their company. Unfortunately, Bella must have someone over whom she can reign. George is a dashedly poor serf."

"So, I assume it was you for whom he was searching."

"Yes, I daresay he saw me coming in this direction. As fortuitous as it is that you were here to distract him, I am certain to be quite in the soup. He will be ever so testy now, and I expect Bella will have a minor tantrum when he returns without me." Chloe dropped her chin onto her fists. "Why is it that I seem destined to fall into one bumble bath after another?"

Vivian tried not to laugh as she patted the girl's drooping shoulder. "I expect it is because you are an irrepressible spirit."

"Like you?"

"Good heavens!" This time she did laugh. "I am beginning to consider myself rather more misguided of spirit than irrepressible."

"Fustian!" Chloe tossed her head. "You are quite splendid! I have certainly always thought so. Why, George even said so himself." A wistfulness came over the piquant face. "He has never called *me* awe-inspiring, nor even unique. When he refers to me at all, it is usually as a damned nuisance."

There was no jealousy in the girl's tone, only a deep

longing. Vivian promptly draped her arm around her shoulders and squeezed. "I promise you," she said emphatically, "that one day you shall inspire something far more enduring than awe, and it will be in a man far more worthy than George."

"Do you really believe so?"

"Without a qualm!"

Chloe sighed. "It is hard to imagine anyone more clever than George. Or more romantic." She looked up. "You wanted to ask him if he is Newstead, did you not?"

"Yes, I did." Vivian ran her free hand over her eyes. "You see, suddenly I need very much to know."

"I imagine you would. Has the attention been very hard on you, Vivian?"

"Hard? I am not sure that is the word I would choose. It has been excessive at times, absurd, and certainly unwanted. But not precisely *hard*."

"Well, I feel for you, regardless. I am certain such was not the poet's intention. For my own part, however, I would give every last penny I possess to have someone write of me in the way George writes of women."

Vivian stared at her. "Do you believe it is Lord Byron, then?"

"Newstead, you mean? He has given no indication of it."

"But what do you *believe*, Chloe?"

The girl shrugged. "I believe he is underappreciated. And I *know* his pockets are not as flush as many would believe. I would be more than happy to help, but . . . Well, you can imagine what his response would be were I to offer him money. He would toss me headfirst into the Thames, probably with one of his beloved ancient stones tied to my feet."

"Sometimes the hardest thing for a person to do is accept help, even when it would make all the difference."

"I would venture to agree with you there." Chloe bounced to her feet and Vivian watched as she forced a bright smile. "I suppose it is safe enough for me to venture out. Perhaps I shall lurk about the dance floor for a time and then give myself up." She gave her skirts a resolute shake, sending a small collection of leaves and twigs onto Vivian's feet. "Shall I send word to you should anything interesting happen? Before my surrender, of course."

"Chloe . . ."

"It rather looks as if Meriton will offer for Delia Courtland, though not here, of course. And then there is always the requisite number of trysts in the gardens. I should have made a very good spy, I think. I quite pride myself on invisibility. Yes, if I happen to overhear anything of note, I shall certainly share it with you. You cannot expect to find much amusement in here, after all."

"Chloe!"

"Yes? I am sorry, Miss Redmond. I do tend to prattle on. Was there something you wished to say?"

You will be fine. You will be cherished someday. But something in the girl's expression stilled the words on Vivian's tongue. Instead, she said, "You have azalea petals in your hair."

"Do I?" Chloe reached up to brush ineffectually at the untamed curls. "We cannot have that. Bella will think *I* have been trysting with some unsuitable bounder in the gardens, and there would be hell to pay with Father then. And, of course, George would merely laugh."

Vivian rose to her feet and removed the petals. "Much better. Now, I shall accompany you. We can lurk together for a bit."

"Smashing!" Chloe declared, and bounced from the room.

As always, Vivian was forced to hurry even to keep the other girl in sight. She entered the main hall just in time to see Lord Byron reach out and snare the erstwhile fugitive's arm as she passed. Whatever he said a moment later must have been stinging indeed, for Chloe's face flushed miserably and she hung her head. Vivian strode forward, determined to intervene, but by the time she reached the spot where they had been, they were gone.

The orchestra seemed far more proficient with Scottish

reels than Bach, its lively music swelling through the hall. Squaring her shoulders, Vivian prepared to reenter the festivities. Her time in the isolated wilderness of the solarium had been lovely in its way, but it was over. She was ready for another round of Society's games.

With that thought in mind, she nabbed a glass of champagne from a passing footman and resolutely circled the ballroom in search of Carlton Burroughs. She found him after a time, skipping merrily about the floor with Grace. Both seemed to be enjoying themselves immensely, and Vivian found herself offering a toast to the old gentleman. He might have, as Lady Fielding had reported, spent the years following his wife's death in relative seclusion, but he now seemed to be living life to the fullest. Vivian thought there were a good many people less than half his age who would do well to follow his example.

He danced with Aurelie next. Vivian wandered across the room to stand with Jason and Rafe. Noel, she noticed, was nowhere to be seen. Nor was Lydia Burnham.

"Impossible," she muttered.

"I beg your pardon?" Jason queried.

"Passable, I said. The music."

"Mmm. Yes, far better than the Concertos."

Rafe chuckled. "How would you know, Tare? You slept through them."

"And how would *you* know that?" his friend shot back. "You did too."

"Touché." Rafe turned to Vivian. "Have you reconsidered my proposal, my love? I confess I am not sure of the proper amount of time one should wait after a refusal before having another go."

Vivian tried to glare at him but knew it was useless. "What would you do if I were to accept? You might find yourself with a marchioness."

"Ah, a gracious woman to brighten my mornings, enliven my afternoons, warm my ... slippers ..."

"And most likely murder you in your sleep," Jason added dryly. Then, to Vivian, "Ignore him. He is foxed."

"Am not. I've merely been plying old Hel with liquor. *He* is foxed. I am merely—"

"About to choke on your own loose tongue." Jason shook his head. "We have tried to leave him behind on countless occasions, Vivian, but he always manages to turn up nonetheless."

Vivian nodded absently. She was far more interested in Rafe's loose tongue. "Why are you plying Lord St. Helier with liquor, if I may ask?"

Rafe opened his mouth to reply, then closed it abruptly with a wince—almost as if he had been kicked in the shin. Vivian darted a glance back at Jason, but he was gazing out over the floor. After a moment, Rafe said, "Just a gentleman's pastime, of course. It is a matter of honor among us to see who can drink the most and still remember the steps to the Ecossaise."

"I see."

He proceeded to flash his most engaging grin. "So, are you going to marry me or not, Vivian? If you refuse me now, I shall have ample time to propose to someone else before the night is over. Just wanted to give you first crack and all."

"Feel free to go forth and propose," Vivian replied blithely, giving up on the matter of Noel. Rafe was a careless creature at times, but she knew better than to underestimate him. "I am all but betrothed, you remember."

"Ah, yes. Daniel."

"David."

Rafe thought for a moment, then nodded. "David. Right. Well, we shall all miss you when you go." He peered at her. "Last chance, Vivian . . ."

She laughed. "You do not want to marry me, Rafe."

"No, I don't suppose I do. But I don't especially want you traipsing back across the Atlantic either. We've grown rather used to you here."

"Oh, Rafe." She placed her hand on his arm. "Thank you. I shall miss all of you, too." *More than I can say.*

Aurelie appeared at that moment, a grinning Burroughs by her side. "Vivian! We thought we had lost you."

"We *are* losing her, goose," Rafe said with a dramatic sniff. "She is leaving us for David."

"Daniel," Aurelie corrected.

"Er . . . Daniel. Right."

Realizing her own gaffe, Vivian directed a brilliant smile at Burroughs. The splendid man did not disappoint her. "May I have the honor of this dance, Miss Redmond?"

"It would be my pleasure, sir."

He led her into the set and she noted with some relief that it was a minuet. He was certainly fit for his fifty-odd years, but she rather expected skipping about three dances in a row would take its toll.

"You are looking pensive this evening, young Vivian. Is there something on your mind?"

Asking him if he had been writing poetry about her was not an endeavor to be taken lightly, and certainly not in the midst of a minuet. So she smiled and replied, "Nothing that needs to be addressed immediately, sir."

"Well, good, good. We cannot have you weighed down by heavy thoughts on such a splendid evening."

They spent the remainder of the dance engaging in nothing more than inane pleasantries. When the music ended, Burroughs led her back toward Rafe and the Tarrants. "I do believe the card room beckons. These old bones cannot handle as much dancing as they used to."

"Sir"—Vivian grasped his sleeve,—"there *is* something I wish to discuss."

"Ah? Yes, I did suspect so. You are a bit less vivid than usual tonight."

There was that blasted word again. Vivian guided the older man to a relatively quiet spot and took a deep breath. "I wish to talk about . . . poetry."

"Poetry?" He gazed at her intently. "I see. Well then, was there a particular work you wished to discuss?"

The kind blue eyes revealed nothing. Vivian silently cursed her seeming inability to get straight to the point. She came as close as she could. "I thought perhaps we could talk about *Heart's Notions*."

"My goodness!" Burroughs chuckled. "Why would you want to do that, my dear? From what your charming hostesses have said, I would have thought you past tired of the entire affair."

"I am, sir. In fact, all I wish is to put the matter behind me." She peered at him closely and saw only mild amusement. "But you see, I must know who Newstead is."

"Is it not the general consensus that it is young Byron?"

"Perhaps, but I am not sure . . ."

"Let me ask you this, my dear. Why is it so important that the man's identity be known?"

Vivian twisted her hands in her skirt. This was not going at all as she had hoped. She had meant to be the one asking the questions. "Someone is writing poetry about me, sir."

"You are certain it is you, then?"

She felt herself flushing. "I confess I was not at first. Even now I suppose it could be someone else, but"—she released her grip on the muslin and gestured expressively—"I cannot deny the similarities. There are too many."

"Hmm." Burroughs rubbed his chin and nodded. "And you feel this great need to know?"

"I need some certainty in my life!" she blurted out, drawn by his fatherly warmth. "Everything else is so . . . precarious. I need something of which I can be sure, something that is mine without question." She looked up miserably. "Does that make sense?"

There was a moment of silence. Then Burroughs reached out and patted her cheek. "May I give you a bit of advice, Vivian my dear?"

"Of course."

"Take this gift, this eloquent verse, as something that *is* yours. You need not know who wrote it. In fact, I am certain it is better that you do not. We spend so much of our life looking past the gifts—trying to see what is behind them. Sometimes they are given out of a deep and meaningful emotion, a desire to make a difference in the recipient's life . . . and sometimes merely out of the giver's need to prove something in his own."

He smiled gently. "As it is, my dear, you can have either one. Leave it so. The truth might not leave you any better off than you are now. It is rather like gambling, after all. Best to know when to keep the cards you have been dealt." His eyes twinkled then. "Now, I am off to see what cards shall be delivered into these old hands. Go off and dance, young Vivian. You deserve as much joy as you can get."

Vivian watched him head toward the card room, his stride that of a much younger man. Her own steps were far slower as she sought out a bench in a shadowed alcove. Was she truly better off not knowing? The wisdom of Burroughs's words was undeniable. No gift was ever given without some reason behind it. And sometimes knowing that reason diminished the pleasure. She just could not convince herself that the cantos were really a gift. More than anything, they had become a paper albatross.

Love seemed the same sort of burden. When welcomed, it was the greatest gift imaginable. When unwanted, it weighed heavier than any ancient stone. Vivian sighed and leaned back against the reassuring solidity of the wall. Of late, even the simplest of her thoughts seemed to make her head spin. And she needed to think.

It was quite some time later when she looked up to find a familiar figure standing in front of her. As ever, her heart skipped in her chest. "Hullo, Noel."

"Hullo, Vivian." His hair was more tousled than usual, and his cravat knot sat at an interesting angle to his jaw. "I have been looking for you."

"Have you?"

"We need to talk, you and I."

She gazed into the silver eyes and felt something twist within her at the hardness she saw there. "I cannot," she whispered. "Not now."

"Damn it, Vivian . . ."

"Please, Noel. Not now."

To her slight relief and great regret, he did not try to stop her as she rose to her feet and slipped past him. Nor did he follow as she walked slowly from the room. It was, she tried to convince herself, a good thing. She wanted more than anything to be near him, but she did not think she could handle those words she expected him to say. Besides, she had a great revelation to ponder.

She knew, with utter certainty, who Newstead was.

16

NOEL ENDED HIS session at Gentleman Jackson's a good deal sooner than he had originally planned. He had felt well in control of his champagne consumption the previous evening but was fast coming to the conclusion that he had been utterly deluded. At present, his head felt as if it were on the verge of toppling from his shoulders. The sparring had certainly not helped matters. In fact, one more blow to the chin, padded though his partner's fist might have been, would have sent more than just his head crashing to the mat.

He cursed Rafe fluently as he struggled into his coat. The bounder had been behind the bottle all evening, making sure the glasses never grew more than half empty. And all the while, he had been proselytizing on the merits of love. As if Rafe knew anything about the subject. Noel would have abandoned his company with pleasure, but whenever he tried to leave, Lydia Burnham materialized in the vicinity. He wondered if they had been conspiring.

Vivian had been conspicuous in her absence throughout much of the evening. He had not particularly wanted to speculate on where she might have been. In fact, he had not particularly wanted to think about her at all. So, in the end, it had seemed most reasonable to remain comfortably in one place, swilling champagne. Eventually, he had made it into the card room for a bit of faro, but he had not had the wits to stay in a game.

Every time he had been dealt a hand, he had seen Vivian's face among the cards.

A groom greeted him outside the boxing club and handed over his horse. Noel allowed himself a soft groan. Had he known how the brisk ride from home would all but shake his eyes from their sockets, he would have taken a hack. No, he would have turned right back around and gone back to bed. He mounted gingerly, ignoring the groom's quick smile. He could not be bothered by the fact that he appeared a clod who had gotten his clock cleaned in the ring. His energy was better put to making sure he stayed in the saddle.

It took twice as long as it should have to get home, courtesy of the slow, even pace to which he was forced to set his horse. Even then, he was feeling decidedly queasy by the time he got both feet back solidly on the ground. A hot bath was the first order of business, and, if he could resist the urge simply to stick his head under the water and leave it there, he would follow it with a good, stiff shot of brandy.

He entered the house and crossed the hall carefully as the impact of each step on the marble floor jarred his teeth. Whatever had possessed him to have a go at sparring? He was unquestionably a prime candidate for Bedlam.

Yes, that was just it. He was in possession of perhaps half of his wits, and if he did not do something about it soon, he would no doubt lose the rest.

It was almost sooner than expected. An ungodly shriek echoed through the hall, piercing his eardrums and quite chilling his blood.

Seconds later, it came again, followed by "Off with his head!"

Falstaff. Apparently his mother had brought the creature downstairs. Had Noel had the strength, he would have wrung the wretched bird's neck, consequences be damned. As it was, he merely steeled himself for more of the infernal noise and headed for the drawing room. The parrot only shrieked those particular words when his valet was around. With any luck, Tavis could be dispatched for hot water and brandy posthaste.

It was not to be.

"Good morning, dear," his mother greeted him as he entered the chamber. "You look terrible."

"Thank you, Maman," he returned dryly. "It warms my heart to know you love me enough not to pay court to my ego."

"Your ego functions quite splendidly without my help. You inherited it from your father's side of the family."

Noel grunted and peered through the back doorway. "Where is Tavis? He must have been here a moment ago."

"Yes. The dear man was kind enough to assist me in bringing Falstaff downstairs."

The parrot, preening in the sunlight, lifted his head and gave a distinctly smug sounding squawk.

"Where is he now, Maman?"

"I have no idea. He left in rather a hurry."

The parrot squawked again and Noel winced. Leaving the room sounded like a very good idea. Unfortunately, he was not up to doing anything quickly. His mother stopped him as he was trudging laboriously to the door.

"I have had an interesting note from Lady Fielding this morning."

"Oh?"

"Most interesting." Lady St. Helier peered at her embroidery frame as if it, too, contained something of great interest. Noel ground his teeth and waited for her to continue. "Apparently there has been some flux in the feather market. Something about an unexpected glut of ostrich plumes."

Knowing Lady Fielding's enthusiasm for both high fashion and the 'Change, Noel surmised that she was probably quite beside herself. "Fascinating," he murmured.

"I am certain you will think so, dear, when I tell you . . ." His mother lifted her embroidery again and studied it closely. "Oh, bother. I *did* miss a stitch. I thought I might have." She then proceeded to dig through her sewing basket for some sharp implement or another.

Noel knew he was not going anywhere until she had finished her tale, and decided he might as well have the brandy first and the bath later. Followed, most likely, by more brandy. He poured himself a glass at the sideboard.

"Now, what was I saying, dearest?"

"Ostrich plumes, Maman."

"Oh, yes! Well, it seems that Vivian will not be staying until the end of the Season, after all. She is to be on a ship back to Boston in just a few day's time."

Noel promptly showered his shirtfront with brandy. "*What? Why, in God's name?*"

"The feathers, of course. Her father has been blessed with a far larger supply than expected. The ship carrying them from Africa will be making an unscheduled stop in England after France to deliver some of the surplus, and it seemed to make the most sense for Vivian to be on it when it returns to America."

"Sense to whom?" Noel shouted. And winced as his head protested mightily.

"Her father, I suppose. It cannot be practical for him to send his ships sailing about expressly for the purpose of transporting his daughter . . ." She paused as Noel went to the door and yelled for the butler. "Whatever are you doing, dear?"

"I am ordering the carriage readied." He did just that, then collected his hat from where he had dropped it on the settee.

"Noel, sweetheart?"

"Yes, Maman?"

"You seem to be in rather a hurry, but do you not think you should postpone your departure a bit?"

"Why on earth would I want to do that?"

"Well"—his mother smiled at him fondly—"not to put too fine a point on it, but you do look a bit worse for wear."

"I do not care," he began, but she held up her hand.

"And there is the matter of the brandy, dear. I might be mistaken, but I do not believe you wish to arrive at your destination smelling as if you had just climbed from a cask."

Noel cursed fluently as he stared down at his ruined shirt. His mother was right. This time, his hat landed on the floor. "Tavis!" he bellowed, forgetting his sore head as he headed for the stairs. "Get me hot water. Now!"

It was over an hour later when he arrived at the widows' townhouse. His mother, ever clear of head, had countermanded his order for more brandy and had sent coffee upstairs instead. He was feeling decidedly more human, if not entirely himself, as he descended from his carriage.

Stevens greeted him at the door with his usual reserve. "Good day, my lord. May I take your h—"

"Where is Miss Redmond?" Noel was already heading for the parlor.

"Miss Redmond is not here, my lord."

"Not here?"

"No, my lord."

"Where is she?"

"I am afraid I do not know. She left some time ago for a visit. I shall certainly inform her that you called . . ."

"Lady Fielding, then."

"Her ladyship is not here either."

"Not here either."

"No, my lord."

Noel took a deep breath. "Mrs. DeLancey?"

"Mrs. DeLancey is here, my lord."

"Fine." He started again across the hall.

"But I am afraid she is not receiving."

"Not . . ."

"No, my lord."

"Stevens, would you be so kind as to inform Mrs. DeLancey that I am here and that it is most imperative that I speak to her." It was not a request.

The butler regarded him apologetically. "If I could, my lord. But she was most emphatic on the matter."

Counting ten helped somewhat. Another deep breath helped a bit more. "Tell me this, Stevens," Noel said calmly. "Is there any brandy to be found here?"

The man blinked at him. "Certainly, my lord. In the drawing room."

"Splendid. I shall wait there."

"For whom, my lord?"

"For whomever becomes available first," Noel muttered as he stalked toward the drawing room.

Aurelie stood with Vivian, surveying the dense ivy covering her garden wall. "Are you certain this is necessary?"

"Quite certain. I have thought it out carefully." Vivian tugged at the ivy. "Yes, I think this will work."

Aurelie sighed. "Could you not just use the door?"

"No. I do not wish to be seen. It is most important that no one know where I have gone."

"Including me?"

Vivian gave her friend an apologetic smile. "I am sorry, but it is better that you do not know either. This way, should anyone ask, you may claim innocence with no deceit."

"I am liking this less and less every minute. What if something should happen to you? You could meet with some . . . injury, and we would have no idea where to look."

"You are being overly dramatic. I am merely trying to afford myself a bit of anonymity, not embarking on some spy mission." She straightened her oversized hat. "How do I look?"

"Like a second-rate spy. Really, Vivian, are you quite certain . . . ?"

"You may stop fussing. I shall be just fine. Now, if you would be so kind as to give me a leg up, I shall be on my way."

Aurelie sighed as she complied. "How am I ever going to explain this to Jason?"

"You will not have to." Vivian levered herself to the top of the wall. The men's breeches made such endeavors ever so much easier. "I shall have his clothing back by teatime."

"Do not be a goose." Aurelie gazed at her from below,

concern etched on her lovely face. "The clothing does not matter. It will not be missed. You would."

Vivian grinned and sketched a jaunty salute. "Fear not, fair lady. I shall return. And, should I not, I bequeath to you my copy of *Heart's Notions*." She laughed at her friend's responding frown. "Yes, well, I would not want it either. Oh, Aurelie, leave off. I shall be fine. If it makes you feel any better, I will tell you that I am not going far at all."

"That helps a bit. I still do not like this, but I have faith in your resourcefulness—if not your wisdom." Aurelie sighed. "I shall miss you when you leave, Vivian."

Sudden tears prickled behind Vivian's eyes. "And I you," she murmured. Then she forced a smile. "Now, off to meet my Destiny!"

"Do be careful!"

Vivian waved. "Just remember," she called as she dropped over the other side of the wall, "should I not return, Newstead is yours!"

Newstead, she thought as she made her way down the alley, was in for a bit of a surprise. She could only hope she would not be turned away from the house. Her garb was decidedly ill-fitting, and not in the least proper, but she wanted anonymity. It would not do at all for her hostesses to hear that she had walked bold as brass up St. James Street on her way to an unaccompanied visit.

She pulled up the collar of her borrowed coat, pulled down the hat, and did her best to affect a male swagger. As it turned out, nobody looked twice at her, and she was feeling quite confident when she finally bounded up the stairs to the house.

The butler who greeted her did not so much as blink at her appearance, but he did balk a bit at her request. "I am afraid I must have a name . . . er, madam, if I am to announce you."

"It is all right, Jerrod," a voice said from behind him. "I am familiar with our guest." The butler bowed and disappeared. "This is an unexpected pleasure, Miss Redmond. Shall we . . ."

Vivian followed the gesture into a sunny parlor. "I apologize for arriving in this manner, but it was imperative that I see you, and I did not wish to be . . ."

"Accompanied? Trust me, I quite understand. Would you care for some tea?"

"No, thank you." Vivian removed her hat and dropped it onto a chair. "I must not stay long."

"What a shame. I get so little of your delightful company as it is. Are you certain about the tea?"

Vivian nodded and seated herself. "I would like to discuss poetry."

"Poetry?"

"Yes. *Heart's Notions,* to be specific."

"How curious."

"Not in the least. I understand why you did it, you know." There was really no sense in circling the subject. "And I must say, Mr. Newstead, you have achieved your purpose. You ought to be quite proud of yourself."

There was a moment of silence. Then Lady Chloe Somersham dropped into the facing chair with a sigh. "Pride has very little to do with it, really."

"No, your intentions are far more noble. George would not accept your money, but he cannot very well complain about his increased book sales due to the Newstead situation."

"Actually, he is rather amused by the whole thing."

"Yes, I expect he would be. I take it he has never suspected it is you."

Chloe shook her head. "He thinks it Carlton Burroughs, I believe. How did you figure it out? I worked so hard at cloaking my identity."

The girl looked so crestfallen that Vivian had to smile. "You did a splendid job. I should probably never have known had we not had our discussion last night."

"What did I say?"

"It was a combination of things, really—your concern for the effect the cantos had had on me, your desire to provide George with funds, your pride in your 'invisibility.'

211

Then, later, it occurred to me that you were in Cambridge when I was and arrived in London at much the same time." She shrugged. "I just *knew*."

Chloe nodded, her usual vitality dampened. "Are you very angry with me?" she asked, her voice small and lost sounding.

Vivian promptly jumped from her seat to kneel at her side. "Chloe," she said softly, taking her hand, "I am not angry at all."

Hopeful eyes met hers. "Truthfully?"

"Truthfully. But I am sad. For you. You do have talent, and you have more spirit and ingenuity than anyone I have met. I think it wonderful that you used it to help someone you care for, but I cannot help but be saddened by the fact that you will see so little for it."

"You are wrong there." The other girl gave a wry smile. "I have benefitted. The world might never know who wrote those cantos, but it has certainly paid handsomely for them."

"But you said George would not accept money."

"The money is not for George. It is for me."

"For you?" From what Vivian knew of Chloe's father, she could not believe the girl was in want of funds.

"Yes, I can tell what you are thinking. But my fortune is in my father's hands. I shall not see a penny of it until I reach thirty. Or," she added with a grimace, "until I marry a man of his choosing. When I wrote the first canto, and the money began pouring in, I realized I was having a hand in my own fate. It was a heady thought, I must tell you."

"I would imagine it was." Vivian sat back, filled with admiration for this young woman who had managed, with a pen and clever mind, to take her future into her own hands. She frowned then, thinking how little she had done to see to her own fate.

Chloe, clearly misreading her expression, leaned forward and cried, "I do not mean to imply that I put you through such discomfort for money!"

"Oh, Chloe . . ."

"It is just that I admired you so when I saw you in Cambridge. You seemed so confident, so self-assured, so ... vivid. I envied you your character, and your beauty. George spied you across the street one day and commented on you." She sighed, a heart-rending sound. "I thought if I could but capture just a bit of it all on paper, I might absorb it into myself."

"Oh, Chloe." Vivian ached with sympathy. "You do not need to absorb anything, except perhaps a bit of the freedom you so desire. You are lovely and so very vivid in your own, unique way. And you must not think that others do not see it."

"You are being very kind," Chloe replied, unconvinced.

"And you are being very hard on yourself. George is not a bad man, nor is he as careless, I think, as everyone wants to believe. But he is too busy searching his own soul for completion to see the vitality in others. You *will* be recognized for what you are, and you will be treasured for it. What is most important, however, is that you learn to treasure yourself first!"

"Do you, Vivian? Do you treasure yourself?"

"Yes" was her reply, then, with more conviction: "Yes, I do. Not at every moment, to be sure. I can be a regular mess at times. But I know my value, Chloe, and I will not allow anyone else to diminish it."

To herself, she thought that was truly only part of the equation. The far greater part, certainly, but still not complete in itself. She had her self-esteem, and her pride, but she was missing something crucial. Noel had her heart.

"Vivian?" Chloe's voice brought her out of the bleak contemplation. "Are we still friends, then?"

Vivian forced a puckish smile. "That depends on whether you are planning on writing more cantos about the Vivid One."

"Oh, no! I have quite finished with that business. Newstead shall be retired immediately." This time it was Chloe's turn to grin. "Unless, of course, I find myself needing him again."

"Then we are most certainly friends . . . unless, of course, Newstead finds himself needing a subject again."

Chloe promptly enveloped her in an enthusiastic hug. "You *are* splendid, Vivian! I daresay we shall be friends forever. We shall share the most delicious gossip about the ton behind its back, dance with only the most gallant of men, and you shall help me avoid the leash . . ."

"Chloe." Vivian gently disengaged the girl's arms. "You will have to share your gossip through letters, I am afraid. I depart for Boston in a few days' time."

"What? No!"

Vivian nodded sadly. "I have to go home rather earlier than originally planned." She sighed. "Something to do with feathers."

"Feathers?"

"It is of no consequence. I shall be happy to be home. But I shall miss you. We will write often and"—she managed a grin—"should the leash become too much for you, you can use your well-earned money to visit me in Boston."

Chloe was silent for a moment. Then she announced firmly, "I should like that."

"Good. I shall count on it." Vivian glanced at the mantel clock. "Now, I must go before I am missed."

"I miss you already." Chloe grasped her hand as she rose. "You have helped me more than I can say, Vivian. I will never forget that."

"Nor will I forget what you have done for me," Vivian teased. "I expect Newstead will be waiting for me in Boston."

The girl's face fell. "Oh, I am so sorry . . ."

"I am jesting with you. Pay it no heed."

"Still, I am sorry." Chloe rose to her feet. "Will I see you again before you leave?"

"I shall be at Almack's tonight."

"Well, I most probably will not. I am quite in Coventry for my disappearance last night. Bella was less forgiving than usual and George was like a bear with a sore head."

"If I do not see you tonight, I shall call before I leave. How is that?"

"Thank you," Chloe said gratefully. She retrieved Vivian's hat from the chair. "I rather like this. Perhaps I shall raid George's wardrobe."

"I would not advise it," Vivian replied with a smile. "Borrowing his writing style is one thing, his clothing quite another."

"I suppose you are right. I am quite finished with taking anything from George. From now on, he will have to give!"

Vivian left her standing there, a decidely confident smile on her face.

Noel had finished off the brandy and was in the process of counting the tiles in the hearth when Lady Fielding swept in. She did not seem in the least surprised to find him there and promptly waved him back into his seat.

"I assume you are here to see Vivian."

He shrugged. The brandy had gone a long way toward easing both his gut and his mind. "I was. She is not here."

"Not here?"

"No, my lord . . . er, my lady. So I thought I would just wait until someone showed up." He stifled a yawn. "You have above eighty-six."

"I beg your pardon?"

"Tiles, madam. In the fireplace. I had just reached eighty-six when you arrived."

"I see." Lady Fielding looked at him closely and smiled. "I have been thinking on how nice a strong cup of tea would be. Would you care to join me?"

"Might as well," Noel murmured. Then, remembering his manners, "Forgive me, my lady. I do not seem to be myself today."

"I am not surprised." Lady Fielding rang for tea. "She is leaving, you know. The ship sails Monday."

"Yes, I know."

"What are you going to do about it, boy?"

"I was not aware I was supposed to do anything. Short

of scuttling the ship, I am afraid I can do little to prevent its departure."

"Do not be dense. The ship may bloody well sail around the world so far as any of us are concerned. We simply do not want Vivian to be on it."

Noel sighed and counted a few more tiles. "Ninety-three."

"Really, dear. You are not being helpful."

"No? Should you ever decide to redecorate, you will know precisely how many tiles to order."

Lady Fielding chuckled. "You always were a bit of a rogue. I was prodigiously fond of you as a child."

"And now, madam?"

"I am still fond of you, but I am beginning to have questions about your intelligence."

"Madam, *I* have no such questions. I know I have lost what wits I once possessed."

"Well, you shall have to get them back. And I shall help as best I can."

"I am grateful beyond measure."

The older woman swatted at him with a copy of the *Weekly Political Register*. "Be serious and listen to me. We shall all be in attendance at Almack's tonight."

"Marvelous," Noel muttered. "My favorite place. Do you suppose they will remember to put sugar in the lemonade?"

Stevens arrived with the tea tray. Lady Fielding smiled as she poured Noel a cup. "Perhaps I am doing the girl a disservice," she announced dryly. "You really have become the most impossible adult."

"Yes, well, that is not news to me, dear madam. Vivian tells me so all the time."

Sometime later, he clambered into his carriage and headed for home. He felt wretched. Lady Fielding's potent China Black tea was doing battle with France's finest brandy in his stomach, and his mind was whirling with dizzying speed. If this were to be the way of things with Vivian in his life, he might just as well spare himself the continuous agony and put a gun to his head.

So she was to be at Almack's. He supposed he would have to be there, too. At least there was no liquor to be found on the premises. He might damn well feel nauseous, but it would have nothing to do with drink.

He had never, in his darkest imaginings, thought he would end up confessing his deep and undying love to a woman on the warped floors of the Assembly Rooms. But that love had quite taken over his heart, becoming a consuming and inexhaustible pressure. It was high time that he gave it away, and he had no choice but to give it to Vivian.

He simply had to do it quickly, before she sailed off across the sea, leaving him alone to bear the affliction for the rest of his life.

17

"YOU DO REALIZE that I hold you in the greatest esteem, do you not?"

Noel shifted his weight, trying to find a comfortable position. "I have never doubted it."

"I am glad. Then you will understand that what I am about to say is put forth with every attempt at compassion and civility."

He arched a brow, having a rather unpleasant feeling about what was to come. "Of course."

"And you will endeavor to take it with the spirit in which it is offered."

"I shall make every effort to do so."

"Good." There was a brief pause. Then, "You are a blithering idiot, Lord St. Helier, undoubtedly in the running for Greatest Fool in England!"

"Now, how did I know something like that was coming?"

Aurelie was not amused. "I am quite serious, Noel! You must not let her go!"

"You presume much in thinking I could stop her." He shifted again. Discomfort caused by the drink had been replaced by soreness from his unfortunate sparring session, and the Tarrants' elegant parlor chairs, while ordinarily perfectly comfortable, seemed hard as marble at the moment. "Who chose your furniture, Aurelie? The Grand Inquisitor?"

Aurelie promptly gave a strangled oath and threw up her

hands. "Just as I predicted!" she said to her husband. "*You* say something."

"*Et tu, Brute?*" Noel muttered.

Jason shrugged. "She is right, you know. You have become something of an imbecile as far as Vivian is concerned."

"What would you have me do? Get on my knees and profess my undying admiration? Beg for hers? Why do you not just shoot me right now and be done with it?"

He could, of course, tell his friends that he was more than willing to profess and beg from here to eternity. Anything to make Vivian stay. But the interference was decidedly annoying, even as it was well meant, and he was in no mood to offer further encouragement.

"Noel"—Aurelie had clearly decided to have another try—"you really must desist with this foolishness. She cannot very well leave if she is to marry you. Go to her now!"

His present opinion was that a proposal might very well send Vivian running for her ship days early. The thought brought a miserable tightening to his gut.

It occurred to him that he really had no idea what he could possibly say to make her consider shackling herself to him for the rest of her life. His foot seemed to gravitate toward his mouth with impressive speed whenever he tried to discuss their relationship.

Jason would probably be a very good person indeed to ask for advice on the matter. He had, after all, obviously said something right to Aurelie. As it was, however, Noel had no intention of giving the man the satisfaction of the request.

"All right," he said wearily, rising to his feet. "I am going."

"To Vivian?" Aurelie asked.

"To White's. I find myself in the mood for a bit of peace and quiet."

He ignored the couple's blustering and let himself quickly out of the house. Rafe was just coming up the stairs. "I would not advise going in there," he advised. "They will have you beaten and betrothed in minutes."

219

Rafe chuckled. "Been at you about Vivian's departure, have they?"

"Like pit bulls on a badger."

"And you snapped and scuttled for cover, I take it. What a pity."

Noel studied his friend's face. "Not you too."

"She is a smashing creature, Hel. Make any man a fine wife."

"Then you marry her!" He regretted the words as soon as they were out, but could do no more than console himself with a fierce scowl.

"It occurred to me," Rafe shot back blithely, "but I am rather fond of life."

"There, you see? You expect she would drive you to an early grave!"

"Not at all, my friend. I expect *you* would. I do not fancy having your hands around my throat."

Noel used his hands to cram his beaver hat low on his head. "Pit bulls," he muttered. Then, ignoring Rafe's insolent grin, he stalked away.

The walk to St. James Street cleared his head somewhat. He intended to make damn sure that Vivian was not on the blasted boat, but he was going to do it his way, with no one leaning over his shoulder like some crazed Cupid. He had a few hours before returning home for the requisite knee breeches—plenty of time to come up with the perfect plan.

He had just passed Boodle's when a figure launched itself at him. Startled, he took a step back from the whirling pink muslin.

"You are leaving, and the ship must stop her!"

"I beg your pardon?" he asked politely.

"Oh, do not be obtuse! It must not be allowed to happen!"

"Lady Chloe"—he raised the urge to place his hand atop her head to cease the bouncing—"St. James Street is hardly the place for a well-bred young lady." He glanced about. "Especially one alone. Where is your chaperone?"

The girl gave a dramatic sigh, then pounded one tiny fist

220

against his waistcoat. "At home, of course. I could not very well bring the Midge along on a mission of such importance. Now, are you going to stop her?" The brilliant curls were in even greater disarray than usual, and the color in her cheeks quite rivaled the coral muslin.

Noel was, despite himself, thoroughly amused. "The Midge?"

"No, you clodpated ninny! Vivian! Boston will not do at all!"

He patted her on the head. "Go home, Chloe, before you are missed."

Knowing she could not very well follow him into White's, he strode off at a quick pace. She stayed right behind him.

"She will leave, St. Helier, and you will be prodigiously sorry!"

"I shall take that under advisement." The club's front door swung open. "Summon a hack, please, Gidding."

The man blinked. "Are you leaving, my lord?"

"Not at all." Noel jerked a thumb over his shoulder. "She is."

"St. Helier!"

He paused. It would not do at all for young Chloe to make a scene in full view of the club. The chit was going to have a hard enough time finding a man daft enough to marry her as it was. "Yes, my lady?"

"If you allow Vivian to leave on that ship, I shall make your life quite miserable. I will dog your footsteps, haunt your haunts, and generally make a nuisance of myself! Do you hear me, St. Helier? A damned nuisance!"

As Gidding closed the door behind him, Noel decided that even if he were not rather overwhelmingly in love with the woman in question, Chloe's threat would be more than enough incentive to get himself wed at the first opportunity. He actually found himself grinning as he dropped into one of the library's deliciously overstuffed chairs.

Perhaps had he not consumed a year's supply of liquor in the past day, and his nerves not beleaguered to the point of sheer exhaustion, he would not have fallen asleep. When he woke, pained anew by countless hours sprawled in the chair, the club's lamps were lit and there was an ominous darkness outside the window.

The Duke of Marlborough, dozing comfortably near the fire, jerked upright with a muffled shout as Noel all but sprang upon him.

"Beg pardon, your Grace. I must know the time!"

The elderly man scowled. "Damme me, St. Helier—"

"The time, sir!"

"I believe"—the duke leaned around him—"the clock says ..."

Noel spun about. "Bloody hell!" he bellowed, and rushed from the room.

Marlborough grunted and glanced about. There was no one else present. "Young fellows today," he complained to the marble bust on the mantel. "Not a shred of sense among the lot."

Noel got himself into his knee breeches and out of his house within minutes. Deciding a carriage would only slow him up, he set off for Almack's at a jog. The street was ominously deserted when he reached the entrance.

He cursed as he pounded on the heavy doors. Willis, the Assembly Rooms' redoubtable proprietor, appeared an eon later. "Good evening, my lord." Noel nodded and tried to push his way past. Willis did not budge. "I am sorry, my lord, but it is after eleven."

"I know what time it is, man! I must get in."

"Again, my lord, I am sorry, but you are aware of the rules. No one is allowed in after eleven o'clock."

Noel took a deep breath. "Willis, the woman I am trying to marry is inside. I must see her."

The man bowed. "Congratulations, my lord," he offered sincerely. And shut the door in Noel's face.

His first impulse was to bang on the wood until the lout returned, but he knew it would be a waste of time. Prinny himself would not be admitted after eleven. So, cursing fluently, and feeling no better for the effort, he turned and wandered down the street. "A minor setback," he muttered to himself as he walked. "Nothing more. I shall simply call on her tomorrow . . ."

He continued the one-sided conversation as he went, not paying attention to where he was going. In the way of serendipity, he had just been afforded another twelve hours with which to prepare his speech. "Vivian, I implore you . . . Vivian, I implore you . . . Oh, hell. Let's see . . . Vivian, you must realize that I hold you in the highest esteem . . ."

He did not notice the figures until they were directly in front of him.

"Whadda we got 'ere, lads?" he heard. "Must be a fug'tive from Bedlam . . . talkin' to hisself like that."

There were three. By the looks of them, they were not likely to have been partaking of the sour lemonade at Almack's. By the smell, they had not been partaking of much wash water, either.

"Nah—jes' a gentry cove takin' the air," another announced.

"What say you we be takin' 'is purse?" the third suggested with a guttural chuckle.

The leader took a step forward. "What say ye to that, guv'nor? Sounds like a right good idea to me." The other two moved in behind him and Noel saw the club gripped in one's fist. "Let's do it, lads."

Noel sighed. "Gentlemen, I would not advise it."

"Ye wouldn't, would ye?"

"No, I would not." His fingers tightened around his own walking stick. "You see, gentlemen, I have just had a bit of a disappointment, and I am not in a particularly agreeable mood. I suggest you go avail yourselves of someone else's generosity."

"A disappointment, 'e says, lads. Ain't that jes' too bad? Get 'im!"

"Well, hell." Noel sighed again and rolled his eyes heavenward. "It cannot be said I did not warn them."

* * *

"Hell," Vivian whispered, "would be a vast improvement."

"What was that?" Jason queried.

"Nothing of import." She scanned the room yet one more time. "What time is it?"

"Five past eleven. Ten minutes since you last inquired."

"Jason!" Aurelie scolded. "Do not be rude!" She gave Vivian a sympathetic smile.

Hell would, in fact, have been an improvement on the evening. It had become abundantly clear that Noel was not present, and now there was no chance of his arriving. True, there would still be more evenings—four to be exact—but that did not signify. He would have heard of her imminent departure; it seemed all of London had. And had he been even in the least bit distressed by the news, he would have been there.

She had been surrounded by well-wishers from the moment she walked through the door. Some of the words had been unquestionably sincere. Others, like Lydia Burnham's, had been spoken with thinly disguised delight. Even more, she decided, had been motivated by sorrow at losing the Season's best entertainment. Little did the ton know that both the Vivid One and Newstead were things of the past.

Chloe was not present, nor was Byron. Vivian could but hope that they were not in the same place. The girl deserved far better than his snide attention. Carlton Burroughs was not in attendance either, and Vivian was sorry for that. She would have very much liked to thank him for his kindness. She supposed a letter would have to suffice.

At her side, Aurelie was whispering something to her husband. Vivian caught something that sounded rather like ". . . St. Helier to hell!"

Yes, well, she was not feeling pleasantly disposed toward the man either. Not that she was angry, or even bitter—instead, she was tremendously sad, and more than willing to curse him for it. It was not his fault that her love for him tore at her heart, but she could not like the fact that he was most likely off somewhere else, laughing his careless laugh with no idea that she was quietly bleeding inside.

"Vivian?"

She looked up to find Grace regarding her intently. "Hmm?"

"Are you all right? You look a bit . . . pale."

"I am fine." She forced a smile. "Merely wondering how I shall ever get through Wednesdays without Almack's."

"Oh, Vivian!" The girl's topaz eyes sparkled with tears. "It certainly will not be the same without you!"

It looked very much as if she were going to burst into tears on the spot. Vivian wanted to take her into her arms and comfort her. To her astonishment and delight, Rafe took it upon himself to do just that.

"Come along, Gracie, and dance with me."

Grace went willingly into his embrace, resting her head briefly against his chest. He stroked her hair for a moment before gently leading her onto the floor. Vivian smiled and offered a heartfelt prayer that Rafe would come to his senses before Grace slipped from his grasp.

Her friends' sadness was almost more than she could bear, and Aurelie's sympathy only made it worse. Bad enough that she had to suffer Noel's desertion; far worse that Aurelie knew of her suffering. Unable to help herself, Vivian patted the other woman's hand. "Everything will be all right."

If she could find no comfort, she could at least try to offer some.

She managed to endure another hour in the stuffy rooms before she could stand it no longer. Pleading fatigue, and past caring if anyone believed her, she collected her hostesses and left for what had become home.

"Very disappointing," Lady Fielding grumbled as the carriage pulled away from the door. "Very disappointing, indeed."

Vivian did not need to ask. She knew exactly to what the woman referred. Or rather, to whom. It seemed that everyone had expected Noel to dash onto the scene like some

225

romantic hero and carry her off to a castle in the clouds. Everyone except Noel, of course—and Vivian herself, who had hoped with all her heart, but never expected.

The sight of the partially packed trunks scattered across the floor of her bedchamber did nothing to improve her spirits. She really was leaving, and nothing short of a miracle was going to change that.

The first glimpse of her father's letter had brought a wide smile to her lips. Reading had brought an unbearable pain to her heart. She could not fault him for arranging her early return. It made perfect sense, after all, for her to take passage on the soon-to-be-departing ship. His business was not based around seeing to her preferences. So, instead of cursing her father, she allowed a stinging mental tirade against the ostriches whose prolific feather production had caused her sorrow.

She brushed angrily at the tears dampening her cheeks and blew out the candle with unnecessary force. She really ought to be cursing Noel, but she did not have the heart. In fact, her heart was not up to thinking about him at all. As sleep evaded her, she stared up at the bed canopy and tried to count cherubs. Between the tears and the darkness, the blighted little creatures blended together in such a way as to make counting them impossible.

Her already beleaguered heart nearly stopped altogether when the shadow loomed over her. Her cry was effectively staunched by a heavy hand descending onto her mouth.

"Damn it, Vivian. If you scream, I fear I will be forced to throttle you." *Noel.* "My nerves could not take the strain."

The hand lifted. There was a muffled scratching and the guttered candle sparked into life. The sight that greeted her made her gasp.

He looked terrible. His face and clothing were rumpled and filthy, there was a jagged tear in the white shirt and an egg-size bruise over his right eye. "My God! What happened to you?"

226

"Have pity on me and do not ask," was his terse reply.

It was difficult, but she managed. After a moment, she queried, "What are you doing here, Noel? Should anyone discover you . . ." The words were lost in the swell of hope. He had come to her.

"Ah, Vivian." He sat down heavily on the bed. "It has been the most hellish night of my life."

"I . . . I am sorry."

"Are you?" His eyes glittered silver in the light. "Are you willing to take responsibility for it?"

She could barely speak. His nearness, as always, was doing terribly strange things to her breathing. God, how she loved this man! "I do not understand."

"Perhaps I shall tell you about it, after all." He leaned close, so close that she could see the pulse ticking in his jaw. "I have been snubbed by the mighty Willis, been set upon by footpads, spent an extremely unpleasant hour in the shadows of this house's garden, and suffered the thorns of the most vicious vine known to man while climbing the wall to get in here."

"F-footpads?"

"Dispatched them."

"Garden?"

"Endured the damp and cold."

"Climbed the wall?"

"With my bare hands." He placed one against her cheek and she could not help but press her face against the glorious roughness. "And it is all your fault, Vivian."

Some faint vestige of spirit roused itself at his imperious tone. "I did not ask you to do any of those things," she replied, but her voice lacked its customary strength.

"No, you did not. But I had no choice. I have a gift for you, and I could not let you leave without it."

A gift. He had come to give her a farewell gift. Vivian's hopes took a mighty dive. "I see."

He felt her pulling away and promptly slid his hand through her soft curls to hold her still. "You are an odd woman, Vivian Redmond. Are you not even curious as to what I have to give you?"

"A piece of memento jewelry?" she asked dully.

"No."

"A book of verse?"

"No. Any more guesses? I sincerely hope not. You are depressing me." He pulled her face closer to his. "As a matter of fact, I have come to give you something I no longer care to possess."

"I . . ." She tried to pull back again, and again he held her still.

"I have come to hand over my heart, Vivian. It is no longer of any use to me, you see. It belongs entirely to you and by all rights now rests in your hands."

There was a moment of heavy silence. Pain lanced through him as he decided his gift was about to be shattered into countless pieces. Then, with a breathy sob, Vivian hurled herself into his arms.

"Oh, Noel! Say you are not teasing me! I could not bear it if you were!"

He clasped her to him with tender fierceness. "Do I sound like a man who is teasing?" he asked, letting all his love spill into his voice. "My God, Vivian, if I were any more serious, I would expire from the sheer force of it!" She began shaking against him and he could not tell if it were with laughter or tears. "Can I take this to mean you will accept my paltry gift?"

She lifted her face and he could feel the fire of the emerald eyes searing him. "Only if you will take mine in return. I no longer have any use for my heart either. It has belonged to you for the longest time!"

"Ah, my love!" He decided then that words were a rather monumental waste of time. Kissing her would do far better.

So he did. And she kissed him back with a passion that made his very bones melt. She smelled like flowers, tasted like fine wine, and felt like heaven itself. He knew he was going to spend the rest of his life kissing this woman, and would have begun the rest of his life right then had the room not suddenly been flooded with light.

"Good heavens!" Mrs. DeLancey gasped, the log-size candle in her hand wavering.

"Well, I'll be damned" was Lady Fielding's contribution.

Noel lifted his head reluctantly and smiled as Vivian scuttled to the opposite side of the bed. "Good evening, ladies."

"Evening?" Lady Fielding snorted. "It is the middle of the night and you are in Vivian's bedchamber. I certainly hope, young man, that you are planning to propose marriage."

"As a matter of fact," Noel began, and Vivian watched as he slowly lowered himself to one knee beside the bed, "I was just getting to that when we were . . . interrupted."

"Hmph." Lady Fielding made a thoroughly unsuccessful attempt at a scowl. "I suggest you get on with it, then. Come along, Felicity. Let us leave the dear boy to it." She grasped her sister's arm.

"But, really, Constance! In her bedchamber! We would be sadly remiss as guardians if we were to allow . . ."

"Oh, shut up, dear." Lady Fielding got her sister into the hall and pulled the door shut behind them.

"Vivian . . ."

She turned to see Noel regarding her seriously from the other side of the bed. "Yes?"

"Come here, please. I would like to do this properly."

"I do not think . . ."

"Please don't. If you think, you might refuse me." When she did not move, he gave an eloquent sigh. "Oh, very well." Still on his knees, he shuffled his way around the bed until he was before her. "Would you do me the very great honor, Miss Redmond, of becoming my wife?"

He grunted as she landed on top of him, sending them both flat to the carpet. "This is familiar." He tempered the teasing words by wrapping his arms tightly around her waist. "I sincerely hope that was a yes, sweetheart. Otherwise, I fear Mrs. DeLancey would feel obligated to cosh me with that torch she was holding for compromising her ward."

Vivian silenced him with a fiery kiss. "Yes," she said, before kissing him again. "Yes, and yes, and yes!"

Seconds later, without having any idea quite how she got there, she found herself trapped beneath him. He gazed down at her with a devilish grin. "What about David, my love? Or was it Daniel?"

She felt herself blushing. "You know as well as I that there is no David. Or Daniel."

"Yes, I do. I just wanted to hear it from you."

"Well, you've heard it. Will you kiss me now, please?"

"What of Boston, and your place in your father's business?"

"Oh, Noel, my place is with you! Now, will you please . . ."

"With pleasure." He lowered his face—then, to her great displeasure, pulled back. "There is just one more thing . . ."

"Yes?"

His beautiful mouth thinned. "That damned poet. I believe I shall have to have a talk with him in the very near future. Should I figure out who he is, of course."

Vivian laughed. "I fear that might be a bit difficult, my love."

"Oh? And why is that?"

She anchored her fingers in his hair and tugged. "I will be more than happy to explain. Just not right now. I would rather not talk, if you do not mind."

He obediently let her pull him close. "Not at all." His leonine grin sent warm shivers all the way to her toes. "From now on, you will reserve your vividness for me alone. Understood?"

"Certainly, my lord." Her grin fully matched his. "I shall

make every attempt to be as unvivid as possible. I promise to be the most docile, unobtrusive of wives."

She thought she heard him groan as she captured his lips with hers.